# When I'm Old and Grey

# When I'm Old and Grey

*Ted Darling crime series*

*'When a killer strikes close to home'*

**L. M. Krier**

ISBN 978-2-901773-04-7

# Contents

# About the Author

L M Krier is the pen name of former journalist (court reporter) and freelance copywriter, Lesley Tither, who also writes travel memoirs under the name Tottie Limejuice. Lesley also worked as a case tracker for the Crown Prosecution Service.

The Ted Darling series of crime novels comprises: *The First Time Ever, Baby's Got Blue Eyes, Two Little Boys, When I'm Old and Grey, Shut Up and Drive, Only the Lonely, Wild Thing, Walk on By, Preacher Man.*

All books in the series are available in Kindle and paperback format and are also available to read free with Kindle Unlimited.

# Contact Details

If you would like to get in touch, please do so at:

tottielimejuice@gmail.com

facebook.com/LMKrier

facebook.com/groups/1450797141836111/

https://twitter.com/tottielimejuice

For a light-hearted look at Ted and the other characters, please consider joining the We Love Ted Darling group on Facebook.

# Discover the DI Ted Darling series

If you've enjoyed meeting Ted Darling, you may like to discover the other books in the series:

The First Time Ever
Baby's Got Blue Eyes
Two Little Boys
When I'm Old and Grey
Shut Up and Drive
Only the Lonely
Wild Thing
Walk on By
Preacher Man

# Acknowledgements

Thanks to all those who helped with this third book in the DI Ted Darling series, Beta readers Jill Pennington, Emma Heath, Kate Pill, Chris Bellamy-Brown, Claire Godfrey, additional editing Alex Potter.

Thanks to the Stockport Memories group on Facebook who helped with local knowledge, especially Paul Jenkins and Jim Savage for their input about the River Goyt and the Stockport Hydro, which did not exist when I last visited Stockport, the town where I grew up.

*To Jill Pennington*

*my alpha beta reader*

*who encourages me to keep writing*

# Chapter One

'Ted? Bill here,' a familiar voice greeted DI Ted Darling when he answered the phone on his office desk. 'There's a woman at the front desk, asking to speak to you. She won't give a name or say what it's about, but she's adamant she wants to speak to you and only you. What have you been up to?'

Ted chuckled. Bill was a uniform branch sergeant who had known Ted long enough and well enough not to stand on ceremony with rank. He also knew that Ted was in a stable, long-term relationship with his partner, Trevor, so was not likely to have been up to anything, especially with a woman.

'Any other clues?' Ted asked.

'None at all,' Bill replied cheerfully. 'She doesn't look particularly dangerous, though. Not that you can ever really tell.'

Ted looked at the pile of paperwork on his desk which, despite his best efforts, seemed to be breeding in his in-tray whenever he took his eyes off it. He knew that he needed to be in court later that morning to give evidence in a complex case which he and his team had finally managed to bring to trial. It was tempting to take the opportunity of a break. Doubtless, though, the woman would turn out to be another time-waster, wanting to confess to a crime she had not committed, just to get some attention. Such instances were all too common in modern society.

'I'll be right down, Bill,' Ted said, as he rose from his desk.

Before he left his office, he carefully adjusted his tie to

cover the fact that his top button was undone, as usual. His friend and former boss, DCI Jim Baker, had always been relaxed about dress code for his CID officers. His replacement, the formidable Superintendent Debra Caldwell, universally known as the Ice Queen, was much less tolerant.

As Ted reached the front desk, he could see a woman sitting on a chair opposite it, nervously clutching a bulky handbag in front of her and looking ill at ease. She appeared to be well into her sixties, the lines on her face indicating clearly that life had not always treated her kindly. She had light brown hair, verging on chestnut, in a cut which was neither flattering nor skilfully done. There was something familiar about her which Ted could not immediately place.

As he moved over towards her, she jumped hurriedly to her feet, looking even more anxious.

'I'm Detective Inspector Darling,' he said, by way of introduction, in his usual measured tone. 'I believe you wanted to speak to me?'

The woman's eyes filled suddenly with tears. Her right hand moved upwards and out towards Ted, almost as if she wanted to touch his face. Ted, highly trained in several martial arts, instinctively raised his left forearm to block any possible attacking movement, then realised there was none and let it fall again, a little embarrassed.

'Teddy? My little Teddy?' the woman asked, her voice quavering uncertainly.

Ted felt himself go cold.

'Is there something I can help you with?' he asked formally.

He could see the hurt in her eyes at his tone, but she carried on, in spite of it.

'I came to tell you that your Grandma Jones died suddenly last night,' she said.

'I'm sorry to hear that, and sorry for your loss. Was that all you wanted?'

Ted's voice was totally professional, devoid of any warmth.

'They said it was natural causes, Teddy, but I don't think it was. There's something not right, not right at all, and I thought you'd know what to do ...' Her voice trailed away into silence.

'Please don't call me Teddy,' he said stiffly, then he softened slightly. 'All right. I can't give you long, I have to be in court later this morning. Come up to my office and you can tell me all about it and explain why you don't accept that it was natural causes.'

Bill was watching them from behind the desk, clearly intrigued but not listening in on what was obviously a private conversation. Ted gave a curt nod in his direction, then guided the woman up the stairs to his office. Bill seemed to grab all the shifts going. He appeared to be almost always on duty. Ted suspected that filling his days with work was better than being at home alone for the widowed officer.

'I only have green tea or coffee to offer you in my own office, but I can arrange something else, if you prefer,' he told her as they made their way through the main office. Most of his team were out, several already at court, while others were following up on enquiries. Only DC Maurice Brown was at his desk, plodding reluctantly through his own pile of paperwork.

'Just ordinary builders' tea would be lovely, if it's not too much trouble,' she said.

They both paused as Ted said, 'Maurice, would you be kind enough to rustle up a cup of tea for ...' he broke off, not yet ready to acknowledge her as his mother, '... for this lady, please.' Then turning back to her, he surprised himself by asking, 'A cloud of milk and two sugars?'

Tears started to her eyes once more as she said, 'You remembered.'

'Right you are, boss,' Maurice got to his feet, clearly pleased to have the distraction from his work.

Ted showed her into his office, installed her in the spare chair and placed the mug of tea, which Maurice had rapidly produced, in front of her. He then sat down and said courteously, 'All right, tell me everything, from the beginning.'

'Your grandma has been in a care home for years. She has – had – dementia and I couldn't cope with her at home any more. I've been living with her since … since I moved out,' his mother began. 'Physically, she was very well, still very active, which was the problem. She would go outside, wander off, even get on a bus. You couldn't tell by looking at her that there was anything wrong with her. She always dressed nicely and did her hair tidily.

'I always used to visit her every morning, then go on to work. I'm a home carer, afternoons and evenings. I was with her yesterday morning and she was absolutely fine, nothing wrong at all. Then the care home phoned me very early this morning to say Mam had been vomiting violently in the night and her heart had just stopped because of it. Their doctor signed a certificate to say it was natural causes. But I don't believe it was.'

Ted tried to curb his mounting impatience. He had not seen either his mother or his grandmother for years, not since he was a little boy and his mother had walked out on him and his disabled father. He was sorry to hear of the old lady's death, but so far he'd heard nothing which made it a police matter.

'She must have been well into her eighties, though, surely? I would imagine that a sudden virus at that age could easily prove fatal for a frail, elderly person.'

'She was eighty-four, but she'd never had a day's illness in her life,' his mother replied. 'The home said she was the only one who'd been ill, no other sickness among any of the other residents. And there's something else that doesn't add up at all, something not right. They told me she'd been fine in the afternoon and had had a nice time eating cake and chatting to her granddaughter.'

'You had other children, then, with the man you left Dad for?' Ted asked neutrally, trying to keep any note of bitterness out of his voice.

She looked puzzled.

'But there never was another man. That's not why I had to leave. And there were certainly no other children. I had a bad time when you were born, Teddy. I nearly died. They had to operate on me. There could never be any more children.'

'So you have no idea who this supposed granddaughter might be? ' Ted asked and she shook her head, still looking bewildered by it all.

'I don't know who she is, but the home said she often visited Mam in the afternoons. She may have been one of the last people to see her before she died, and she was giving her cake just before she took ill. I don't understand it, it doesn't seem right to me.'

'But you say there's a death certificate saying natural causes? Well, it may just be possible to get a post-mortem in spite of it, if there are sufficient grounds to classify it as a suspicious death,' he was almost speaking to himself. 'Where is she now?'

'She's still at the home in Marple,' his mother told him. 'I've just come from there. I'm meant to be making the arrangements for the undertaker to take her to the Chapel of Rest. I came straight here, because I thought you'd know what to do.'

'How did you know I was here?' he couldn't resist asking.

'I've followed everything about you that's ever been in the local papers. I was so proud to read about your career and your promotions,' she told him, her eyes shining.

'Marple's on my patch, that's a good start. Right, give me all the details and I'll just make a few quick phone calls,' he said, his tone brisk, professional and impersonal. He was a policeman, talking to a member of the public who had reported a suspicious death. Nothing more.

His first phone call, to the home, was to advise them of a possible post-mortem examination, in spite of the death certificate, without going into any details. His next call was to ask a massive favour.

'Bizzie? It's Ted. I wondered if you could possibly help me out with something which is way above and beyond the call of duty on your part. That is, unless you're too busy?' he added, then groaned. 'Sorry about the appalling pun, I bet you've heard it a few thousand times before.

Professor Elizabeth Nelson, the senior pathologist, gave a throaty chuckle of delight.

'Good morning, Edwin. How very intriguing. And no, since only family and very close friends use my nickname, the pun has not been overused to date. What can I do for you?'

Ted smiled. The Professor was the only person, apart from his partner, who even knew Ted's full name, let alone used it.

Ted briefly outlined what his mother had told him and added, 'I know it's a bit irregular and that I should go through the senior coroner, but he's never been my number one fan. I wondered if there was any way you could have a word first, prepare the ground for me a bit? I'd be eternally grateful.'

She laughed again.

'I'd be delighted to. Give it twenty minutes or so then call him yourself and we'll see what can be done. I'm sorry to hear of your grandmother's demise and I do hope there is nothing sinister about it. I'll try to arrange to carry out the post-mortem myself. I take it you're suspecting a possible poisoning?'

'I'm not sure that I'm suspecting anything untoward at the moment. It does just seem a bit of a coincidence that an unknown visitor is feeding cake to her one minute then she becomes seriously ill enough for her heart to fail shortly after. It's certainly worth looking at a little more closely,' Ted replied. 'Thanks, Bizzie, I really am grateful. You must come to dinner in payment one of these days.'

He hung up the phone and turned to his mother.

'That's as much as I can do for now, but if you leave me your contact details, I'll be in touch to let you know what the post-mortem shows, if the coroner agrees to allow one.'

'Does that mean I can see you again?' she asked, hopefully.

'I'll be in touch,' he repeated, distantly, jotting down the details she gave him in his notebook. He then rose to show her politely out of his office and possibly out of his life once again.

# Chapter Two

Ted was proud of his team. He had one detective sergeant, four detective constables and a TDC, a trainee detective constable. They were one member down on the full team complement at present, and he was constantly reminding the Ice Queen of that fact. All his team members worked together with efficiency and mutual respect. Between them and Ted, they had an enviable crime clean-up rate.

Sometimes though, despite all their best efforts, circumstances conspired against them to bring a case crashing down around their ears. Unfortunately, today had been one such day. Late that morning and completely out of the blue, a key prosecution witness had suddenly changed his testimony. The Chief Crown Prosecutor tried everything he could but the witness, who was clearly scared for his life, resolutely contradicted his earlier statement.

Without his critical eyewitness account and identification of the suspects, the prosecution case was in tatters. By early afternoon, it had collapsed completely. The jubilant accused men headed out to freedom with air punches and noisy cheers from their friends and family, both inside and outside the courtroom.

Ted knew he should head straight back to the station to debrief the Ice Queen, but it was the last thing he felt like doing. He tried his best to boost the rock-bottom morale of his team, promising them a round of drinks in their usual watering hole at the end of the day. Then he told his sergeant, Mike

Hallam, that he had somewhere to be for the next hour or two, but would be back in his office as soon as possible.

He fully expected the post-mortem on his grandmother to confirm that her death was due to natural causes. Bizzie Nelson had done a good job of softening up the coroner for him. With his usual brusque manner, he had agreed to Ted's request for one to be carried out, without comment.

But Ted had decided to start initial enquiries before the autopsy findings, as he would for any such death which was suspicious. It gave him a valid reason to be out of the office for a while, and he felt he needed one.

His mother had given him the address of the care home, near to Marple. At least it was on his patch, so he could feel some justification in going to check it out. It was a newish single storey building, functional but completely devoid of any character, with an antiseptically tidy front garden. A sign by the entrance announced it as 'Snowdon Lodge – High Quality Care for the Elderly'.

Ted wondered if his mother had chosen it for her mother simply because of the name, as she was Welsh.

He parked his elderly Renault in the visitors' car park and sat for a moment, observing. Another car pulled up alongside him and what looked like a family got out. Mother, father, two teenage children. The boy was glued to some sort of hand-held gaming device. Ted was a complete technophobe and knew little about such things. The girl was wearing earphones, her head nodding and twitching in time to some music only she could hear. From the looks on their faces, a visit to an elderly relative in a home was not what they had in mind for an afternoon in the school holidays.

Ted fell into step behind them, heading for the front door, interested to see what, if any, security measures were in place at the home. He discovered that there were, in fact, two doors. The outer one was unlocked and led into a small entry hall, where a visitors' book was spread out on a shelf. The man wrote in it while the woman rang the bell of the inner door, which was locked.

Ted took the pen when the man offered it and made a show of writing his name, although in fact he wrote nothing. He noticed that the man had written 'Adams Family' and wondered if that was ironic or was really their name.

They were kept waiting for some time until finally a rather harassed-looking member of staff came to unlock the door. She gave the Adams Family a cursory greeting but totally ignored Ted, trailing in their wake.

Once inside, the family headed off down a corridor, clearly knowing where they were going. Ted didn't know, so he stood for a moment in a light and airy vestibule, looking around. Seeing him standing there, one elderly woman in an armchair near to the door called out to him, raising a gnarled, blue-veined hand to attract his attention.

'Sid! Sid! I'm dying for a wee. Can you take me to the toilet, Sid? Hurry up, I'm bursting.'

From the all-pervading smell of urine, Ted thought that it was likely to be too late already, but he looked around hopefully for a member of staff. The elderly woman reached out her hand again, with its paper-thin skin, and tried to catch hold of him.

A younger woman was sitting nearby, next to an old man who appeared to be asleep in his armchair.

'You could try pushing the call button on the wall just there,' she said helpfully, pointing. 'With any luck, someone might appear in the next half hour or so, but I wouldn't count on it. Are you a relative?'

Ted took a discreet step back from the clutching hand and said, 'No, I'm, er,' he hesitated. 'I'm here to talk to the manager.'

The woman gave a short laugh. 'Good luck with that,' she said. 'Most of us never get to see her.' She pointed again. 'You might get lucky if you take a walk down that corridor. There may be one of the carers there. I've seen a few of them going that way. I think something must be going on.'

Ted thanked her and headed down the corridor, which had bedrooms opening off on either side of it, most with their doors open. The smell was considerably worse as he progressed and was not confined to urine.

With his martial arts training and small stature, Ted could move extremely quietly. His team called it his stealth mode. He would have made no sound even without the carpet, with its old- fashioned, dirt-disguising, swirling pattern, which reminded Ted of a budget hotel's décor.

As he neared the end of the corridor, a short, rather plump woman was backing out of one of the rooms. She was talking quite loudly to whoever was inside it, her tone disagreeable.

'And for God's sake, get the Jones woman's room cleaned up quickly. We need more bums in beds as soon as possible, if you lot expect to get paid this month.'

Turning, she saw Ted standing, quietly motionless, near to her. Instantly, she stretched her face into something resembling a smile and asked, 'Can I help you?'

'I'm looking for the manager,' Ted replied.

'I'm the manager,' she said briskly. 'What can I do for you? As you can see, I am rather busy at the moment.'

Ted noticed that she did not give her name. She hadn't offered it over the phone when he had called her earlier in the day.

'We spoke on the phone this morning. I'm Detective Inspector Darling. I'm here to talk to you about Mrs Gwen Jones.'

She looked flustered. 'Has there been a development? I know you said there would be a post- mortem but ...'

Ted interrupted her. 'Could we perhaps go somewhere more private to talk, rather than standing in a corridor, Mrs ...?'

'You better come to my office,' she said, still not giving her name. She swept along the corridor in front of him, not affording him a backward glance. They went through the vestibule and into another corridor on the other side. She led the way through the first door on the left, pointing ungraciously towards a spare chair, which Ted sat in, taking out his pocketbook.

'Can you start by giving me your name?' he asked, at the same time retrieving his warrant card from his pocket and showing it to her to confirm his identity.

'Rawlings,' she told him brusquely. 'What did you want to know?'

'First of all, have any of your other residents been affected by similar symptoms to those of Mrs Jones?'

She shook her head. 'Not so far, but these things flare up all the time. Mrs Jones was elderly. It's unfortunate, but it seems the sickness was too big a strain for her heart.'

'I understand a member of your staff told her daughter that Mrs Jones had spent some time yesterday afternoon with her granddaughter?'

'Yes, I think so. Her granddaughter came quite often, I believe. They seemed to get on well. She always called Mrs Jones something that sounded like Nine. She said it was Welsh for grandma.'

'*Mamgu*,' Ted said, to his own surprise. 'Mrs Jones was from South Wales, where the word for grandma is *mamgu*. *Nain* is what they say in North Wales. No family member would ever have called her that.'

In his head he saw a smiling, rosy-cheeked face, plump arms outstretched, as a voice said, 'Come here, Teddy, *bach*. Come and give your *mamgu* a kiss.'

He recalled vividly the smell of wonderful baking on her apron as she folded him into her embrace.

'Would you be surprised to hear that Mrs Jones didn't, in fact, have a granddaughter?' he continued. 'What can you tell me about the person who claimed to be hers?'

The woman looked bewildered.

'But Angie has been visiting her regularly. I'd often see

them sitting together in the vestibule, chatting away and laughing.'

'Do you not keep some sort of record of relatives? Would no one have thought it strange that Mrs Jones was being visited by someone claiming to be a granddaughter she didn't have?'

'We have a lot of residents,' she said defensively. 'We can't possibly check up on everyone who comes to visit. Sometimes the residents tell us a visitor is their daughter or granddaughter when they aren't really. A lot of them are very confused.'

'Tell me about when Mrs Jones was taken ill. How soon after the visit of this Angie did that happen?'

'I don't yet know all the details, I'm just catching up with everything myself.'

Again the defensive tone.

'There may be more detail on her file, or in the day book.'

She started pushing paperwork around her desk, clearly looking for something to help her answer Ted's questions.

'Yes, here it is. Mrs Jones went to her room to lie down just after Angie left and said she didn't want any tea as she'd had cake. Later that evening she started being violently sick and had diarrhoea.'

'What time was a doctor called?' Ted interrupted.

'Later on,' came the evasive reply. 'The night carers would have seen to her on their rounds then, when she wasn't showing any signs of improvement, they called out Dr Patel. It seems Mrs Jones deteriorated rapidly and her heart failed, from what the doctor said.'

'What can you tell me about this Angie? Do you have any information on her? Can you give me a description of her?'

'Ordinary,' came the unhelpful reply. 'Mid to late thirties, perhaps. Maybe a little older. Brown hair. Not very tall. Nothing striking that sticks in my mind. I know she told one of the carers she didn't get on with her own mother so didn't visit at the same time as her. She said she didn't want to bump into her.'

'Do you know her surname?'

'I assume it was Jones, like her grandmother and her mother.'

Ted noted that his mother had obviously gone back to her maiden name after she'd left his father.

'One more thing, Mrs Rawlings. Do all visitors have to sign the book in the hallway? If so, can you come with me and show me where this Angie signed herself in, as that should surely tell us her surname.'

With barely concealed impatience, she went with Ted to the entrance hall and looked at the book, skimming through the signatures for the previous day. Each visitor was meant to note not only their name but that of the person they'd come to visit. She clearly didn't find the name she was looking for, so she started to turn back the pages, scanning each in turn, her finger tracing down the list.

After she had gone back several weeks, she looked at Ted in confusion.

'I don't understand,' she said. 'I can't see anyone who could have been this Angie signed in to visit Mrs Jones. Her only visitor recorded seems to have been her daughter, Annie Jones, who came most mornings.'

She took one more defensive shot as she said, 'But then you don't seem to have signed yourself in either, Inspector.'

# Chapter Three

Ted's partner Trevor was in the kitchen cooking when he got home. The smells wafting from the saucepan were delicious and Ted realised he was ravenously hungry. He hadn't felt in the mood to eat at lunch time, with the worry of how the case was going, and hadn't had time for anything since.

Trev returned Ted's kiss then put a spoon of sauce in front of him and said, 'Taste that, it's a new recipe.'

Ted did as he was told and rolled his eyes in delight.

'That is fantastic,' he said. 'Is that what we're having for supper?'

Trev laughed.

'Well, I didn't make it for the cats,' he said, as six purring felines wound their way round both men's legs, totally ignoring their newly-filled feed bowls. 'So tell me, how was your day?'

Ted leaned against the sink so he could watch his partner at work. Trev loved to cook and was brilliant at it. Ted's repertoire didn't rise much above a chilli con carne or the occasional Thai green curry. The two were just back from a rare fortnight's holiday in the Italian Apennines and Trev was darkly tanned and finely toned from the many miles they'd walked.

'Strange,' Ted replied, frowning slightly as he recalled the morning visit. 'My mother turned up, out of the blue, to tell me my gran had died and that she thinks she may have been poisoned.'

Trev put down his spoon and folded his arms round Ted,

hugging him protectively close.

'Oh, that's awful! I'm so sorry. How did it make you feel, seeing your mother again after all this time?'

Ted hesitated. He had always found it hard to talk about his feelings, even with Trev, unless they were out walking in the Peaks or mountains where he felt more relaxed. He had recently agreed to start counselling to deal with demons from his past, but was only just learning how to express emotions in the close confines of a room.

'Confused,' he said eventually. 'I wanted to hate her. I've hated her since she walked out. But she looked older than she should and a bit vulnerable, as if life has treated her badly. And she denied going off with another man, which is what my dad always told me she did.'

'Why does she think it was a poisoning?' Trev asked over his shoulder, going back to stirring the sauce.

Ted outlined everything his mother had told him, what he had found out so far and how Bizzie Nelson had helped him arrange a post-mortem.

'You started the enquiry yourself? On a relative?' Trev asked, surprised. 'What's the Ice Queen going to say about that?'

'I haven't told her anything about it yet,' Ted admitted. 'I thought I'd wait for the PM report before I mentioned it.'

After years of working with the easy-going DCI Jim Baker, his replacement had proved difficult for Ted to get used to. After a shaky start, they'd settled down to a level of mutual respect, though not yet the trust and ease he had known with Jim.

Ted was of short stature. The towering Ice Queen, with her dazzlingly white impeccable uniform shirt and implacable demeanour, usually made him feel awkward and rather stupid. She was always assuring him that she was not his enemy and had proved it on a recent difficult case, but he still felt the need to tread carefully around her.

She had proved surprisingly supportive over the collapsed case that day, though, stressing repeatedly that the unfortunate outcome was no reflection on him or his team. Even so, he knew he would have to be careful how far he took this current enquiry before briefing her on it, and particularly mentioning his personal involvement.

'Dinner is nearly ready,' Trev told him, 'if you want to get changed before we eat.'

He was already freshly showered, dressed in a pink polo shirt, crops and leather sandals, obviously still in a holiday mood.

'I will do, but first tell me how your day was.'

Ted loved to ask, just to watch Trev's eyes light up with real passion when he talked about the motorbikes he spent his days fixing and playing with.

'Brilliant!' Trev replied, with his customary enthusiasm. 'Geoff has a list of some shows and exhibitions he wants to go to in Europe. He wants me to go with him, to translate. Would you be okay with that?'

'Of course.' Ted said immediately. 'You'd love it, go for it. Don't worry about me and the cats. We'll be fine. I'll just be here alone, crying into my pillow, hugging one of your shirts for comfort …'

He broke off as Trev threw a damp tea-towel at him, which he deftly dodged. He then sprinted upstairs to change out of the hated suit and tie which the Ice Queen insisted he wore in preference to his preferred casual clothes.

He wondered, as he frequently did, with a passing glance in the mirror, why an attractive, vibrant, intelligent, younger man like Trev stayed with someone as dull and damaged as he considered himself to be. But their relationship had survived eleven years and, apart from a small wobble during a recent difficult case, they were still happily together.

Trev was just dishing up supper on the table outside the back door when Ted came lightly back down the stairs, also in crops and a polo. They were both keen to profit from the last of the late summer sunshine, and being outside was always Ted's preference. There was fresh pasta with the sauce Trev had made, with the last of the ham and Parmigiano Reggiano which they'd brought back from Italy.

'So, when do I get to meet the mother-in-law?' Trev asked smilingly, as they began to eat.

Ted immediately stopped eating, his face darkening, jawline tense.

'She gave up any right to be my mother when she walked out on me,' he said sharply. 'She's certainly not your mother-in-law.'

'Hey,' Trev reached across the table and put a gentle hand on Ted's arm. 'I was kidding. It was a light-hearted remark. I'm sorry if it upset you.'

Ted shook his head.

'No, I'm sorry,' he said more softly. 'It just touched a raw nerve. I shouldn't have snapped. But you know that she walked out on me when I was eight, Trev. Not long after my dad broke his back in the mine and was paralysed. What kind of a mother does that?'

'Perhaps you need to listen to her version of events?' Trev suggested diplomatically. 'If she says there was no other man, maybe you need her to tell you exactly why she went?'

Ted sighed.

'Can we just drop it for now, please? This meal's too good. I'd rather just enjoy it and forget about her for this evening.'

Trev had not yet finished. His concern for Ted was driving him on.

'Will you promise me something, then I'll drop it?' he asked, looking directly into Ted's eyes.

He knew the power his blue eyes had over his partner, who found it hard to resist their effect. Ted tried to look away, to concentrate on his food, but it was useless. Trev had him, and he knew it.

'All right, what is it?' he said resignedly.

'Will you talk to your counsellor about all of this, whatever happens?' Trev asked him, still holding his gaze. 'Whether your gran's death was sad but natural causes, or something more sinister. Please? Because I'm worried how this is going to affect you.

'If someone killed your gran, your mother is going to need you, as a son, not just as a copper. Then, if you agree to let her tell you her version of events, it may make you see your father in a totally different light, perhaps not a very good one. And I know how much you idolised your dad.'

# Chapter Four

Professor Nelson had been true to her word in doing an early post-mortem examination on Ted's grandmother, and getting the toxicology results back in record time.

Ted had attended the PM, never his favourite activity, made all the harder by the fact that the woman on the table was his grandmother. He could hardly get over the change in her appearance in the thirty or so years since he had last seen her.

In his memory she was plump and jolly, apple-cheeked and always smiling. The body on the steel table seemed to have wasted away to skin and bone, although it appeared that she'd still been straight-backed. He remembered his mother saying how much she had started to roam and wondered if her constant activity was a factor in her weight loss.

He could see no obvious signs of injury or illness, other than being much thinner than when he had known her, his observations confirmed by Bizzie Nelson as she began her examination.

Ted had shared his customary bag of Fisherman's Friend menthol lozenges with her before she started. They were his way of coping with the smells and sights that went with his job. He was never without a packet in one of his pockets, never knowing when the next body might confront him.

Ted bitterly regretted not having kept in touch with his grandmother. He'd always liked her and she had been his only surviving grandparent. But when his mother walked out, he lost all contact and his father refused to have anything to do with her. He supposed it was only natural that she would take the side of her daughter when his parents split up.

The Professor kept up a running commentary for the tape as she worked. Ted had to look away for some of it. It felt obscene somehow, to be standing looking at the naked body of an elderly relative. He contented himself with listening to Bizzie's voice and looking at various instruments within the autopsy suite. He preferred not to think about the purpose of some of them.

'Right, that's me done for now,' Professor Nelson said finally. 'There's not a lot left in the way of stomach contents but I will send what there is, plus bloods, of course, for toxicology testing. I'll let you have the results as soon as I possibly can. I'm sorry for your loss, Edwin, even if you hadn't seen her for some time.'

He was surprised and pleased by how soon she got back to him about the toxicology tests. The call came early one morning, as the Professor always seemed to start work at the crack of dawn. As usual, there was no preamble, no time wasted on salutations. She just launched in, almost mid-sentence.

'You certainly have got an interesting one on your hands here, Edwin. I almost didn't believe the results, it's so unusual. This was definitely a poisoning and the toxins used are really a rare finding. There were traces of both aconitine and aconite, from the garden plant *aconitum napellus*, sometimes called monkshood or dog's bane.

'The effects are rapid and often lethal. The victim suffers violent vomiting and diarrhoea and it can quickly lead to heart failure, especially in someone elderly or frail. This lady would have been very ill indeed in the time before her death ...'

She stopped suddenly and there was an awkward pause.

'Edwin, I am so sorry, how dreadfully insensitive of me. In my enthusiasm for a rare toxin, I completely forgot this poor lady was your grandmother. I do apologise for my lack of sensitivity.'

'It's fine, really,' Ted said. Tact and diplomacy were not qualities he associated with the brusque and efficient, though decidedly eccentric, pathologist. 'So is it possible that this could have been accidental? My mother said my grandmother wandered a lot, because of her dementia. Security at the home seems a little haphazard. Could she have gone out into the garden and eaten some?'

'Extremely unlikely,' came the prompt response. 'It has a very bitter taste, so accidental poisoning is most uncommon, although not unheard of. I must also say, though, that sometimes people suffering from some types of dementia tend to lose their sense of taste and smell. But I would still say accidental ingestion would be unlikely. There have been cases of people being affected by handling it, but there are no lesions on her skin, which would have made that a more likely scenario.'

Ted was thinking about the mystery visitor, Angie, the bearer of the cake which his grandmother had eaten shortly before her death.

'What if it was in something very palatable, like a cake, or something sweet?' he asked.

'Possible,' came the reply. 'Especially if the victim was a bit of a cake eater.'

'She loved to bake,' Ted said fondly. 'There was always something baking away in the oven whenever I visited. If someone had come to see her, bringing cake, I'm sure she would have eaten it. I know dementia changes people, I understand that, but she was always kind enough not to say anything if she was eating something she didn't really like the taste of.'

'I'll be sending my full report to the coroner. My conclusions are that this was very unlikely to involve an accident. I would say that someone cynically and deliberately poisoned your poor grandmother,' she said. 'Once again, I'm sorry for your loss, and I apologise once more for my thoughtlessness.'

'Honestly, think nothing of it,' Ted told her. 'Now, I promised you a meal, at the very least, in thanks for all your kind help with this case. What do you like to eat? There's a fair chance Trev can cook anything you fancy.'

'Oh, I'm very easy to feed, a proper trencherman,' she said. 'The only thing I don't like, I think, is tripe. Oh, and summer pudding, which has always seemed to me to be a waste of even the most stale of bread.'

Ted couldn't help but laugh. 'All right, no tripe or summer pudding,' he promised. 'Now, when are you free? What about this weekend?'

'That would be lovely. I have nothing on.'

From the way she said it, Ted suspected she did not exactly have a full social calendar.

'If you have a Significant Other, you're very welcome to bring them along,' Ted said tactfully, having no clue as to the Professor's domestic circumstances.

'My only partner is my old Staffie, Monty, and his farts are so noxious I wouldn't wish him on my worst enemy,' she told him.

'Shall we say Sunday lunch? If you'd like to have a glass or two of wine, I'll happily collect you and run you back home so you don't have to drive. I never drink.'

'That's far too much trouble for you,' she said immediately. 'I'll get a taxi both ways.'

'Not at all,' Ted said, 'I wouldn't dream of it. Come in a taxi if you prefer, but I'll certainly run you home. It's the least I can do after you've gone to so much trouble for me.'

There was a pause then the Professor said, 'Could I ask you a small favour? It's going to sound very strange.'

'Go on,' Ted said, intrigued.

'Well, I know your partner has a motorcycle, and I assume you also know how to drive it,' she said hesitantly. 'It's just that,

ER

I've never been on one, and it's on my … what do they call it these days … my bucket list? Things to do before I die? Could you possibly run me home on that?'

Ted suppressed a grin. He had a fleeting mental image of the short and rather stout Professor Nelson, enveloped in a billowing cloak, astride the bike, looking like Hagrid on his way to Hogwarts.

'Consider it done,' he said.

When he rang off, he headed into the main office to find his team for the usual briefing with which they always liked to start the day. It was time to open an enquiry into what was now officially a suspicious death, at the least.

The team members were all in on time. It was rare for any of them to be late, out of respect for their boss. Ted was fair and easy-going but still managed to run a tight ship, leading by example. It was out of their respect for him that the team members chose to call him either boss or sir, rather than being on first name terms, which often happened with other teams.

'Right, listen up,' he said, calling them to order. 'We have a suspicious death on our hands. A poisoning, and a very unusual one at that.'

He briefly outlined all that he knew to date, without yet mentioning his relationship to the victim. As he spoke, he was writing keywords on the white board which would help them coordinate the new case.

'So, at the moment, we have nothing much to go on. No motive, no real suspect, just someone unidentified who may have been one of the last people to see the victim alive. Where do we start? Steve?'

He looked at his young TDC, always keen to encourage him and give him the chance to voice an opinion.

'Immediate family, sir,' he said. 'Statistically the most likely suspect in a murder.'

'Very good,' Ted nodded. 'Now, here's the complicated part. The victim was my grandmother. Her only surviving family

24

members are my mother, and me. So clearly, someone else needs to start this enquiry, and I'd like you to do that, Mike,' he said to his sergeant.

'Luckily, I have a good alibi, as I was here at the time when she was probably poisoned. But Mike, I'd like you and Sal to go and interview my mother first of all. I'll give you her contact details. I should just say at this stage that I haven't seen my mother or my grandmother for about thirty years.

'So, I'm not the poisoner, and I'm hoping my mother isn't, either. Are there any other theories? Where else should we be looking for suspects, until we can trace who this Angie is and either eliminate or arrest her?'

'What about the doctor, boss?' Mike Hallam asked. 'An overworked GP with too many old grunters ...' he broke off abruptly. 'Sorry, boss, no disrespect intended. Too many old people on his hands, wanting to get rid of some of them?'

'Another Dr Shipman, you mean?' Ted asked. 'I sincerely hope not, not on our patch. But it's worth checking. Put someone on that, please. Anything else?'

'One of the carers, boss?' DC Dennis 'Virgil' Tibbs suggested. 'I'm sure your granny was a lovely old lady, but maybe if one of the carers thought she was a bit of a nuisance...?'

'She might well have been,' Ted conceded. 'I haven't seen her for a long time, and she did have dementia. She might not have been very nice at all lately.'

'Personal revenge against you for something you've done?' DS Hallam suggested.

Ted shrugged.

'Even I didn't know where my grandmother was.'

'That wouldn't stop some of the people you've dealt with lately from finding her if they wanted to, boss,' Mike said. 'Something we can look at if we draw a blank on everything else.'

'Boss, should we be checking to see if there have been any

other similar deaths in the area recently?' It was the turn of DC Abisali 'Sal' Ahmed to voice his thoughts. 'I imagine that it's not that out of the ordinary for old people to die in homes. Probably not at all unusual for a virus to be suspected in a sudden death. But maybe there have been other isolated cases, where no one else was affected.'

'Yes, I was coming to that,' Ted said. 'Steve, that's a job for you. Pull off a list of all the care homes in our area. I'm not sure what else they're called. Nursing homes, perhaps? Give it to Maurice and you and he work together to see if any of the others have experienced anything  similar. As Sal said, we're looking particularly for any cases where only one resident was affected, where it may have appeared to be nothing more than a virus.

'Once we have that information, we need to find out if any other home had a visitor who looked anything like this Angie person. It goes without saying that we also need to find her, sooner rather than later.'

'Money's a common enough motive, boss,' DC Rob O'Connell began.

'I doubt if my grandmother had any,' Ted interrupted.

'Yes, but I understand it costs a fortune to keep old people in a home. It starts to be quite a burden on family members who are having to pay,' Rob continued.

'Good point,' Ted nodded. 'Mike, that's one for you to check out when you interview my mother. Who pays the care home fees? Are there any arrears? Check too, while you're at it, whether the house is still in my grandmother's name. I know they're often sold to pay elderly care fees.

'There's just one more thing. I haven't yet mentioned this case to Superintendent Caldwell, and certainly not yet my personal connection to the victim.'

Six pairs of eyes looked at him, eyebrows raised. As ever, it was Maurice Brown who spoke first.

'Bloody hell, boss, you like to live dangerously.'

Ted smiled, in spite of himself. 'I just didn't want to take it any further until I had the tox results back from the Professor. I didn't expect anything like this. I really did think it would be natural causes. I can't discuss it with the Super today, she's out at a conference all day, not back in until tomorrow. So just for now, please keep that information under your hats. That is, if you still want to keep me as your boss and not see me thrown to the wolves or sidelined to an admin post.'

He knew that he could trust every one of his team members implicitly. They, in turn, all knew the unwritten rule. The boss was there to watch their backs and stop any flak from higher up heading their way. He could, and would, protect them physically as well if he needed to. In exchange, they all thought the world of him and would do anything he asked of them.

# Chapter Five

Both Ted and the Ice Queen were always in early every morning. He found her in her office first thing the following day, despite her long conference the day before. He wondered again how she managed to look so impeccable always. He smothered a grin at the mental image of the Ice Queen's traffic inspector husband ironing shirts for his wife and senior officer.

'Come in, Inspector, take a seat,' she said pleasantly enough, although she looked tired.

'Thank you, ma'am,' Ted said, always at pains to be formal and polite with his boss. 'How was your conference?'

To his surprise, the Ice Queen said, 'Oh dear,' and looked at him searchingly. 'As I can't imagine you being remotely interested in divisional budgetary planning matters, I have to conclude you are either being polite or you have something to tell me which you think I'm not going to like. So which is it?'

This time Ted laughed aloud and relaxed slightly as he sat down.

'You have my measure, ma'am,' he said.

He outlined the facts so far on his grandmother's death, not attempting to hide his involvement to date, but then said, 'As soon as it was confirmed as a suspicious death and not just natural causes, I handed the enquiry over to DS Hallam. He's on his way now, with DC Ahmed, to interview my mother. I have already provided an alibi for myself.'

'I see,' she said in a measured tone, from which Ted couldn't deduce whether or not she was disapproving. 'Well, as ever, keep me posted and please ensure you stay out of the enquiry so as not to compromise it. Although of course, I don't need to remind you of that.

'Do you have any indications at this stage that this is anything other than a one-off?' she asked, then hastily added, 'Not that I am in any way belittling the loss of your grandmother. And please accept my condolences on her passing.'

'Thank you. Actually, we lost touch more than thirty years ago, when my mother left home,' Ted told her. 'At this stage no, nothing, although Mike Hallam has already raised the spectre of another Harold Shipman.'

The Ice Queen appeared to shudder.

'I do hope not, and certainly not on our patch. Please keep me informed of any developments at all, as and when they happen.'

Dropping the 'ma'am' and 'Inspector' from their conversations, as they were doing now, was about as informal as it ever got between them, certainly in the work place.

'One thing I know I don't need to remind you about is the fact that we are still a person down on the team. If this does turn out to be more than a single case, we'll certainly need another pair of hands ...'

The Super interrupted him imperiously.

'As you say, you don't need to remind me of that and I am working on it. Anything else at this stage?'

'Nothing else. I'll leave you to the delights of your budgetary planning,' Ted smiled and left the office.

Back in the main office, Maurice was looking pleased with himself.

'Got another possible, boss,' he told Ted as soon as he walked in. 'Recent, only a couple of days ago. An old lady, same symptoms, lots of vomiting, then heart failure.'

'Right, we need to go and get some more details. Whereabouts is it?'

'It's out towards Mellor, boss, I've got the address.' Maurice hesitated then continued, 'Er, shouldn't we wait for the sarge? I thought he was leading on this one, because you're personally involved?'

'I have no involvement in this latest enquiry, as far as I know, and we aren't even sure yet if they are linked,' Ted told him. 'Time is important in this. If there needs to be a PM, it needs to be carried out as soon as possible.'

'But boss, haven't you already told the Ice Queen you'll stay out of it …' Maurice protested.

'I've reminded you before, it's Superintendent Caldwell to you, Constable, or the Super at the very least. Don't let me have to remind you again,' Ted said sternly.

'Right, boss,' Maurice grinned, but he might just as well have said 'yeah, whatever' for all the sincerity in his tone. 'Just trying to watch your back for you, like you do for us. We'd better go, then. Your car or mine? And before you say anything, since I've got Steve as a lodger, mine is pristine and a smoke-free zone.'

Ted was surprised but pleased to hear it, so he opted for Maurice's car. True to his word, it was cleaner than Ted had ever seen it. Steve Ellis had moved in as Maurice's lodger after he was badly injured working on a case. The arrangement seemed to suit them both well and he was clearly helping Maurice deal with his smoking addiction and the compulsive eating which affected him whenever he tried to quit.

This time the care home they arrived at was much smaller than Snowdon Lodge, where Ted's grandmother had died. It looked like a large house, clearly not purpose-built as a care home. The front area was surfaced with tarmac for parking but the flower borders all around it were a riot of colourful flowers. Ted mused that it must have made a nicer view for residents looking out of the windows here than that at Snowdon Lodge.

There was only a single door inside an open porch. A sign gave the name as The Poppies, illustrated by bright, vibrant paintings of the eponymous flowers. As Ted and Maurice approached, ready to ring the bell, the door opened and an immaculately dressed elderly woman came out, a large handbag over her arm. The two men instinctively stepped aside as she swept on her regal way, heading for the roadside, where a bus had just pulled up.

Hard on her heels was a young man, wearing a pale blue tunic with a name badge pinned to it which said 'Stacy'. Ted noticed that he was wearing eye liner and had long hair pulled back into a pony tail. He excused himself as he hurried past them, calling out, 'Elizabeth! Elizabeth! Hang on a minute.'

He just managed to intercept her as she was about to board the bus. Ted and Maurice heard him apologising to the driver as he steered the woman skilfully back towards the front door.

'Come on now, put your leg in bed and let's go and get you a coffee,' he smiled at her, holding out a crooked arm which she obediently slipped her hand through and went with him, seemingly meekly.

'If you gentlemen would like to follow me and just wait a couple of ticks till I get Elizabeth settled, you will have my undivided attention,' he told the two men, who followed him in through the front door.

'Boss, is he ...' Maurice began as the young man disappeared.

'Yes, Maurice, he certainly looks like one of the care staff to me,' Ted said ironically.

Stacy was soon back with them, apologising for the delay.

'Sorry about that. Elizabeth is a little tinker. She's learned how to open the front door so she's always going walkabout. We'll have to change the lock again. What can I do for you gentlemen?'

'I'm Detective Inspector Darling, this is Detective Constable Brown,' Ted told him, as they both held up their warrant cards. 'We were hoping to speak to the manager.'

'Ah, bit tricky just at the moment, I'm afraid. She's in a

meeting with someone, not to be disturbed unless really urgent. Is it anything I can help you with?'

'DC Brown spoke to her earlier today about the recent death of one of your residents,' Ted began, then looked at Maurice to supply the name of the resident.

'A Mrs Margaret Tyler,' Maurice said. 'Can you tell us anything about it?'

'Oh yes, happy to help. Maureen said you might be coming in at some point and that if you did, I was to help you with your enquiries,' Stacy replied. 'That's what they say, isn't it? Helping the police with their enquiries? Would you mind if we just sit here in the lobby, so I can keep an eye on the door in case Elizabeth makes a break for it again? She really is a monkey if we don't watch her all the time.'

He indicated a sofa and an armchair at one side of the tastefully decorated vestibule. Ted noticed that everywhere smelled clean and fresh, so unlike the other home. One or two residents were dozing peacefully in chairs and there were no unpleasant smells hovering about them either.

Ted was feeling mischievous so he quickly took the armchair, leaving Maurice to lower his bulk into the small space next to Stacy. He knew Maurice was fine with him and Trev, but he would doubtless feel uncomfortable in such close proximity to someone he had obviously decided must be gay since he used kohl pencil around his eyes and had long hair in blonde dreadlocks. He nodded to Maurice to lead the questioning, having promised to take a back seat.

'What can you tell us about Mrs Tyler, please?' Maurice asked, notebook and pen at the ready.

'Our Maggie? Well, she was certainly one of a kind,' Stacy began. 'She could moan for Britain, that's for sure. But the poor old thing took very ill a couple of days ago. Mostly violent sickness and diarrhoea. We called the doctor but her heart just gave out and she passed away before he arrived.'

'Which doctor do you use here?' Ted asked and Maurice

looked daggers at him for not keeping quiet.

'It was Dr Patel who came that evening. He said it was probably a virus and was happy to sign the death certificate as that being the cause. He told us to keep a close eye on the other residents, but so far no one else has come down with anything similar. Thank goodness.'

'Would you know if Mrs Tyler had had any visitors on the day she died?' Maurice asked.

'Her family never came to see her. Well, only once in a blue moon. She did sometimes get a visit from a former neighbour of hers. A woman called Angela. In fact, I'm pretty sure she was in that day.'

'Can you describe this Angela for me, please?' Maurice asked.

'Bright, bubbly, curly blonde hair, big glasses with different coloured frames to match her various outfits. Often bright pink. Late thirties, early forties perhaps? Always very friendly and cheerful. Though how she stayed that way talking to our Maggie, I have no idea.'

'Are you saying Mrs Tyler was not very popular?' Maurice pursued.

Stacy laughed.

'Well, let me just say that if it turned out that somebody had bumped her off, it would take me all day to list the possible suspects.' Then his hand flew up to his face and he looked horrified as he continued, 'Oh, good gracious. I am so stupid. That's why you're here, isn't it? Two detectives, asking about her death. You think someone may have killed her, is that it?'

'We're just making initial enquiries at the moment,' Maurice told him. 'But perhaps you could tell us how you felt about her?'

Stacy looked from one to the other. He clearly saw something more sympathetic or approachable in Ted's face as he concentrated his attention on him as he spoke. '

I know one should never speak ill of the dead, but dear

Maggie was a thoroughly disagreeable and unpleasant woman and I'm sure everyone would tell you the same thing.

'Always complaining and criticising. She never had a kind word for or about anyone. And constantly putting on airs and graces. I can honestly say none of us here will miss her. She was utterly thankless to look after. I'm sorry if I'm speaking out of turn but she really was. It's why her family hardly ever came near. They said she'd been like that all her life, even before the dementia.'

Ted couldn't stay quiet. He asked, 'Yet this neighbour, this Angela, chose to come and visit her? How did she put up with her?'

'She was an absolute saint,' Stacy replied. 'She just used to carry on smiling and ignore all Maggie's vitriolic rantings. I don't know how she did it.'

'Did she ever bring in cakes or other treats for Mrs Tyler?' Ted asked, ignoring the black looks Maurice was throwing at him.

'Oh yes, definitely,' Stacy replied. 'She'd always have like a little picnic for her. Cakes, biscuits, a flask of tea. In fact, they were sitting here on this very sofa sharing a picnic just a short time before Maggie took ill and died.'

Maurice shifted uncomfortably in his seat at the thought. He and Ted exchanged knowing glances, then Ted spoke again.

'When she's free, could you please inform the manager that we will be treating Mrs Tyler's death as suspicious. Arrangements will be made to carry out a post-mortem examination without delay. Thank you for your time and all your help.'

As they headed back to the car, Ted pulled out his mobile to make a call.

'Morning, sir, it's DI Darling. We have another suspicious death on our hands and I'd like you to authorise a post-mortem, please,' he said, before giving the details to the senior coroner.

Maurice Brown was slightly older than Ted and had known

and served with him for some time. He was always the one who pushed the boundaries and took liberties. Occasionally Ted had to jump on him, but generally speaking their relationship was good.

'Boss,' he said as he pulled out of the driveway into the main road. 'You were supposed to keep it zipped. If you can't stay out of this like you promised, at least until we've eliminated your mum from our enquiries, I'm going to have to report you to Her Royal Highness the Ice Queen.'

Ted had to laugh.

'Yes, Maurice,' he said meekly.

# Chapter Six

Ted waited until the end of the day, when everyone was briefly back in the main office, to fill the team in on his visit to the second care home with Maurice. As he spoke, he wrote the name of the latest potential victim, Maggie Tyler, on the white board.

'I've phoned the coroner to ask for a PM. It is just possible that it's all coincidence and the two deaths are unrelated, but I think that's unlikely. Everything is similar, including the visits from a mysterious woman called Angela,' he told them. 'So, where are we up to with the first death?'

'Annie Jones has a watertight alibi, which we've checked out, for the time covering the illness and death of her mother, Gwen Jones,' Mike Hallam said, deliberately not referring to them as Ted's mother and grandmother. 'She seems genuinely mystified by the whole thing and she has no idea who this person Angie is. She's certainly not a known relative'

Ted joined in at this point, not wishing to step on the DS's toes but anxious to make suggestions as they occurred to him.

'I think what we need to do now, without spreading alarm, is to ask all the homes within our area to report any further unexpected deaths, especially when they're sudden. That's a simple ring-round job, for whenever anyone has a spare moment.

'Steve, can you be in charge of coordinating the list, make sure all the homes know the information we're looking for,' he said. 'We also need them to look again at their records for any past deaths that they may just have dismissed as natural causes.'

'Should we ask the hospitals too, boss, on our patch and close to?' Rob O'Connell asked. 'They must get a lot of old people through their doors. Should we be checking if any of them have died suddenly and unexpectedly?'

'Good thinking, worth a try. Steve ...'

'Printing the list now, sir, I had the same idea,' Steve told him.

'Next up, we need to get round all the homes, and the hospitals if necessary, to ask about an Angie or an Angela,' Ted continued. 'The two descriptions we have of her are completely different. Is she the same person who changes her appearance? Or two people with similar names? In either case, where is she, or where are they?'

'That's going to be a lot of leg-work, boss. Any signs of another team member?' Mike asked.

'I have reminded the Super yet again,' Ted told him. 'She says she's on it. In the meantime, I'll talk to Inspector Turner, see if he can lend us some Uniform officers to give us a bit of a hand. Anything else?'

No one had anything to add, so there was a general gathering of belongings and most of the team began heading for the door. Ted went back to his own office to collect a few things. Mike followed him.

'Can I have a word, boss?' he asked in a measured tone.

'Of course. Have a seat, Mike,' Ted replied, sitting down himself.

'Do you think I'm not up to handling this case?' Mike asked bluntly.

'Of course I don't,' Ted assured him. 'Is this because I went to the home today instead of waiting for you to finish with my mother?'

Mike nodded.

'That, and more or less taking over just now. You said you

were stepping back from it because of your family involvement and you really need to, if you don't mind me saying so. At least until we know a bit more about what's going on.'

Ted leaned back in his chair and laughed.

'I've already been thoroughly told off by Maurice and I consider myself duly reprimanded once more. You're right, of course, Mike, and I apologise. I just thought it was important to act quickly, before our second victim was buried or cremated and we lost the chance for detailed analysis.

'Do you want to tell me how it went with my mother?'

It was Mike's turn to laugh. 'Sal and I loved all your baby pictures, boss. Or should I call you Teddy?'

He knew the DI could take a joke, although Ted pretended to be angry.

'If you start calling me that at work, I might just have to remind you that I hold black belts in four martial arts.'

'Seriously, though, boss, even without the alibi, there's no way I would suspect your mother of any involvement. It's really knocked her for six to hear that she was right and someone seems to have done this to her mother deliberately.'

'I'd better go and call on her myself tomorrow morning, now she's no longer a suspect,' Ted told him. 'Just to make sure she's all right, see if she needs help with the funeral or whatever. I'll be in a bit later than usual, so brief the team and get them started, please. Thanks, Mike, and sorry if you thought I was overstepping the mark we agreed on. It won't happen again.'

When Ted stopped his Renault outside his grandmother's house the following morning, he looked nostalgically at the tiny mid-terrace cottage, with its pocket handkerchief-sized front garden. It was smaller than he remembered from boyhood visits, but there was still a climbing rose around the rickety, rustic porch. He didn't know if it was the same one.

His mother had said she worked afternoons so he hoped to find her at home, as Mike and Sal had done the previous day. He rapped the brass knocker, worn smooth by the touch of many hands over the years. He remembered being too small to reach it, either his mum or his dad having to lift him up to it, as he always wanted to be the one who knocked.

His mother's expression was of surprised delight when she opened the door to him.

'Teddy! You came. Come on in. I was just putting the kettle on. Do you want a cup of tea?'

Ted knew it would be strong tea, like treacle, which he'd long since given up in favour of his preferred green tea. He nodded acceptance anyway and followed her in.

Inside, the cottage was dark and seemed minuscule to his adult eyes. He looked around, noting all the photographs of himself, just as Mike had mentioned. His gaze fell on one of him in a pram which looked far too big for one small baby boy.

His mother saw him looking at it and smiled fondly.

'You were such a bonny baby, with all that lovely strawberry blond hair. That's why I used to call you my little Teddy Bear.'

She must have sensed his discomfort as she swiftly changed the subject.

'I'll just make that brew. I know it's early, but would you like a piece of cake? It's only a *teisen lap* but I remember how much you used to love that, and I still use your gran's recipe.'

Again, the memories which immediately sprang to Ted's mind were so vivid he could almost taste the moist flat cake, baked on a plate, which his grandmother used to make whenever he visited.

His mother anxiously fussed around, bringing him tea and cake, offering milk and sugar, having no idea of his tastes as an adult. Ted tried hard to control the feelings of resentment which threatened to overwhelm him. Despite his usual strict self-control, he found that he could not.

'Why did you walk out on me?' he blurted.

'Oh, Teddy,' she said, and once again her eyes were full of tears. 'I never walked out on you. I never wanted to lose you. I just couldn't stay with your dad any longer, not the way he was.'

'It wasn't his fault he broke his back,' Ted said, through gritted teeth, feeling anger rising in him at her words. 'He needed you. I needed you.'

'Drink your tea, *bach*,' she told him, taking a mouthful of her own. 'And eat your cake. The officers who came yesterday wouldn't have any of it.'

In spite of the circumstances, Ted almost laughed. His mother was clearly too naïve to realise that police officers coming to interview a possible murder suspect in a poisoning case were highly unlikely to accept any food from them.

He took a bite of the cake. It was just as he remembered, fruity and delicious. Its sticky, sweet familiarity helped to calm his mood as he savoured each mouthful.

'This is very hard for me to talk about,' his mother began. 'But you have a right to know the truth. Your dad was always such a lovely man, kind, thoughtful, intelligent. But after the accident he changed completely. He couldn't … he wasn't …'

She was struggling to express herself, then said in a rush, 'He wasn't a proper man any more. We couldn't … things weren't like they had been. He wanted me to do things. Things I wasn't happy with. And when I refused, he started to hit me.'

Ted put down his plate of cake, suddenly incapable of eating any more. It was the last thing in the world he had expected to hear.

She saw his stunned expression and continued, 'We kept it from you, of course. He never left any marks. Not where they could be seen, that is. But they were there, all right. Bad ones. He hated himself afterwards, ashamed of what he'd done. So he started to drink. Then things got worse. He just got more and more violent towards me. It was the frustration, you see.'

'So you left a little boy alone with a violent man? A drinker?' Ted asked, horrified by what he was hearing.

'Oh, Teddy, I knew he would never harm one hair of your head,' she said. 'He worshipped the ground you walked on, especially as we could never have any more children. He would never, ever have been violent to you, or harmed you in any way.

'Do you remember when he used to take you fishing? Up at Roman Lakes? You would sit there for hours, freezing to death, never catching anything. Joe used to suck those little menthol sweets he liked.'

Wordlessly, Ted reached into a pocket and pulled out his own packet of Fisherman's Friend. It brought tears to his mother's eyes again.

'Couldn't you have got help for him? Or for you?' Ted asked.

She shook her head. 'Back in them days no one talked much about such things. I told my mam, when I asked if I could come back here to live, but that was all.'

'Didn't you worry that the extra strain of looking after me on his own might just tip him over the edge? There was only him and me after you walked out. Just that carer that used to come during the day to see to him.'

'Oh, she saw to him, all right,' his mother spat bitterly. 'She saw to his every need, gave him the things I couldn't.

Ted was staggered by what he was hearing. He felt his world unravelling around him. He'd always been told that his mother had left with another man. It was the reason why he'd never attempted to trace her.

'All right, if you had to leave Dad, I can understand that, after what you've just told me. But what about me? Why didn't you keep in touch with me? Send a letter or a card at least, even if you couldn't visit?' Ted asked, hoping he didn't sound too pathetic.

There were tears running down his mother's face now. She

41

L. M. KRIER

made no attempt to wipe them away. The silence thickened between them as she struggled to find the right words. It was some time before she could speak.

'When you never replied to any of my letters, I thought you wanted nothing more to do with me. You never even sent a thank you for the presents I sent for your birthdays and for Christmas. And you were always such a good little boy, always had all your thank you letters written and in the post by Boxing Day.'

It was Ted's turn to find difficulty in speaking. He looked away, fighting a lump in his throat, as the full extent of his father's betrayal hit him. Not only had he lied about her reasons for leaving, it seemed he had also kept her letters from him. He had grown up hating his mother, without knowing the real reasons behind his parents' break-up.

'I never got them,' he said eventually, in a hollow voice. 'None of them. All these years, I thought you'd gone off with another man and never given me a second thought.'

Gently, his mother reached out a hand and took hold on one of his. She gave it a little squeeze. After a moment, Ted squeezed hers in return.

'Never mind,' she said briskly, drying her tears with her other hand. 'We're back in contact now. Tell me a little bit about yourself. I've read everything that's ever been in the paper about your career, but I don't know anything about you, your personal life. Are you married? Do you have children?'

'I have a partner. No children. We have cats.'

Ted wasn't sure why he was evasive about Trev. He was comfortable with his sexuality, proud of his long-standing partnership. For some reason, he felt unable to tell his mother anything personal about himself. Not yet, at least.

'I'd love to meet her some time, if that would be all right?' she said. 'You always did love cats. Do you remember Snowy, that we had when you were a little boy? And your gran's cat, Puss *Fach*?'

Ted looked at the hearth rug, almost expecting to see his grandmother's small tabby stretched out in front of the fire, as it always seemed to be whenever he visited.

'Look, I have to get to work now, but here's my card. Let me know if I can help you with gran's funeral, or with anything else,' he said, standing up and handing her a card with his contact details. 'Have you got a mobile phone?'

'I have to have one for work. I never remember the number,' she said apologetically.

'There's a way to get it to show you, but I'm no good at this sort of stuff,' Ted said. 'Give me your phone. I'll ring mine from it, then I'll have the number.'

Once he had done so, he headed for the door. He was struggling hard with his emotions. He could tell that his mother would like to hug or kiss him before he left, but he could not yet bear the thought of being close to her again, emotionally or physically, after all the lonely, bitter years.

As he was leaving, he steeled himself and took hold of one of her hands, saying quietly, 'I'll come for the funeral. And if you need anything, anything at all, you just have to call me.'

# Chapter Seven

Mike Hallam was the only one in the main office when Ted got back from visiting his mother. He looked up from the pile of paperwork on his desk when Ted came in.

'Just a possibility we may have yet another one, boss,' he said. 'Not recent though, this time. From about three months ago. The team are all out on the knock, trying to find out more about this Angela woman. I'm ringing round and I've just been speaking to a home down near Davenport where they had a death a while ago, which seems to fit the pattern.'

'Are you on your way there now?' Ted asked and when Mike nodded, he said, 'Mind if I tag along?'

Mike sighed and gave him what Ted would describe as an old-fashioned look.

'Boss, number one, shouldn't somebody stay at home and mind the shop? Number two, what happened to you backing off and leaving me to it?'

Ted grinned guiltily.

'Think of me as the Elephant's Child, Mike. I have an insatiable curiosity.'

Ted was not a great reader himself but his father had been. He remembered fondly long winter evenings by the fire with him, listening as he read aloud the Just So Stories.

They went in Mike's car. It was a short drive but long enough to catch up a bit and to kick some ideas around. When they parked and before they went into the home, Mike elicited from Ted a promise to observe and say nothing.

It was another former private house, converted into an elderly care home. Its sign called it Turnpike House. A large detached residence in a mock half-timbered style typical of the area. The off-road parking ran the length of the front of the building. The only greenery around comprised gloomy evergreen trees and some rhododendrons, which probably provided a splash of colour at the right time of year.

The door was opened by a young woman in a lilac tunic. Her name tag identified her as Sally. Mike produced his warrant card and asked to see the manager, saying his visit was expected. Ted meekly remained quiet, though his keen eyes were busy checking out the security arrangements.

'Oh yes, Mrs Williams said you would be coming,' Sally told them. 'Would you like to come with me?'

She led them through an entrance lobby in which an elderly man was sleeping in a wheelchair, and two blue-rinsed women were deep in conversation, ignoring their passing. They walked down a carpeted corridor, at the end of which Sally stepped aside to let the two men into a small office, where a woman was sitting at a desk, just finishing a phone call.

Sally mouthed to her, 'It's the police,' then backed out to return to her appointed tasks.

Mike identified himself again, not referring to Ted, who got the message, loud and clear. Observe, but don't interfere.

'Mrs Williams, you mentioned to me on the phone that about three months ago, one of your residents died very suddenly after a bout of violent vomiting. Could you tell me a little more about the circumstances?'

'Yes indeed. It was our Mrs Protheroe,' she began. 'Lilian Protheroe. She was one of our younger residents, comparatively speaking. Seventy-six, but sadly affected with dementia. Very confused, which was why she was with us. She was in quite good physical health, so we were rather surprised at how quickly she went downhill and died.

'She hadn't shown any signs of being ill, but late one

afternoon, she complained of feeling dizzy. Then she said she had a bad stomach ache and started vomiting violently. We called the doctor straight away but there was nothing he could do. There wasn't even time to get an ambulance. She started having difficulty breathing, then her heart just gave out.

'The doctor signed it off as natural causes. He thought it was probably some sort of a virus, although luckily no one else came down with it. It was very sad, we were all very fond of our Lilian. She was a real sweetie, apart from being confused all the time.'

Ted was itching to ask questions but he had promised to keep quiet. He knew he could safely leave it to Mike, who asked, ' Which doctor was that, Mrs Williams?'

'Dr Evans,' she replied promptly. 'He's our usual doctor. He's very good with our residents, so kind and understanding, and very patient.'

'Did Mrs Protheroe have any family, and did they visit her?' Mike asked.

'Not many,' she replied. 'I think some of them live abroad. There was a son who came occasionally, and I think a younger sister, but she wasn't local. I know it was a long journey for her so she came for celebrations like birthdays when she could.'

'Any other visitors?' Mike persisted.

'There was a woman who came to see her sometimes. I think she said she had been her carer at one time, when she was still living at home.'

'Do you know her name?'

'Ange,' she replied. 'I'm not sure that I ever knew her second name. Perhaps Morton, or something like that?'

'Can you describe her, please?'

'A real hippy type,' came the prompt response. 'Henna red hair to her shoulders. Hippy clothes. You know, swirly skirts, sometimes short ones over leggings. Not very tall. Dressed quite young for her age, I always thought. She must have been into her forties. She always smelled of that flower power stuff, you know, that patchouli oil.'

'Do you know where she lives? Do you keep any kind of record of the visitors who come to see your residents?'

She shook her head.

'No, we don't really. Not all the visitors. We just have details of family, next of kin, that sort of thing. It's just so nice when our residents get visitors at all. So often elderly people in long-term care get a bit forgotten about.'

Ted could see that Mike was getting ready to leave, so he shot him an apologetic look and asked, 'Mrs Williams, did this Ange ever bring food in for Mrs Protheroe? Cake, or anything like that?'

'Brownies,' she replied. 'She always brought chocolate brownies for her. She handed them round to the staff, too. I tried one but it was disgusting, tasted very bitter. We all had a good laugh about it, we wondered if she was putting something in them. You know, drugs of some sort. But then Lilian seemed to enjoy her company and she used to eat them happily enough with no ill effects.'

'Mrs Williams, do you happen to know if Mrs Protheroe was buried or cremated?' Mike asked her.

'Buried,' she said. 'The family were insistent on that, something about their beliefs.'

As they were walking back to the car, Ted started to apologise but Mike cut him short.

'No, it's just as well you did, boss. I almost forgot to ask her about cakes and stuff, pillock that I am.'

It wasn't like his DS to be forgetful, or to swear in front of him, so as they got into the car, Ted asked, 'Is everything all right, Mike? Nothing on your mind?'

'No, not really,' Mike said, as he started the car and turned it round. 'Well, yes, there is. The missus is coming home next week. The hospital say she's fine now, as long as she takes her medication. It's just, when someone's been ill like that, in that way ...' he hesitated before continuing, 'well, you rather

L. M. KRIER

wonder if it's all going to start up again.'

'Do you need any time off?' Ted asked. 'Is there anything I can do to help? You know my door is always open.'

'Thanks, boss, I really appreciate all you've done to help already. We're just taking one day at a time for the moment, see how things go. Now, back to the case. What do we need to do next?'

'Well, I need to talk to the coroner, and to the Super. It looks like we'll need an exhumation order and I hope to hell the press don't get hold of that. Last thing we need now is to start people panicking, thinking we have a mad serial killer on the loose, randomly poisoning pensioners.'

'But what if we have?' Mike said. 'I know you don't like coincidences any more than I do, but we must surely be past that stage now with this Angie, whoever she is.

'We've got a different doctor this time, so she's the only common denominator left, isn't she? But how do we even start to find her, from the information we've got? No second name, no address and a completely different description every time she's surfaced. Also, what possible motive can she have for going round bumping off old people she's not even apparently related to?'

'Maybe we need to look for possible motives first, which might in turn lead us to the killer,' Ted suggested. 'At the moment, I don't have any other answers or suggestions. Let's hope the rest of the team come back with some more leads. In the meantime, I'll talk to Inspector Turner about perhaps getting some more help from Uniform. And I'll also chase the Super yet again about another DC.'

Ted headed in search of Inspector Kevin Turner, his opposite number in Uniform, as soon as he got back to the station. He briefly outlined the information they had so far, then asked him if he could spare any officers to help.

'Bloody hell, Ted,' Kevin replied, clearly deeply concerned. 'My dad's in a home, the poor old sod. Not been playing with a full deck of cards for a long time now. Shocking to think of someone going round picking off defenceless old people like that. You know how short of manpower I always am, but I'll certainly try and find you a couple of spare bodies for this one. Sorry to hear about your gran, by the way.'

Ted shrugged.

'Thanks. We weren't close, we lost touch thirty-odd years ago. But I was fond of her when I was a kid. Haven't seen my mother for years, either. She came in here to tell me about it.'

'So that was your mother? Bill told me there'd been a mystery woman at the desk, asking for you. Surely the Ice Queen doesn't want you on this case if it's a relative, even one you've not seen for years?'

'I've mostly handed it over to Mike. I'm taking a bit of a back seat, but still watching from the sidelines. This could be a very tough one to crack. We need everyone we can muster working on it. You know as well as I do how hard it is to catch a random killer.'

# Chapter Eight

Late Wednesday afternoon. Ted was staring at the carpet. It was a rather nice carpet, in a soft shade of green which he liked. He had a shirt in a similar colour. He had spent rather a lot of time staring at the same carpet in the past weeks. It was good quality. Pure wool, he felt sure. That was probably so that it didn't generate static electricity.

Sometimes it bothered him that there were indentations in the carpet, from the feet of the chair he was sitting in. Sometimes he felt he should move the chair, so that its feet were back in exactly the same marks and not causing new ones. He never did. He felt the action might be misinterpreted.

The chair was surprisingly comfortable. It was also good quality, probably real leather. Ted had been relieved to find a chair to sit in. He had spent a long time worrying that he might be expected to lie on a couch to talk.

Ted was sitting in his usual posture. Legs apart, elbows resting on his thighs, hands clasped between them. Studying the carpet as if he was going to be tested on what he knew about it. Occasionally he spoke. Sometimes he even managed to look up as he spoke.

His therapist, Carol, was patience personified. She constantly reassured him that there was no pressure at all, no deadline which had to be met.

'It's not an exam, Ted,' she repeatedly told him. 'You don't have to find the answers within a certain time.'

Lately she had started asking him to evaluate his progress.

To give himself a mark for where he felt he was now compared to where he had been when he started the sessions. Ted was not normally a negative person. Except when it came to himself. He wanted to award zeroes. With her encouragement, he had tentatively marked himself as a five on one occasion.

He had at least managed to talk to her about the dark episode in his childhood which had recently surfaced to haunt him. It was the main reason he had finally consented to counselling, under pressure from both Trev and DCI Jim Baker.

'I met my mother again this week,' Ted began, his first words in the current session, after a lot of carpet studying. 'I think I told you, she walked out on me and my father when I was small, when I was eight. After my dad's accident.'

His therapist said nothing, waiting for him to continue. All her patients were different, with individual needs. To date, Ted was the one who required the most time and greatest patience to get him to externalise his feelings.

Ted was good with facts. He was trained for presenting them. The perfect witness in any Crown, magistrates', or coroner's court. His delivery was always flawless, without a stumble, seldom requiring notes to jog his memory. He looked up now with a steadying breath. Then he launched into professional mode as he told her all about how his mother had come to see him and the facts which had emerged about his grandmother's death. He maintained eye contact with her throughout.

'And how did that make you feel?' she asked, when he had finished.

The carpet became magnetically fascinating once more. Ted had known she would ask that question. He should have been better prepared for it. He tried to remember what he had said to Trev on the subject, to see if he could use that again.

'Confused,' he said eventually, recalling his conversation with Trev. Then he surprised himself by continuing, 'Betrayed.

51

Lied to. Let down. I spent my whole life believing my mum walked out on me. Now she tells me she didn't and that my dad was the one who lied to me my whole life.'

'Will you see her again?'

'At the funeral. Perhaps before. I said I'd help her to organise things if she needs me to.'

'And will you tell her how you feel?'

This time he made eye contact.

'I doubt it. I haven't even told her yet that I'm gay. She asked if I was married. I just said I had a partner.'

She was so used to him by now that she always knew the precise moment to wind things up, until the next time. She also knew he would go straight on to his martial arts evening and that would, as usual, help him to deal with any feelings which had emerged during the session.

She stood up and showed him to the door. As he always did, Ted shook her hand warmly and gave her a dazzling smile. His relief at the end of each session was always palpable. She wondered if he knew how attractive he was. As ever, she asked herself with a mental sigh why all the best ones were either married or gay.

Trev was just putting something in the oven when Ted got home.

'Your kitbag's ready in the hall, and this is a Lancashire hotpot for when we get back,' Trev told him. 'Do you want anything before we go?'

Ted shook his head.

'Just some water, thanks.' He tried to peer past Trev at the dish going into the oven. 'Are there oysters in the hotpot?'

'No, there aren't, so you can stop leering like a randy billy goat,' Trev laughed. 'They're out of season and there's no R in the month, as you know perfectly well. How did your session go?'

Ted made a rueful face.

'Two out of ten. I tried to tell her how I feel about what my mother told me, but I failed miserably, as usual.'

Trev gave him a hug.

'You know what Carol always says. It's not an exam, there's no pass or fail. Anyway, as hard as it is for you, at least you now know both your parents loved you and tried to do right by you. Even if what they did was misguided.'

He added bitterly, 'What do you think my parents would have to say if they suddenly reappeared after fourteen years? Trevor, you know how, when you came out and told us you were gay, we said that you were disgusting and to get out and never darken our doors again? Well, hey, we were only kidding. Love you really, son.'

Ted felt ashamed of himself.

'I'm sorry. I know I'm being a bit self-obsessed at the moment,' he said.

He got himself a glass of water, drained it quickly, then went to pick up his kitbag for their judo session that evening.

'Right, I'm ready. Are we walking, as usual?'

'The exercise will do us both good. Blow a few cobwebs away before the serious stuff, on the mat.'

Trev's mood had lightened again. They were seldom at odds for long. They strode out briskly together, heading for the gymnasium near Davenport which housed the judo club they attended, as well as the self-defence group for children which they ran jointly.

'Anyway, you know what they say. Don't speak of the devil or he will appear,' Trev said. 'If we talk about my parents, they might suddenly pop out of the woodwork, like your mum did.'

Ted grimaced at the mere thought.

'Statistically unlikely though,' he said. 'Unless parents are like buses? You wait ages for one to come along, then two appear at the same time?'

'Not impossible, though,' Trev countered. 'Remember Rich and Andy's mothers both died on the same day, within a few hours of one another, at opposite ends of the country. Anyway, please let's not talk about my parents. I'm better off without them.'

They walked on in silence for a short distance.

'I need to take you clothes shopping again,' Trev said, changing the subject.

Ted looked aghast.

'Really? It seems only five minutes since we went last time. What do I need new clothes for?'

Trev laughed and shook his head.

'Honestly, Ted, what sort of a gay man are you that you don't like clothes shopping? I despair of you sometimes. Don't forget we're going to Rupert and Willow's wedding very soon. Mixing with the Cheshire set. We might even get our photos in Tatler.'

Ted groaned at the very thought.

'Can't I just wear one of my work suits?' he asked plaintively.

'No, you can't, certainly not if you're coming with me,' Trev said firmly. 'And don't forget there's Rob O'Connell's wedding coming up too.'

Ted had one last go.

'What about a work suit, freshly dry cleaned, with a new shirt and tie?'

'Out of the question. Shopping it is. Now come on, hurry up. I have a good feeling about judo tonight. The first throw will definitely be mine. Down is where you are going, uncle,' he added in a phoney accent, quoting a line from a film which they'd both enjoyed watching.

He upped his speed to a steady jog. Ted smiled and shook his head, marvelling again at his partner, then broke into a short sprint to catch him up.

# Chapter Nine

Professor Nelson arrived for Sunday lunch full of profuse apologies to Ted, as she'd not had the time to carry out the post-mortem on his second victim. That meant there were no results back yet from toxicology testing.

'We've been very busy this week. People seem to be dying inconveniently and keeping me from your lady,' she said. 'And I want to do this one for you myself, as it's such an intriguing case.'

As she was anticipating a motorcycle ride home, she had come dressed in trousers, rather than the old-fashioned tweed skirts Ted was used to seeing her in. They were in some sort of hounds-tooth check and looked more functional than fashionable.

'I had no idea what to bring as you told me you don't drink, Edwin, so I settled for some elderflower cordial. It's home-made, but not by me. Mummy still makes things like that, although these days I have to pick the blossom for her as she can't get about,' she said as she thrust the bottle awkwardly at Ted.

'Thank you, Bizzie, that's very kind. Can I introduce you to my partner? This is Trevor. Trev, this is Professor Elizabeth Nelson, our new senior pathologist.'

'Do please call me Bizzie, as Edwin does,' the Professor said, as she pumped Trev's hand enthusiastically in an iron grip. 'I'm delighted to meet you, Trevor. It's so kind of you to invite me. What a treat.'

'You're very welcome, Bizzie,' Trev replied. 'Would you like a little aperitif outside before lunch? I wasn't sure of your taste but I've made a small jug of Pimm's for the two of us, if that interests you? Ted can have the cordial, it will make a nice change for him.'

He smiled warmly as he ushered her through the house and out to the small patio beyond the kitchen, picking up the jug and glasses on his way. He turned back to Ted with a wide grin, raised his eyebrows and mouthed, 'Edwin?' He, of course, knew Ted's full name but never used it himself, except in fun. Bizzie was the only person he'd ever heard use it.

Ted fixed himself a glass of the cordial, just to be polite, but was then agreeably surprised at how refreshing it was. He went out to join the others. Trev already had Bizzie firmly under his spell, as he generally managed to do with everyone he met.

'Ted tells me you want a ride on the Triumph,' he was saying. 'I'd be delighted to take you myself, so I promise not to drink any more than just this one Pimm's. Ted could take you, of course, but he's very staid and I expect you would enjoy something more exciting, more adventurous.'

He winked at Ted, who had come outside to join them. Ted glared back.

'Just behave yourself,' he said. 'It would be embarrassing enough for me at work if you picked up a speeding ticket, but I'd never hear the end of it if you were pulled over with the Professor on the pillion.'

Lunch was a resounding success. The Professor, who had always seemed a little socially inept to Ted, even more so than himself, was completely relaxed in their company. She kept them both entertained and amused with surprisingly racy stories from her days as a medical student.

As she was preparing to leave, clutching Ted's helmet in gleeful anticipation of the bike ride home, she said apologetically, 'It's scant recompense for such a delightful lunch, but what if I meet you at the hospital at seven-thirty tomorrow morning, so that I can fit your lady in before the start of the day?'

'That would be absolutely brilliant, Bizzie, thank you so much. It can't be me, I'm afraid. I'm having to take a bit more of a back seat on this enquiry, as my grandmother was a victim, and we now know that hers was a suspicious death. Let me just phone my sergeant, Mike Hallam, and see if he can cover for me.'

He took out his mobile and dialled Mike's number.

'Mike? Sorry to disturb your weekend. I'm with Professor Nelson and she's very kindly offered to do our outstanding PM early doors tomorrow. I know you're determined to keep me off this case, so I wondered if you could cover for me? Seven-thirty sharp, at the hospital?'

Mike laughed. 'I walked right into that one, boss,' he said. 'Yes, it's fine, tell the Professor I'll be there. You're with her now? Is it another death?'

'No, a social occasion. Thanks, Mike, I appreciate it.'

'I'll fill you in as soon as I get back. Well, I'll probably stop for a quick bacon sandwich on the way from the hospital. If I eat anything before a PM, I'll only lose it.'

As in the case of Ted's grandmother, the post-mortem revealed little which was immediately conclusive, although the Professor observed that the cardiac ventricles were dilated. They would have to wait for toxicology results for anything more definite, and to see if there was a link between the two cases.

Once again, the Professor was quick to phone Ted back with the results, as promised. She called his mobile early one morning a couple of days later, when he had just arrived at his desk, ahead of his team.

'Fascinating, Edwin, absolutely fascinating,' she positively boomed down the phone. 'I had to call in an enormous number of favours to rush results through, but this is definitely another case of poisoning. This time, however, the toxin is different. It's again plant-based. Toxicology tests revealed traces of various cardiac glycosides, notably digitoxin and digitalin.

'The plant is from the *Scrophulariaceae* family, most probably *digitalis purperea*, which you might know better as...'

'Foxglove,' Ted interrupted triumphantly. He didn't know a lot about plants, but he and Trev had thoroughly researched which ones were poisonous to cats before planting anything in their garden.

'Exactly. It's an unusual choice once again, in that, although it can be lethal in very small doses, it has a strong emetic effect. Anyone ingesting it is often so violently sick they expel much of the poison before it can do any harm. It initially causes a rapid rise in heart rate but it can then slow it down to the point where a heart attack can occur, which was the case with this lady.

'And in case you are going to ask me again if this could have been accidental, then once again I would have to rule that very unlikely. If our victim were to have been skipping around the garden munching on the leaves, she would probably have made herself instantly extremely sick but would very likely have gradually recovered. Administered in a higher dosage, however, in something like a cake, could well end in fatality, as in this case.

'I hope that's helpful to you? It is, of course, up to you to say whether the two deaths are connected, and if it amounts to murder. But I would say you need to be looking at people with an extensive knowledge of plants and herb-lore. Quite a specialist knowledge too, with regard to specific lethal doses.

'By the way, thank you so much for Sunday. I did enjoy myself, and your Trevor is absolutely delightful. I had such fun on the back of his bike.'

Ted smiled to himself. Trev had returned grinning widely,

eyes sparkling, telling him how, once the Professor had discovered the in-built intercom system on the helmets, she had spent much of the short journey encouraging him to go faster. It was only a short distance to her large house in Davenport Park so, after taking her twice round the block, Trev had offered to take her for a longer spin sometime soon.

'He enjoyed it too, Bizzie, he loves showing his bike off. I'm sure he'll be happy to take you out any time you fancy it. Thanks again for this. You know we're looking at a possible exhumation for the next one?'

'Yes indeed. Bad business, this. Three so far? I'm sure you're hoping as much as I am that there are no more.'

He thanked her again, then rang off and waited for the team to appear. As usual, no one was late. Ted was impressed at the difference he was seeing in Maurice since he had a lodger. Maurice was a natural parent who missed his daughters dreadfully since his divorce, although he still saw them most weekends. Treating Steve more as a son than a lodger was doing him a power of good, especially now that Steve had finally got him to stop smoking. The girls were delighted to have suddenly gained a surrogate older brother and a healthier, smoke-free father.

'Right, Mike, I'm not hijacking your briefing, I just want to fill everyone in on the latest I have from Professor Nelson,' Ted began apologetically. 'As you know, the PM itself showed very little but she phoned me first thing with the tox results. Mrs Maggie Tyler was also poisoned, also with a plant-derived toxin. From the foxglove, this time.

'It's similar to monkshood in the way in which it works. It normally first causes sickness then affects the heart and often leads to a heart attack. And once again, it's extremely unlikely to be an accidental poisoning.'

He nodded to Mike to take over while he perched quietly on a desk to watch his team at work.

'So, are these deaths connected? That's the million dollar

question,' the DS began. 'We need to look at the similarities between the cases, including Mrs Protheroe, even though there has been no PM on her yet and no tox report. But we also need to look at any differences between them, balance the two. Coincidences do happen. We shouldn't assume they're linked without positive proof.

'So, similarities first? Common denominators?'

He looked questioningly round the team. A chorus of voices chimed in, 'Angela.'

'Yes, but Sarge, she counts as differences too,' Steve spoke up. 'The name is similar each time but the physical description is totally different every time. Shouldn't we be careful of just assuming it is the same person?'

Mike nodded encouragingly. He started two columns on the white board, labelled them Similarities and Differences and put the name Angela under both headings.

'Same doctor for the first two, different for the third,' Sal offered, while Mike scribbled on the board.

'Are days of the week significant, Sarge? Can we establish any sort of a pattern from that?' Steve asked.

'Good, Steve, check it, please.'

'The fact that all three had few visitors,' Virgil Tibbs added.

'This is going to sound daft,' Maurice began hesitantly, unusually for him, as he normally opened his mouth before engaging his brain. 'Is where the victims sat in the home significant?'

The rest of the team looked at him questioningly. Mike nodded at him to continue.

'Well, when I went to that home with the boss, the young lad there said Mrs Tyler always sat on the sofa, in the lobby place, just as you go in. And boss, you said there was no real security at the home where your gran was.

'What if, and I hope to hell I'm wrong, we've got a random killer going round, just wandering in to homes and poisoning the first old lady they find sitting by themselves near the doorway? Well, targeting them first, coming a few times to avoid suspicion, then bam! Eat this, granny.'

He realised what he'd said and looked apologetically at Ted.

'Sorry boss, that was tactless, even for me.'

Ted waved away the apology.

'It's fine, Maurice. I wonder if you have something there. What do you think, Mike?'

'It's an interesting theory, Maurice,' Mike said. 'Now all we have to do is find someone with a motive to fit a crime of that nature. Should be a piece of cake – pardon the dreadful pun.'

# Chapter Ten

Trev got his way about clothes shopping at the weekend. Once he had made his mind up about something, Trev got his way on anything he wanted. Ted had never learned to say no to him.

They'd spent the afternoon at what to Ted was a shopping centre, although Trev had assured him was a designer outlet. As far as Ted could see, that just meant the prices were higher, especially as they were in Cheshire. Trev had insisted, saying it was the place to shop if they were to mix with the Cheshire set.

Trev adored shopping. Ted hated it and was there very much under sufferance. But he had promised to make an effort for Willow's wedding. They'd not known Willow and her fiancé Rupert for long, but had become close friends with them both. Ted was particularly fond of Willow, who had helped him through a tough time recently.

They had made an occasion of the outing by enjoying an early evening meal at a small French bistro nearby, which was excellent. They'd left Ted's now shopping bag-laden Renault in a side-street a short walk away, wanting to avoid the manic crush of cars all trying to leave the outlet's car park at the same time.

They were strolling back to the car after their meal. As they walked past a pub on the corner of a road junction, a group of young women came round the corner towards them. One at the front of the group almost bumped into Ted, who, ever the gentleman, stepped back and to the side, his hands raised in a gesture of appeasement, and apologised.

The women were all in various bizarre outfits. One was wearing L-plates. It looked like a hen party. It also appeared that they were already a long way into a well-oiled pub crawl.

'Oy, watch where you're going, mate,' the one who had almost collided with Ted said, her voice loud, the tone aggressive.

'To be fair, we both rather walked into one another,' Ted said mildly. 'And I have already apologised.'

The woman was about Ted's own size, which was to say not very tall. She had spiky hair, dyed a bright shade of shocking pink. She also had a formidable array of piercings. Both ears were full of rings, as was one eyebrow. She had a big, black labret stud, which looked like an over-sized beauty spot, and a nose ring.

To Ted's surprise, instead of continuing on her way, the woman suddenly clenched both fists and started bouncing round on her toes. Unlike most of her friends, she was wearing flat shoes. Drunk as she clearly was, she certainly knew how to move.

Ted took a careful step back, assessing the way she was weighing him up, trying to work out which martial art was heading his way. He had an answer to most of them.

Left jab. Right cross. Back roundhouse kick. Classic basic kickboxing moves. It would probably have taken down anyone who was not expecting it. Only none of them found a target. Ted moved on the balls of his feet with a speed which made the young woman look as if she was wading through treacle. Her target was simply no longer where she had aimed the blows.

Trev stepped out of the way, chuckling softly to himself.

'Please don't do that,' Ted said pleasantly.

The young woman bounced a bit more on the spot to focus herself. She tucked her chin in with determination. This time her opening jab was followed by an uppercut, then a front kick. But Ted moved so swiftly out of her range that her own momentum took her staggering forward. She would have fallen into the road in front of the passing traffic, had Trev not extended a powerful arm to block her.

'Don't make him angry. You wouldn't like him when he's angry,' Trev said, laughing.

'No, really, please don't do that,' Ted repeated. He could sense the situation was about to turn nasty. With four black belts in martial arts, Ted knew that he was more than capable of stopping her. But despite being a fervent believer in equality, he did not relish the thought of fighting a woman, especially in the street.

The rest of the drunken women were starting to shout encouragement to Pink Hair, who was still bobbing about in front of him. One of them yelled, 'Go on, Jezza, lamp him one!' Some of the others were chanting, 'Fight! Fight! Fight!' with evident glee.

Ted's eyes often appeared to change colour according to his mood. His team knew to watch out when their usual warm, rich hazel started to flash like cold emerald shards. As Pink Hair circled and bobbed, looking for an opening, Ted sighed and positioned himself for defence.

The speed with which he blocked the first jab this time was barely visible to the naked eye. He let Pink Hair's weight take her forward but this time he went with her. He held firmly onto the arm, not causing her any pain, just effectively immobilising her. To a casual observer, they looked like friends, arm in arm, having a chat.

'Look, I strongly advise you just to go with your friends and enjoy the rest of your evening,' Ted told her quietly. 'I don't want any trouble and I'm sure, on reflection, you don't either.'

He let go of her arm and she stood for a moment, looking at him and breathing hard.

'Nar, I can't be arsed,' she said loudly enough for all her friends to hear. 'Lead me to the tequila slammers. Much more fun.'

Trev was still laughing as the group of women staggered on

their way into the pub. He grinned at Ted and said, 'Wow, what a little hell-cat. You wouldn't want to meet that alone on a dark night.'

Ted now had the exhumation order, signed by the coroner, for the body of Mrs Protheroe. He needed to discuss the formalities with the Ice Queen. He also wanted to talk to her about the direction he intended to take the enquiry in next.

Maurice Brown had come back from one of the home visits with more details of a visitor called Angela, and this time he had a surname to add. Angela Mortice was now written up on the white board. Once again, there was a change of physical description. This one had told staff in the home that she was a solicitor who had got to know the person she was visiting when handling her affairs. So far, there had been no death at that home.

Maurice had learned that she would often appear at the home in the afternoon, wearing a smartly-tailored dark suit. She had black hair, always pulled back tightly in a French pleat, and she wore dark-framed glasses. Maurice had asked about cake and was told she always appeared with a small box of expensive fondant fancies from a nearby cake shop.

'I've got the team contacting all the local law firms in the area to ask if they employ someone called Mortice, but nothing so far,' Ted told the Ice Queen. 'I've been wondering if the time has come to try putting someone in undercover at some of the homes, to see if they can spot this Angela. The trouble is, I don't see any of the current team quite fitting in, posing as a care worker.'

'In which case, I may possibly have some good news for you, in the shape of a new team member. If you want to take her,' the Ice Queen replied.

'Why am I feeling there may be reason why I wouldn't want to?' Ted asked suspiciously.

The Ice Queen smiled.

'You know I believe in being totally open and honest, so I will say at the outset that this young woman comes with a bit of a track record. Academically brilliant, top of her intake at Sedgley Park and Area Training in absolutely everything, was considered for High Potential Development.'

'And the 'but' is?' Ted prompted.

'In a word, attitude,' she replied. 'Now I know you like a challenge, and I know you have an extremely good rapport with all of your team members. I'm not saying this young DC is on her last warning but she has certainly had a few. She is in definite need of the right kind of senior officer to help her to achieve her full potential.

'I think she would be an asset, as she's done a lot of undercover work in her short career so far. She's said to be very good at blending into the background. She can change her appearance very effectively. There's also a note on her file to say she can do accents from, and I'm quoting here, broad Manchester to posh Cheshire.

'So the question is, are you up to the challenge?'

She pushed a personal folder across the desk towards Ted, who picked it up and looked at the name. Jessica Vine.

'Where is she currently serving?' he asked.

'Bolton South.'

'Ah,' Ted said meaningfully. 'From what you tell me, I can imagine her locking horns quite considerably with DI Jill Austin. Her style is a bit more formal than mine, it has to be said.'

'Joining this team could be just what this young woman needs,' the Ice Queen said persuasively. 'There's no pressure on you to take her and you might well want to discuss it with DS Hallam first. Read the file, have a think about it and let me know as soon as you can.'

'I'm presuming that at the moment it's her or no one?' Ted asked with a grin.

'You catch on quickly, Inspector,' she said dryly. 'Now,

what else can you tell me about this case? Are you making any real progress at all?'

'We have the exhumation order now. I'm arranging for it to go ahead as soon as possible.'

'Will you attend yourself?' she asked.

'I was going to do so, yes, with Mike Hallam. Kevin Turner is also providing some Uniform officers to keep curious onlookers at bay. I'm anxious to keep a lid on this as much as possible. The last thing we want is word of it leaking out and causing fear and panic.'

'My sentiments entirely,' the Super nodded. 'I think your involvement can be more hands on once again at this stage, now that we have three possible victims. What you mustn't do, under any circumstances, is start getting involved in interviewing any suspects. Any half-decent defence lawyer would have a field day with that, once your personal connection to one of the victims became known.

'And I concur, we don't want a public spectacle making out of the exhumation. I don't need to tell you that, apart from frightening the public, it is likely to push your killer underground. I hope we can count on every officer in this station to keep quiet?'

'Ma'am,' Ted said stiffly.

There had been leaks on previous cases and their source had not yet been discovered. Ted strongly suspected that those leaks had been external. He trusted all of his team implicitly, even Maurice, who was inclined to speak before thinking. He knew that Kevin Turner felt the same about his Uniform team.

But it wouldn't be the first time a police officer had made a few quid on the side by getting too friendly with the local press. Ted particularly disliked and mistrusted the local newspaper reporter, who was the bane of his life, always sniffing round when there was anything big happening.

Ted rose to go, picking up the file on DC Vine.

'I'll study this in detail and let you know my decision by

tomorrow, if that's all right.'

'I should have mentioned that if you do decide to take her, DC Vine is not immediately available. She is currently on two weeks' enforced leave of absence with a strongly worded recommendation from DI Austin to consider her future very carefully.'

Ted laughed.

'It just gets better and better. I look forward to meeting this DC Vine.'

# Chapter Eleven

'Midnight is a bloody silly time to be hanging round in a graveyard, boss,' Mike grumbled, as he hunched his shoulders against the persistent drizzle.

'Is this your first one, Mike? Exhumations are usually done at night,' Ted said patiently. 'That way there's less risk of onlookers, so it's more likely we can keep it under wraps.'

Ted was not feeling any more enthusiastic himself. At least he was better equipped than Mike, being a keen hill walker. His waterproofs would withstand a lot worse than this and they were breathable, so he was not feeling hot and sweaty inside.

Mike was wearing an ancient waxed jacket, which looked as if it had seen better days and not been re-proofed since he bought it. It was no wonder he was faring badly with the weather. The Professor was in a long waxed coat and matching hat. The way the rain was running off both, it was clear she took better care of her outdoor gear than Mike did.

They were both impressed that Professor Nelson had turned out in person for the occasion. She was not obliged to be there, but as she had explained to Ted, 'You may think me a terrible ghoul but this case really fascinates me. Poisonings are comparatively rare, and ones utilising plant toxins are rarer still.

'I'm hoping to start on this one very early tomorrow morning. Or rather, I should say later this morning, as it's past midnight,' Professor Nelson told them. 'I appreciate that doesn't leave any of us much time for sleep, but I am anxious to get started and get the toxin analysis done as soon as possible. I must warn you, though, that some plant toxins become untraceable after a period of time and I'm not sufficiently au fait with the subject to know off the top of my head which ones, without detailed research.

'So gentlemen, whose turn is it to come to this one?' she asked, looking from one to the other.

Ted and Mike exchanged unenthusiastic glances. Neither of them particularly liked attending post-mortem examinations. With this potential victim having been dead for three months by now, they both fancied it even less.

Mike reached in his pocket and pulled out a coin.

'Toss you for it, boss?' he suggested.

'No, it's all right, Mike, I've got this one.' Ted looked across at the grave, surrounded by screens against prying eyes, with diggers working under arc lights. 'In fact, it looks as if they're nearly done here, so why don't you get off home. I'll go and get a few hours' sleep, then I'll see you at the hospital, Professor,' he said, keeping it formal in front of his DS. 'What time would you like me there?'

'Well, I have a very busy day ahead so would it suit you if I said six o'clock? I generally start work at sparrows' fart,' she replied. 'Then I could get this one out of the way before I start. Or is that too early?'

Ted groaned inwardly but said, 'No, not at all, that's fine, I'll be there. And thanks for hurrying this one through yet again for us, it's a great help. We really appreciate it.'

He waited until he'd seen the newly exhumed coffin safely installed in the hearse and on its way to the hospital ready for the post-mortem before he left the scene and headed for his car. On his way through the gates, he paused to exchange a few words with the two Uniform officers Kevin Turner had provided for the operation. Ted was universally popular in the station precisely because he made time to talk to everyone and accorded the same level of courtesy to all, regardless of rank.

'Thanks for this. It's not much fun for you, especially with this dismal weather. Did you see anyone sniffing about? Any signs of our friend from the local paper?'

'Nothing and no one, sir,' one of the constables told him. 'Is it finished? Can we knock off now?'

'Just wait until everyone leaves and the machinery has gone, if you wouldn't mind. And make sure the gates are securely locked up again. I don't want anyone seeing the freshly disturbed soil, reading the headstone and putting two and two together.'

Trev was already in bed asleep when Ted got in and slipped quietly under the covers next to him. It would have been easier to wake the dead than disturb his deeply sleeping partner, spread-eagled as he was across most of the bed, underneath a heap of cats.

With Trev's patient help, Ted had finally mastered the art of setting the alarm on his mobile phone. He was not a natural with technology. He would get a scant four hours or so of sleep before having to get up again, but he decided it was better than nothing.

He wondered if Bizzie would sleep or if she had gone straight to her autopsy suite. Despite her visit to his house, Ted still knew little about her, outside the professional side he saw when they worked together. But mutual respect and a feeling almost of friendship was slowly building.

It was still raining when he left the house shortly after five-thirty. The drive to the hospital was not long, but Ted hated to be late for anything. He had risked only a green tea with organic honey to start the day. He was usually quite good at post-mortems but he didn't relish being present for one on an older, partly-decomposed body.

He knew that, theoretically, it would be relatively well-preserved but he was still not looking forward to it. He had checked before leaving that he was well armed with his menthol lozenges. Other officers liked to use a smear of pungent vapour rub or tiger balm under their noses during a post-mortem. Ted liked the additional comfort of sucking the throat sweets, which reminded him so strongly of his father. He wondered what his counsellor would make of that, if he told her.

'Morning again, Edwin,' the Professor greeted him brightly. 'Did you manage to get any sleep?'

'A few hours, thanks. Better than nothing,' he said. 'What about you?'

'Oh no, no need of it. I'm a real night owl. I often don't sleep. At the most I get by on about four hours. I'm like Margaret Thatcher in that respect, although I hasten to add that it's the only thing I have in common with that woman. Now, are you well-armed with your sweeties and can I get started?'

Ted took the hint and passed her the packet before she began, before helping himself.

As usual, she kept up a running commentary for the tape. Once again, there was not a great deal to report.

'I'm relying heavily on toxicology for this one, and hoping there is enough with the remaining samples I can take to give us the results. I note that the original death certificate records the cause as heart failure and that would seem to be the logical conclusion to be drawn from what I have seen so far.

'However, we will now have the benefit of tests which the doctor signing the certificate did not have. From what you say about this and the other deaths, there would be really no reason to suspect anything untoward at the time. Sadly, elderly people, especially in communal living, like the care homes, are very prone to viruses and gastroenteritis. Either can easily prove too much for them, even if they don't appear frail.

'It isn't helped by the fact that they are very often dehydrated. They always have the heating up like a tropical greenhouse in those places, and frequently the residents don't get anything like sufficient fluids. Water in equals pee out, of course, which is not always what they want, from a care management point of view. Sudden violent vomiting and diarrhoea on an already weakened and dehydrated system can often be fatal, and very quickly.'

Then she paused for breath and said, 'Sorry, Edwin, I'm on my soap box. Luckily Mummy hasn't had to resort to a home yet, but Daddy was in one before he died. Whenever I went there, I would fling open his bedroom window and give him several glasses of water. I was not popular.'

Ted smiled.

'I can imagine,' he said.

'That's me just about done for now. Would you care to join me for a cup of truly disgusting vending machine coffee, before we both begin the rest of our day? I would welcome some company at this ungodly hour, and the canteen won't be open yet for a halfway decent cup.'

Ted had the sudden impression that she was a lonely person, not good at making friends. He was happy to afford her a few minutes of his time. She was right about the coffee. It was foul.

It turned out to be another intensely frustrating day, with little progress. Steve had been ringing round all the law firms in the immediate area, trying to trace an Angela Mortice.

'She either doesn't work on or near our patch, boss, or she uses a different name at work,' he said, at the morning briefing. 'Always supposing she exists at all, and that really is her name.'

'I think we've been round all the local homes as well now,' Mike told him. 'We've had no more deaths reported and no further sightings of this woman, whoever she is. We haven't started on the hospitals yet. I thought we could do that today. It may mean checking ward by ward, but I highly doubt there is any kind of record kept of hospital visitors. I imagine the staff are far too busy looking after sick people.'

'Sir, what about the cake shop?' Steve suggested. 'The one this Angela Mortice has been buying the fondant fancies from?

It may not be connected, as that home doesn't seem to have had a death yet which fits the pattern. But maybe it's someone setting themselves up to be just an innocent visitor before they strike?'

'Brilliant idea, Steve, that's well worth checking out. If she was a regular and always bought the same cakes, it's possible that they might remember her. Ask the home for the name of the shop.'

'I'll volunteer to go and check it out, boss,' Maurice said quickly, with a wide grin.

The whole team laughed. Maurice was known for his fondness for sweet things, especially since he'd stopped smoking. Although Ted had noticed he was eating less and looking altogether better since he'd had Steve to look after.

'All right, Maurice, just for your cheek, you get that one. Take Steve with you. He might be able to control you,' Mike told him. He was in charge of assigning tasks to the team.

It proved to be yet another dead end. The shop didn't know the woman, just remembered that she came in occasionally for fancies, but they could offer no clue as to who she was or where she lived or worked. At least Maurice and Steve brought back a box of cakes for the rest of the team.

Ted felt completely weary by the time he got home that evening. It was not just having been up late then having to go in early for the post-mortem. He felt he was going round in circles and making no headway. He also had the strong and disturbing notion that he was missing something, something blindingly obvious, in the little information they had already.

He hoped Bizzie would do her best to rush through the latest results, although he feared already that it was going to prove to be another killing, with the same MO.

Trev and the cats were watching the news when he got home. He sank down wearily beside them on the sofa and leaned against Trev, his head on his shoulder. There were delicious smells wafting from the kitchen and he realised just how hungry he was.

'I hope I didn't disturb you when I got back in the wee small hours, or when I staggered out again at the crack of dawn,' he said, lifting his head so he could kiss his partner's cheek, then slumping back against the scatter cushions.

Trev laughed.

'Good grief, we've lived together for eleven years and you still think you're capable of waking me up when you're in stealth mode? No chance. Hard day?' he asked solicitously.

'I feel like we're going round in circles,' Ted told him. He seldom talked about his work at home, but he sometimes briefly outlined a current case. He had spoken a little more than usual about this one as it involved his own grandmother.

'We've got two certain and one possible poisonings and absolutely no suspect at all. Normally we'd have at least one at this stage. The only name that's cropped up to date is this Angela Mortice and we can't get a lead on her.'

'Angela Mortice?' Trev queried, looking at him incredulously.

'Why, do you know her?' Ted asked.

'Ted, I know you're neither a language scholar nor a Catholic. But come on. Angela Mortice?' Seeing Ted's blank look, he continued, 'Angelus Mortis. The Angel of Death? Are you sure someone is not pulling your leg somewhere along the line?'

Ted stared back at him.

'Sometimes, I am just so breathtakingly stupid I astound even myself. Could that possibly be our motive? Someone who's set themselves up to rid the world of old people with dementia? That opens up a whole new can of worms.'

# Chapter Twelve

'Right team, listen up, I have a confession to make,' Ted said at the start of the briefing the following morning. He had already told Mike he had things he wanted to say before handing over to him to assign tasks for the day.

'I am a complete bloody idiot. It's official,' Ted said with a self-deprecating grimace. His team members sat up straighter and looked at him in surprise. It was so unusual for the boss to swear at all, even mildly, that it must be something serious.

Ted was standing in front of the white board, marker pen in his hand, as he continued, 'Our mystery woman is not Angela Mortice, M-O-R-T-I-C-E.'

As he spoke, he crossed out the name Maurice Brown had written there underneath Ange, Angie and Angela.

'It's almost certainly not her real name, but whatever it is, it's more likely to be Mortis, M-O-R-T-I-S.

'I'm too stupid to have realised, but Trev, who as you all know speaks several languages, and who was brought up a Catholic, was quick to point it out. Angelus Mortis is Latin for the Angel of Death. Whoever this woman is, she seems to be having a pretty sick joke at everyone's expense.'

The team members were quiet for a moment, then Maurice Brown spoke up. 'Bloody hell, boss, I'm sorry, that was my fault. I should have checked the spelling.'

Ted shook his head.

'Not your fault at all, Maurice. The home wouldn't necessarily have known the spelling unless she had ever written it down for them. That seems unlikely, since most of the homes don't keep records. Even where there is a visitors' book, she may well never write in it.

'Now this development is worrying. It was disconcerting enough having two, possibly three killings where we've not yet established the connection,' Ted continued. 'But a name like this suggests someone on a mission. And we know just how hard they are to catch. So ....'

He was interrupted by the phone on Mike Hallam's desk ringing. The DS answered it, said, 'Yes, he's here,' and handed the phone to Ted.

'Hello, Ted? It's George,' the familiar voice of the coroner's officer greeted Ted as he answered. 'You've been giving us a fair bit of work of late and it seems there's another possible one for you that we've just been informed about.'

Ted groaned. It was not the sort of news he wanted.

'Thanks for letting me know, George. What have you got for me?'

'There's an elderly woman patient who died at the hospital late yesterday. A sudden, unexpected death. It's been called in as suspicious because the symptoms were out of character with what she'd gone in for. Mr Happy asked me to let you know. I'm just emailing you all the details we have.'

Ted smiled to himself at the nickname. The senior coroner was not known for his sunny disposition, and Ted was not the only one who found him hard to get along with. He often wondered how George had survived working with him for so long.

'Thanks, George. We really didn't want another one, but thanks for letting me know. I'll talk to Professor Nelson about the PM.'

He hung up then looked at his team.

'Sounds like another one,' he said grimly. 'At the hospital this time, which is a worrying departure. Mike, I think you and I should go down there as soon as we can, to establish facts and details while they're still fresh in everyone's minds. In the meantime, do you want to brief the team on what we discussed earlier, please?'

'The boss and I talked about damage limitation, at this stage,' Mike told the team. 'As we don't have a lead on this Angela, whoever she might be, we thought we might go at it from the prevention angle. I want you to get out there, round all the homes, and talk to managers or senior staff about implementing a ban on relatives giving food directly to residents.

'Now, it's not going to be popular. It won't win you any friends. And I imagine most of them will say they can't do it. But I want you to stress to them that they need to try. I also want you to do it without spreading alarm, if you can.

'Get them to say anything they think will sound convincing. They need to test blood sugars or something. I don't know, I'm neither a nurse nor a care worker. But they need to think of something to make sure any food brought in isn't given directly to anyone, until further notice. The boss and I will talk to the staff at the hospital when we go this morning and see if they can impose the same rule, for the time being. It's not much, but it's the best we can do for now.

'The other thing I want you to do while you're out there is to collect lists of staff from all the homes, both currently and for the past six months, initially, so we can start cross-checking. And ask again about visitors, and about any previous deaths which, with hindsight, may be similar. But again, try not to spread panic.

'Rob, can you coordinate things. Divide up the list of homes and make sure they're all covered. The boss and I will get off to the hospital now, to see what we can find out about this latest death.'

On the short drive there, Mike was keen to press for more information on their potential new team member, DC Jessica Vine. Ted had already given him the basic details but Mike was particularly interested in what gave her such a bad reputation for attitude.

'To be honest, Mike, I haven't really gone into it much further,' Ted told him. 'I try to avoid pre-judging people, based on hearsay. I prefer to make up my own mind when I meet them.'

It was a gentle dig at Mike, who had been so on edge on his first day with the team that he'd nearly got off on the wrong foot with Ted. He'd quickly learned that the DI had his own way of dealing with any kind of prejudice, and that the boss was treated with respect by all because he earned it.

'Fair enough, boss, I walked into that one,' Mike laughed. 'From what you've said about her and her abilities, she'll be a good one to send in to the homes undercover, if we need to go down that route.'

As they were walking down one of the long corridors at the hospital, in search of the right ward, a voice behind them called out delightedly, 'Hello, Mr Darling!'

They turned and saw a hospital porter pushing an elderly woman in a wheelchair. He was beaming widely at the sight of Ted, who noticed immediately that he had had his distinctive silver hair cut much shorter since the last time they had met. It suited him.

'Hello, Oliver,' Ted replied. 'How are you getting on?'

'Really well, thank you,' the man said. 'That lady in Human 'Sources you spoke to has been very kind to me. She sorted out for me to get some help with my reading.'

He looked up at the various signs, pointing to different departments, and read haltingly but proudly, 'Maternity. Coronary Care Unit. Orthopaedics. That's where we're going now.'

'Brilliant, Oliver, that's very well done. You'll have to excuse me now, I'm a bit busy and I have to be somewhere. It was nice to see you again, and perhaps we can have a coffee together some time.'

Ted had met the man, Oliver Burdon, when he'd briefly been a suspect in a previous murder enquiry. He had quickly recognised that he was in need of some help and support and had arranged it for him. His kindness was rewarded when Burdon had helped to identify a victim in the case.

'I go on my break in half an hour,' the man said hopefully.

'Great. I'll meet you at the canteen, shall I? Perhaps I can buy you something, like a white chocolate chip cookie, if they have any?' Ted said, remembering Oliver's love of white chocolate.

'That would be lovely,' he said, then bent forward to speak to his passenger.

'Come on, Nancy, sorry to have kept you waiting. Let's get you to your appointment now. I'll have to hurry. Vroom-vroom,' and he set off at a steady trot.

They could hear the delighted laughter of his passenger as she said, 'Oh, Oliver, you are funny. You're a real tonic, the way you make me laugh.'

'Really, boss?' Mike asked as they walked on. 'You're going to take time out to talk to him? You think he may be able to help in some way with the case?'

Ted shook his head.

'Not for a moment. Just sometimes, it's nice to make time for people, because it might make their day better.'

They found the ward they were looking for and headed for the nurses' station. There was no sign of anyone, although they could see some activity further down the corridor. Eventually a woman in a nurse's uniform came hurrying past, carrying a sheaf of paperwork.

'Excuse me,' Mike said. 'DS Hallam and DI Darling. We're here to see the ward manager.'

'Just wait here a moment, I'll try to find her. We're short-staffed and she's up to her armpits.'

After a few minutes, a tall, slim woman, also in uniform, came hurrying out of a side room.

'Sorry to keep you waiting,' she said. 'It's hectic today. I'm two nurses down and the agency staff never showed up. Sorry, you don't want to know any of that. There's a small room just here where we can talk, but I can't guarantee I won't be disturbed if I'm needed.'

'We're not making it widely known yet, so I would be obliged if you would treat this as confidential. We're making enquiries into some sudden deaths in suspicious circumstances and I believe you had an unexpected death on the ward last night?' Mike began.

'That's right. Jane Applegate. She came in from a care home with a UTI,' the manager replied, then, seeing their look of incomprehension, she clarified, 'A urinary tract infection. The scourge of the elderly. She was dehydrated and running a very high temperature. We kept her in and on a drip for a couple of days and she was doing splendidly.

'The care homes often don't give them enough to drink, because it means more toilet trips to make and they're often too under-staffed to cope. But that means the poor elderly people can get very confused, sometimes even aggressive. UTIs are nasty infections which make them feverish.

'Sorry, you don't need to hear all my rantings, I imagine. It's just that if the care homes did a little more caring, the old people wouldn't finish up in here quite so often, taking up beds we really can't spare.

'Anyway, Mrs Applegate was doing well, and we were hoping to discharge her today. Then suddenly, yesterday afternoon, she began with violent vomiting. She was given anti-emetics and we tried to stabilise her but she went into cardiac arrest and we couldn't revive her.'

'What time of day was this in relation to visiting hours?' Ted asked.

'Visiting is two to four every afternoon. She was taken ill about three-thirty, I think and died shortly after seven o'clock. I'd have to check the notes for the exact details.'

'Would you know if Mrs Applegate had any visitors yesterday afternoon?' Mike asked.

She gave a short laugh.

'You know I mentioned being short-handed today? Yesterday was even worse. I honestly wouldn't have had time to notice if a troupe of Morris dancers had come in and performed for her.'

At that moment, the nurse they had seen earlier put her head round the open door and said, 'Jen, sorry, it's Mr Turner, getting very agitated again, trying to pull his drip out.'

'Look, I'm sorry, I have to go. He's another one who's here just because a home didn't make sure he had enough to drink, and now the poor old boy is delirious with fever.'

'Just one quick question,' Mike said, as the two men rose and followed the manager out of the door. 'Did Mrs Applegate have any friends or family who'd been visiting her?'

'As far as I know there was no one. I'll check the files and ring you if I'm wrong but I don't recall ever seeing her with any visitors. Now, please excuse me, gentlemen.'

'Looks like the same MO again, boss, if she did have a visitor that no one noticed,' Mike said as they headed back along the corridor. 'Our top priority now needs to be to work out how and why our killer is targeting the victims, don't you think?'

Ted nodded his agreement and continued, 'Get the team on to those staff records at the homes, Mike. And you'd better speak to the hospital about theirs, see if any names crop up in more than one place.

'You head on back to the nick. I'll jump on a bus or maybe even walk, after I've had my little chat with Oliver. There's just an outside chance he may know about visitors. He's observant, he notices things. And a walk might help me clear my head and give me time to think. There's got to be  something we've missed so far.'

# Chapter Thirteen

Ted knocked briefly and stuck his head round Kevin Turner's door on his way to the Ice Queen's office.

'Have you had the royal summons too?' he wanted to know.

'I have, and let me say at the outset, whatever it is, I didn't do it. I have an alibi. A big boy did it and ran away,' Kevin grinned.

The Superintendent's manner always reduced both men to playground humour. She managed to make them feel like naughty schoolboys, caught smoking behind the bike sheds. It was a long-standing joke between them.

'Seriously, though, have you any idea what it's about?'

'You've not seen the local rag today, then?' Kevin asked him, standing up and trying to ensure his tie was straight and his uniform as tidy as possible. The Ice Queen was always so smartly turned out that it made him feel scruffy by comparison.

'Not the exhumation?' Ted groaned.

Kevin nodded as they headed down the corridor to the Superintendent's office.

'Come in, gentlemen, sit down,' the Ice Queen greeted them, her tone frosty.

Ted had seen an entirely different side to her on a recent case, when they had spent some time together away from the station. She was definitely in formal mode now.

'I take it you've seen today's local paper?' she asked, nodding to where it lay on her desk.

Ted craned his neck and saw the headline, 'Body exhumed

in sudden death mystery,' on the front page lead story. He groaned again, inwardly this time.

'It's very detailed,' she continued. 'They seem to have a lot of information. Have either of you been contacted by the local reporter about this?'

'I only ever say two words to Pocket Billiards, one of which is 'off',' Kevin said frankly then, knowing how formal the Super was, he hastily added a 'ma'am.'

To Ted's surprise, he saw the ghost of a smile flit across the Ice Queen's face. She had encountered the reporter often enough to know why he had the nickname. She would have pulled either Ted or Kevin up short for using it anywhere other than in her office but for the moment, it seemed to amuse her.

'I do hope that is a joke, Inspector Turner?' she asked dryly.

'Sorry, ma'am, probably one in bad taste,' he replied hastily. 'Whenever I do speak to him, which is mercifully not often, I merely refer him to the Press Office.'

'I'm the same, ma'am, and he didn't even bother to contact me on this one because he obviously knew what my answer would be,' Ted assured her.

'So how has he got hold of so much detail?' she asked, looking from one to another.

Ted shrugged.

'I'm no journalist but I would imagine a tip-off about the exhumation from someone who saw something prompted a look to see which grave had been recently disturbed. Then a call to the coroner's office for the name and address, round to the care home for the details and there's your story. I've not yet read it myself, but I'm guessing you could add into that a lot of speculation and a good dollop of scaremongering.'

'As long as no one in this station has leaked anything at all to the press,' she said warningly, looking hard at both of them. 'You shouldn't have to, but please impress once more on your officers how important confidentiality is and what the consequences of any breach will be.'

'Ma'am,' Ted and Kevin said in unison.

'Thank you, Inspector Turner, that will be all for now. Inspector Darling, if I may just have a few more moments of your time?'

Ted had optimistically made to stand up, thinking the interview was over. He sat back down again as Kevin made his exit, with evident relief at getting off so lightly.

'Realistically, is this going to damage your enquiry?' she asked. 'Will it push your killer underground and prevent you from making an arrest?'

'If it does, it also has the effect of preventing any more deaths, which can only be a good thing,' Ted replied. 'Naturally, we want to catch the killer and bring whoever it is to justice, but stopping the deaths would be something, at least.'

'What is your strategy now? How do you plan to take the case forward?'

'I think the next logical step really is to put someone in undercover in the homes, and I wanted to check if you were in agreement with that. I think this is where DC Vine might come into her own,' Ted told her. 'My team are great, I have no complaints about any of them. It's just that I'm having difficulty imagining any of them posing as a carer and looking realistic at it. The killer may well be more wary if they've seen the article in the paper.'

'Could they not simply be visitors?'

'I think our prime suspect, this so-called Angela Mortis, is clever. I also think she watches the homes and chooses her victims carefully. If she suddenly keeps seeing the same person moving aimlessly around or just sitting there, she could well get suspicious. A new carer wouldn't be anything to worry about. She's probably aware that staff turnover is high in the homes.

'As I see it, the way forward is to put DC Vine into the home where our suspect has potentially been laying the groundwork by going in often, armed with harmless cakes. It may be totally unrelated, of course, but I think that unlikely.'

'So you want to take DC Vine on then, having read her file?' she asked. 'Do you think she could fit in with your team?'

'I may be being optimistic, but I do, on both counts. Although her file makes worrying reading,' Ted replied. 'Do we have any clue at all as to why she is as she is? I couldn't see anything in her records to account for it but there must be something, surely? She started out so promisingly and just seems to have gone steadily downhill over the last couple of years or so. It seems a shame. I'd like to try to help, if I can, to reverse the downward spiral.'

'Thank you. It does you credit. I'll arrange for her to start as soon as she has finished her period of leave,' she said. 'Do you need any more officers temporarily? If so, can you liaise with Inspector Turner? I take your point about your existing team. I confess to having difficulty imagining DC Brown making a convincing elderly care worker.'

'To be fair, he is an excellent father, with an incredibly caring side to his nature. And he's doing a wonderful job of getting young Steve back on his feet and helping him to recover from his injuries, both physically and emotionally. But I agree, with his looks, he's not quite the ideal character to blend in anonymously in a care home setting.'

Ted headed back to Kevin's office to discuss with him further the possibility of an extra pair of hands. He explained his dilemma of having a team whose members did not fit the ideal profile of convincing care workers.

'Tell you what, Ted, if the home my dad is in needs looking at, he'd be thrilled to have visitors. He doesn't know who anyone is any more, poor old bugger, not even me. Send in any of your lads and just tell them to sit down next to him and say, 'Hello dad, it's Kevin' and he won't know any different,' Kevin told him. 'Even Virgil,' he laughed. 'Dad won't even notice the colour change.'

DC Dennis Tibbs owed his nickname of Virgil to the films

starring Sidney Poitier as the black detective, Virgil Tibbs.

'It would be doing me a big favour, too. I try to go every day but it's hard finding the time. All they need to do is say 'what about that match last night then, eh?' and he'll rattle on for hours, although it'll be about a match from years ago. Usually the 1966 world cup final, until he falls asleep.

'It's a bastard, this dementia lark, Ted. My dad's not even all that old. His was early-onset. And he can't walk any more, either, after a stroke. I hate to think of some sick bastard going round poisoning old people in the homes like that. The next one could even be my dad,' there was a slight catch in his voice and he broke off for a moment to regain his composure.

'Sorry to hear it, Kev, it must be very hard for you,' Ted said. 'Now, odd question, but relevant. Does your dad like to sit in the lobby or entrance hall or whatever they have at the home he's in?'

'Does that mean he's at more risk? Because he does. He loves to sit by the window so he can see people and cars coming and going, enjoy the sunshine, when it's not raining. There's like a little alcove round to the left as you go in the front door. He usually sits there.

'Is that the MO of this killer, then, targeting the ones sitting near the door? As random as that?' Kevin looked searchingly at Ted, who hesitated, not wishing to alarm him.

'It's a possibility. We've not ruled it in or out at this stage,' he said. 'I'll have a word with Mike, see if we can send some of the team in from time to time to see your dad, keep half an eye on him.'

Kevin beamed with delight.

'Thanks, Ted, I really appreciate it. I owe you one, big time. And I'll see if I can spare you someone, even if it's only occasionally. I imagine anything helps, with a case like this.'

'I might hold you to that favour, one of these days, who knows?' Ted laughed as he headed back to his own office.

# Chapter Fourteen

It felt strange to be standing next to his mother after being apart for so many years. But Ted had promised to be there to support her for his grandmother's funeral and he liked to keep his promises.

There were not many people in the small chapel at the crematorium. A couple of her carers from the home had turned up and seemed nice enough, certainly nicer than the brusque and rather officious manager Ted had spoken to. He was glad his grandmother might have had someone looking after her who perhaps really had cared.

A few of her immediate neighbours had also come, his mother's age, people who remembered his grandmother fondly for her kindness and her baking. If they knew or guessed who Ted was, they tactfully made no comment to his mother.

Trevor had offered to be there but Ted had suggested it might be best not to. He had not yet told his mother he was gay and thought doing so at her own mother's funeral might lack sensitivity. He was not ashamed of his sexuality, nor of his relationship with Trev. He felt that he just needed to pick the right moment.

A priest Ted didn't know, and who had probably never met his grandmother, said a few kind and well-meaning, but rather impersonal, words. In tribute to her Welsh roots, the small congregation sang *Cwm Rhondda*. His mother still had the same fine voice he remembered, just a little more strained now she was older. Ted had a good tenor voice, though he didn't often air it, except alone in his car with either Freddie Mercury or Willie Nelson for company.

From time to time as they sang, his mother reached out and took hold of his hand, tears starting to her eyes. He was not yet comfortable at physical contact with the woman who had abandoned him as a child, whatever her reasons. But he knew there was no one else she could turn to and he did his best to be supportive, returning the contact with a light squeeze. He was rewarded by seeing a sad but grateful smile cross her face each time he did so.

His mother had decided there was to be no sort of get-together after the brief service. She had promised the neighbours she would have them round for tea and cake one day, when she felt more up to it. Instead Ted took her home and spent a bit of time with her, making her a cup of tea and giving her some of the Welsh cakes which Trev had baked specially for the occasion.

'She's a very good cook, your partner,' his mother said appreciatively. 'These are almost as good as Mam's.'

It would have been the ideal moment to tell her, Ted knew, but somehow he couldn't find the right words. He was a good listener but he often had difficulty expressing himself in words.

At Trev's suggestion, Ted had invited his mother for Sunday lunch the coming weekend. He promised to drive up to collect her, then take her home again afterwards. He knew he should tell her in advance that his partner was not a woman, but he somehow couldn't find the way to broach the subject with the mother he felt he hardly knew. As he left to go and collect her, he promised himself he would tell her on the way to lunch.

'What does she like to eat?' Trev had asked him, always keen to serve the perfect choice for a guest.

Ted shrugged.

'No idea,' he said. 'Her tastes may have changed since I knew her, and I was only a kid then, I don't really remember.

She was always a good cook, but nothing fancy.'

'My chicken and ham pie, then,' Trev said decisively. 'That's very traditional, always goes down well.'

Trev's pastry was legendary for its lightness. It was a good choice.

'You have told her about me by now, haven't you?' Trev asked him, anxiously.

'I didn't find the right moment on the day of the funeral,' Ted said evasively. 'I'll tell her when I go to pick her up, promise.'

'You'd better,' Trev said warningly. 'Seriously, Ted, you can't just bring her in and say, you know the woman you think I live with? Well, she's a bloke and here he is.'

But somehow Ted still couldn't find the right words on the short drive with his mother. He decided he would just have to wing it. It had taken some time for him to convince his mother that she looked perfectly fine. She was clearly on edge, nervous about meeting her son's partner, and he didn't want to add to her anxiety.

He was normally a perfect gentleman, who would have stood aside to let his mother go into the house first. In the circumstances, he thought it best to ask her to follow him through the hall and into the kitchen, where Trev was doing his last minute preparations for lunch.

Ted went to him and put an arm around his waist.

'This is my partner, Trevor. Trev, this is my mother, Annie Jones.'

Trev could see straight away by the baffled look on her face that Ted had not told her the truth about his relationship. In a low voice, he said reproachfully, 'Oh Ted, honestly, you promised.'

Ted's mother was looking from one to the other of them, her expression still puzzled.

'But …' she began, then looked directly at Ted and asked, 'Are you happy together?'

'Blissfully,' Ted said, hugging Trev fiercely.

'Mrs Jones, I love your son,' Trev said frankly. 'The fact that I've put up with him for eleven years should tell you just how much.'

'Then that's the only thing that matters to me. That's all any mother should ever want for their children, for them to be happy. And you two obviously are, so there we are, then. Hello, Trevor, it's lovely to meet you. And please call me Annie.'

She held out her arms to Trev, rightly judging that he would be more likely to give her the hug she craved and which Ted felt unable to give her yet.

Ted saw the look of pain which passed briefly over Trev's face and knew he was thinking of how his own parents had treated him. His happiness had clearly not been important to them. Then Trev was folding Ted's mother in a big hug, and happy tears were rolling down her cheeks. Ted knew it was going to be all right.

The meal was a great success. Trev could charm the birds out of the trees and Ted's mother was soon hanging on to his every word. When they had finished eating, Trev was sipping a small cognac, Ted his green tea and his mother her mug of builders' tea.

'Can you think of anyone at all who might have wanted to hurt your mother?' Ted asked.

'Ted,' Trev said warningly. 'You know the house rules. Work gets left at the front door. Stop being such a policeman at the table.'

'I need to ask, though, as her grandson, as much as a policeman.'

'It's all right, Trev, I don't mind answering,' Annie said. 'In fact, I think it would help me to talk about it a bit, if you don't mind. I need to try to make sense of it. No, Teddy, I don't. Even when her mind went wandering, your gran was still a lovely person. It's not as if she was nasty or violent, like some of the others in the home are.'

'And you can't think of anyone called Ange, or Angie, who might have visited her?'

She shook her head.

'The name doesn't ring any bells at all. I've been racking my brains ever since I heard about her and I can't think of anyone Mam knew with that name. And why would the woman say she was her granddaughter, anyway?'

'What about a Margaret, or Maggie, Tyler?'

His mother looked blank and shook her head.

'Or a Lilian Protheroe?'

'Well, Protheroe is a Welsh name, so perhaps there's some connection there to Mam's background? But I don't think I know anyone of that name. Not that I can think of, anyway. Are they your suspects?' she asked.

Ted shook his head. He didn't want to tell his mother at this stage that there were now two, possibly three other victims.

'Just some names that have come up in the course of our enquiries so far,' he said. 'Shall we go and sit down in the other room?' he asked, looking at Trev.

'I should warn you, Annie, that as soon as you sit down on the sofa, the cats will climb on top of you,' Trev told her. 'They have no manners at all. But Ted tells me you like cats too, so perhaps you won't mind?'

Trev took her through to the sitting room, introduced her to the six cats and settled her onto the sofa, before sitting next to her. Ted took the armchair by the window and watched them, looking so happy together. He had never imagined that he would see his mother sitting there, talking to his partner. It was a shame it had taken the death of his grandmother to make it possible.

As promised, Ted drove his mother back to her house. She was full of enthusiasm for Trev, clearly completely under his spell.

'I'm so pleased you have someone so wonderful in your

life, Teddy. I can see how much you love each other. Did your dad know?'

'That I'm gay? Yes, I told him when I was ten. He just hugged me and told me he loved me. He died before I met Trev though, so he never got to meet him.'

'He was a good man, Teddy. I hope you won't feel bad about him that he didn't tell you the truth about me,' she said.

But Ted was struggling to deal with feelings of anger and resentment so strong they surprised him. He could understand why his father had kept the truth from him, but it had robbed him of his mother and grandmother throughout his formative years.

When they reached her house, Ted walked her to the door and saw her safely inside.

'I do hope I can see you again, 'she said. 'And Trevor. He's such a lovely young man, and you're clearly so happy together.'

She stood looking at him, fragile hope etched in every line of her face.

Ted leaned forward and gently pressed his cheek against hers, before he turned and left, quietly closing the door behind him.

# Chapter Fifteen

The following Monday was DC Vine's first day with the team. Except that she didn't turn up at the same time as the others. Even though Ted and Mike held back on starting the morning briefing, there was still no sign of her. Ted was not impressed.

Finally, Mike kicked off the proceedings by allocating tasks for the day. After that, Ted was part-way through a résumé of where they were up to when the door finally opened and the new DC strolled in, seemingly uncaring at her late arrival.

Ted was in his usual place, perched on an empty desk to one side of the room. Mike was in front of the white board, marker in hand, highlighting a point which Ted had made. The new team member wandered over to the DS and said, 'Morning, guv, I'm your new DC.'

Mike frowned but did not correct her. Instead he said, 'Not the best start to your first day, DC Vine.'

She shrugged, unconcerned. 'You know how it is, a new town, finding your way around.'

She didn't seem in the least bit interested in making a good impression.

'Perhaps if you had taken time to find out a bit about your new station, you'd have been on time,' Mike told her. 'You'd also have known that I'm not your new boss. DI Darling is,' he said, nodding to where Ted was sitting, watching his new DC. 'I'm DS Hallam.'

She shrugged again. 'Sorry, Skip,' she said, her tone only

just on the right side of insolence, then turned towards Ted.

'Morning, guv,' she said again, then without being asked, she sat herself down in the nearest empty chair.

The piercings had all been removed. She wore a single sleeper in each ear. The pink hair was now dyed a bright shade of yellow, the colour of sun-ripened maize. She was still unmistakable as the drunken young kickboxer who had tried to pick a fight with Ted in the street. To her credit, if she recognised him at all, she gave no sign of it. Perhaps she had been too drunk to notice what he looked like.

Ted decided to say nothing at this stage, and certainly not in front of the rest of his team. It was clear, though, that he would need to have a few serious words with his newest recruit to establish some basic ground rules.

'Mike, perhaps you'd kindly just give a little recap on what we have so far, for the benefit of DC Vine,' he said to the DS.

Mike glared at her but did as the boss asked, outlining everything they knew so far. DC Vine sat listening, leaning back in her chair, arms folded across her chest.

When he had finished, she announced to the room in general, 'It was the gardener wot done it,' with a note of scorn in her voice.

Ted decided to humour her for now.

'Go on, DC Vine. If you have a theory, let's hear it. We need all the input we can get with this case.'

She sat up a bit straighter.

'Have you looked into who does the gardening at the different homes?' she asked, as if it were the most obvious thing in the world. 'I doubt if, in these cash-strapped days, any of the homes employ their own gardener, so is there a contract gardening company doing the rounds? Quick mow of the lawn, bump off an old biddy, then on to the next one.'

Mike was clearly about to pull her up on the lack of respect but Ted caught his eye and shook his head slightly. He didn't approve of her tone, but it was a valid suggestion, and one that they'd not yet looked at. After all, a gardener would know better than most which commonplace plants were toxic.

'It's an angle we haven't yet explored,' he conceded. 'Mike, can you put someone on to checking that out, please? It's certainly worth looking into. Any other suggestions, DC Vine?'

She looked at him, clearly surprised. If she had been intending to provoke a reaction for some reason, Ted was not about to give her the satisfaction of delivering. The rest of the team were looking at her as if she were some strange alien who had landed amongst them. She merely shrugged in response.

'Right, thanks everyone. You have your assigned tasks, time to get started,' Ted told them and stood up. 'DC Vine, can I please have a quick word in my office before you begin?'

His existing team members grinned at one another. They all knew about the boss's little chats and wondered how this seemingly rebellious new member would fare.

'Come in, have a seat,' Ted told her and sat down opposite her. For the moment, he was a bit at a loss as to how to begin. So far she had looked and acted more like a sulky teenager than the experienced detective her file had suggested she was.

'So, Jessica,' he said by way of an opener.

'Jezza,' she interrupted immediately. 'I prefer Jezza.'

'Fair enough,' he said evenly. 'DS Hallam prefers sarge to skip and I prefer sir or boss to guv.'

She did not react. Neither did she reply. She just stared at him, still looking sullen.

'So,' Ted said again. 'Kickboxing, eh? I do a bit of martial arts myself.'

'You were lucky,' she scoffed. 'I was pissed or I would've taken you out.'

'Jezza, is this your normal behaviour when trying to make an impression with a new team, or is this you on a bad day?' Ted asked her directly.

'What's this, I'm a woman you can't figure out so it must be PMT?' she asked angrily.

She held eye contact with him and her eyes with glinting with anger. Ted noticed she had remarkable eyes, such a pale blue they were almost milky.

He sighed.

'Jezza, I'm a gay police officer. In the CID. Before that, in firearms, an SFO,' he said. 'I am the last person to make any judgement about anyone on the basis of gender stereotyping, or anything else. I'm just trying to find out why you seem to be so angry. Did you not want to join this team?'

She shrugged again.

'Well, here's the thing. We're a good team, we work well together. It's all quite relaxed, but the reason it works is that we all respect one another,' he told her. 'You won't find any sexist, racist or any other 'ist remarks here. But the best way to get respect is to show it. So far this morning, you've demonstrated no sign of that.

'I know you've been on enforced leave to consider your future. I wondered if you'd had time to do so and what you had decided?'

Still the wall of silence. He could see that he was making not the slightest impression on her. She just continued to sit and scowl at him. He tried again.

'From your file, I can see that you're an intelligent officer, capable of working on your own initiative. You have skills which will be invaluable to us, no doubt. But you need to lose the attitude. Seriously, you do. I know you've been told that so many times but I'm telling you again.'

She did not quite say 'Whatever' but her body language as good as did.

'If you have any problems at all, you can always come and talk to me. I'd like us to be able to work together, but you're going to need to meet us halfway if it's going to work.'

He could see he was still making no headway so he said, 'Right, for now, please go and find DS Hallam and see what he wants you to start on. And please try to remember not to call him Skip.'

Without a word, she got up and headed for the door. Ted almost asked her not to slam it, hoping she wouldn't. But she did. Loudly.

He sighed and turned his attention to his paperwork mountain. He hoped to make some inroads into it before the day got away from him.

It was not long before there was a brief knock on his door and Mike Hallam came in, without waiting to be asked. Seeing his face, Ted went to put his kettle on, nodding to the DS to sit down.

'Can I kill her, boss? If I do all the necessary paperwork first? Please?' Mike asked plaintively.

Ted smiled sympathetically.

'Be careful how you try, Mike, she's a kickboxer,' he said, and told him about his first encounter with the new DC.

'Bloody hell, boss,' Mike said. 'What have we done to deserve her? She keeps calling me 'Skip'. It's like an old episode of *The Sweeney*.'

'Does it occur to you that she just does it to get a rise out of us?' Ted asked. 'Perhaps if we simply ignore it and give her time to find her feet a bit, she will get better. You know how the theory goes, as a parent. Ignore the undesirable behaviour, reward the good. On paper, she has the makings of a really good officer. We just need to find out how to handle her.'

'She's like a stroppy teenager,' Mike said. 'I just hope my two aren't going to go through a phase like that. Not sure how I'd cope.'

'Just don't team her up with Maurice too soon,' Ted warned. 'You know how tactless he can be, despite being such a decent bloke, deep down. He's likely to say the wrong thing, not through any malice, but she might just punch his lights out.'

'Is she really what we need right now, with a difficult case on our hands, boss?' Mike asked as Ted handed him a coffee and sat back down with his own green tea.

'She could be exactly what we need now,' Ted replied. 'You know I'm not at all sexist, I hope, although she's already accused me of that. But if we need to put someone in undercover in one of the care homes, can you think of anyone better suited? Can you see Maurice, or Virgil, or any of the others passing for a care worker? Steve might, at a pinch, but he'd be too shy to say anything to anyone.

'She could be ideal, if we can only find the way to manage her. Her file says she can do accents, change her appearance, blend in anywhere. She wouldn't raise any suspicions posing as a care worker, if she'd agree to it.'

'Apart from scaring the living daylights out of the poor old folks,' Mike grumbled. He drank some of his coffee. 'Fair enough, boss, I'll persevere a bit longer.'

'She was right about the gardening angle too, Mike,' Ted reminded him. 'It's something we should have looked at. Have we even checked to see if there are any of the plants used in the killings growing in any of the homes' gardens? Monkshood and foxglove. They sound innocent enough, don't they?'

Mike Hallam sighed.

'Don't you just hate it when someone like that is right?' he asked. 'No, we haven't done so yet and yes, we should have, of course. I'll get Steve to print us off some pictures of the plants and we'll check that angle out.'

'Get Jezza to check it out,' Ted corrected him. 'That's what she tells me she likes to be called, Skip,' he added with a chuckle. 'If it's any consolation, she's obviously intent on calling me 'guv' when clearly none of the rest of the team do and I hate it.

'It was her idea, let her run with it. If nothing else, it will give you and the rest of the team a break from her. She's clearly a lone wolf, so let her run free of the pack for now. At least it will show her we're taking her ideas seriously and valuing her input. That in itself may bring some improvement, if she's not used to such a reaction.'

Mike drained his mug and stood up to go.

'If you say so, boss. At the moment, I can't see anything working with her. But if you've taught me anything, it's not to pre-judge anyone. And she certainly is a she-wolf, that much is true.'

He left the office and Ted went back to his paperwork. He didn't have a clue if they would make any headway with Jezza where other divisions had failed. But he had promised to give her a chance and he was determined to do so.

# Chapter Sixteen

Jezza was late into work again the following morning. Ted was as disappointed as he was annoyed. He had optimistically thought that she might at least have made more of an effort on her second day. They had almost concluded the day's briefing before she appeared.

Again she made no apology but she did say, as soon as she walked through the door, 'Before you say anything guv, or Skip, I have actually been working. I went to a garden centre on my way in, to ask about plants.'

No one had seen her since Mike had sent her out to check into gardeners at the homes the previous morning. Most of the team usually dropped in to the office at the end of the day, just to touch base and find out if there were any updates. It didn't really matter that she hadn't, although Ted did prefer the team to keep in close contact.

'That would be Sarge and sir, or Boss, at the very least,' Mike said pointedly.

It was clearly water off a duck's back to Jezza. She took absolutely no notice, simply continued, 'So do you want to know what I found out?'

Ted looked at her closely. She looked like someone who had barely slept. There were dark rings under eyes which looked bloodshot. He wondered if she made a habit of drinking too much, although surely that would have shown up on her record by now.

'Go ahead, DC Vine,' Ted told her. He wondered if his

formality might produce the same from her, although he doubted it.

'I didn't have time to get round all the homes, clearly, so I started with the ones where there have been deaths. Two of them use the same contract gardener. I have the details, I'll get round there later today when I've checked out more of the homes.'

She was clearly self-confident, used to working by herself. There was no hesitation, and no question of her checking that her chosen route met with approval. Ted let it go for now.

'Also two of the homes, though not the same two, have foxgloves growing in the garden. The one where the victim died of foxglove poisoning and the one where the old Welsh biddy died, but hers was a different toxin, wasn't it?'

There was a stunned silence from the whole team at her choice of words. Mike was the first to speak.

'DC Vine, Mrs Jones was the boss's grandmother.'

'Well, I didn't know that, did I?' she said defensively. 'I wouldn't expect someone related to one of the victims to be involved in their murder enquiry.'

Ted almost smiled. She did have a point.

'It doesn't really matter who she was related to, DC Vine,' Ted said quietly. 'The fact is, she deserves to be spoken of with respect, please, as do all the victims. Go on.'

She did not apologise. She didn't even acknowledge what he'd said. She merely continued, 'I didn't see any monkshood anywhere, although it's a bit early for it to be flowering, apparently.

'The trip to the garden centre was interesting. Anyone can go in and buy any number of highly poisonous plants, like foxglove and monkshood, possibly without knowing how deadly they can be. They're not labelled as dangerous or anything. Well, the foxgloves aren't, the aconite has something about the whole plant being poisonous, but in small lettering at the bottom of the label, which is often sticking down into the soil in the pot. In other words, that would mean you would have to know beforehand that they were poisonous, if you were planning to use them to bump someone off.'

To everyone's surprise, it was Steve who decided to challenge her first. He was usually quiet and painfully shy but he clearly did not appreciate the lack of respect the new arrival was showing to the boss he thought the world of, nor to the rest of the team.

'Anyone who can use a computer can get that sort of information in a couple of clicks. Google it, pick the most poisonous, go out and buy it. That proves nothing.'

'Yes, but, duh. Why go to the trouble?' she came back at him, her tone scornful. 'You can buy enough paracetamol in any supermarket to kill off an old …'

To Ted's surprise, she actually checked herself before continuing, '… an elderly person. Why go to the expense and trouble of faffing about with plants instead?'

Once again, her opinion was valid, Ted grudgingly had to concede to himself. He said nothing, waiting to see where things would go.

'So what exactly are you saying, someone with specific plant knowledge? A botanist or something?' Rob O'Connell asked.

'Well, I've not ruled out the gardener angle yet, I'm still looking into that. Then there's also the question of why the victims are all women,' she continued. 'Is that significant? A grudge against an older woman?'

'Statistically, women live longer than men, so there are far more women in homes than men,' Steve said, clearly not done yet. 'That may be entirely coincidental.'

'And it may not be, which is precisely why we should be considering it,' she countered, then continued, 'Also, sorry to mention this, guv, in relation to your granny, but these were particularly unpleasant deaths. So is that fact significant in the motive for this? Not just killing these old people but killing them in a certain way, making them suffer horribly.'

'We can't really look at motives until we have a suspect though, can we?' Maurice asked her. Ted was impressed that the normally tactless DC managed to keep his tone just the right side of patronising.

'Finding some sort of a motive might lead us to a definite suspect,' she retorted.

'But isn't that guesswork rather than detection?' Virgil Tibbs put in.

'Isn't guesswork all we have so far?' she said scathingly, waving a hand towards the board. 'A woman calling herself the Angel of Death, possibly, under various nicknames, who may or may not always be the same person?'

Ted decided it was time to step in before things got too heated.

'All right, everyone, calm down,' he said, standing up and moving over to the white board. 'This is a murder enquiry, not a debating society. It's also a murder enquiry being headed by DS Hallam.' He was looking straight at Jezza as he spoke. 'Therefore it's his decision which direction it goes in, as well as if and when we move into the realms of pure speculation. Is that clear, DC Vine?'

At that moment her mobile phone rang and she answered it, without even acknowledging him.

'Yes, but can't you …' she started to say and was clearly cut short. She listened for a moment then added, 'I'll be there shortly.' She looked round at the team and said, 'Right, I've got to go, that could be important.'

She grabbed her shoulder bag and was gone before anyone could say anything.

Mike shook his head in bewilderment.

'Is it too much of a cliché to say 'there's no I in team'?' he asked.

Ted's team were all looking at him expectantly, wondering if even their easy-going boss was going to lose his cool in the face of such dumb insolence from a newcomer.

'DC Vine is certainly a little, shall we say, individual. Some of you may be wondering why I've not yet pulled her up on her unusual style. You may even be thinking I'm going a bit soft in my old age. If you are thinking that, I'd prefer you to voice it to my face, rather than behind my back.'

He looked round at the team members. Nobody said anything.

'That's great, thank you. I'd just ask you to bear with me on this for the time being. I'll handle it, but it may take a while. Now, you've got your appointed tasks, please get on with them. And let's not neglect other cases while we concentrate on this one. With luck, we may get further tox results soon on our other victims, which would be a help.

'Mike, have you got a minute?' he asked, as he headed for his office.

Ted went straight for the kettle, nodding to Mike to sit down.

'Coffee?' he asked.

'Give me some of that green stuff you drink, boss, please,' Mike said to his surprise. 'I want to find out how you keep as calm as you do. I just want to slap her face off and I'm not normally the violent sort, with more reason than most.'

Ted laughed.

'I hope that's a joke,' he said, then added, 'I'll put honey in it, it goes down better that way.'

He prepared two mugs, waiting for the kettle to boil.

'The problem is, of course, she does have some good ideas,' he said. 'She's picked up on a couple of angles we hadn't considered and she seems to be working them very thoroughly.'

'Yes, but she's certainly not a team player, boss,' Mike said at once. 'She's only been here five minutes but she comes and goes as she pleases. I don't have a clue where she is most of the time. That's not how we work. And is it just me or did she look well and truly hungover this morning?'

'You know I don't like to judge, Mike' Ted said. 'There could be all sorts of reasons for her to look like that. We've all had stuff in our private lives which sometimes spills over into the workplace.'

Mike had had personal problems when he had first arrived, which Ted had helped him to deal with.

'Fair point, boss, but I hope I was never gobby with it.'

'Never gobby, Mike, no,' he said. 'Let me have another word with Jezza, quietly, and see if things improve.'

'Then can I kill her?' Mike asked hopefully. 'Sorry, boss, only kidding.'

'Let's try her in undercover. According to her file, she really has had some good results. It seems to be her thing,' Ted told him. 'She deserves a chance to show us what she can do. Then, if it doesn't work out, we'll just have to think again. We've always got Inspector Turner's offer of an extra officer from uniform, should we need one, which gives us a Plan B.'

# Chapter Seventeen

'Absolutely fascinating case this, Edwin, really extraordinary.'

Ted was still having his breakfast at home when Professor Nelson called him on his mobile. As usual, she started with the briefest of greetings.

'Morning, Bizzie, do you have some toxicology results for me, then?' Ted asked, pushing aside his plate of half-eaten wholemeal toast. He could hardly be crunching that down the phone whilst the pathologist was giving him details of poisonings.

'Yes indeed. Your poisoner certainly knows their plants and would seem to have been experimenting somewhat with which is the most efficacious, and at what dosage. I will, of course, be emailing you my full report shortly, but I wondered if you would prefer the essential highlights from me first? Is this a good time for you?'

Ted looked wistfully at his breakfast, already going cold and limp on the plate. Depending on how long the conversation was, he would not have time to make more before he needed to leave for work. He sighed to himself. He would just have to pick something up on the way in, to eat in his office.

The most senior of the cats, Queen, sensing his abandonment, had already jumped on to the table and begun licking the butter off the toast.

'Yes, it's fine, Bizzie. Thanks for taking the time to call me. What have you got for me?'

'I now have the two outstanding sets of results. Both deaths were the result of ingestion of toxins from plants, as before. Regarding the toxins used, we have two new ones this time. First, your hospital lady, Mrs Applegate. This time the poison used was *taxus baccata*, from the yew tree. Not at all hard to find. Traditionally, most churchyards had, and sometimes still have, at least one.

'It's quite a poisonous plant but - and this is where I think it tells us something important about your poisoner - the leaves are actually the most toxic part. That is to say that the concentration of the toxins is higher in the leaves than in the berries, contrary to what many people think.

'In fact, the berries themselves are harmless and edible. The stone inside is lethal, but only when crushed so the toxin is exposed. It's why these trees self-seed so easily. Birds eat and digest the fruit, leaving the stone to pass out undigested, thus preventing the birds from being poisoned. Please tell me if I'm boring you?'

Ted smiled to himself. The Professor was inclined to get a bit carried away with her own enthusiasm, but so far what she was saying was useful. He encouraged her to go on, at the same time lifting Queen off the table before she started on the toast itself, having finished the butter.

'Now, I had some stomach contents to go on with Mrs Applegate, so I can tell you that the leaves were used. I would expect most people to go for the berries under the mistaken belief that they are the poisonous part. In addition, I was able to test other fluids like bile, brain tissue, urine ...'

She broke off abruptly. 'Oh, I am sorry, Edwin, I do hope you're not in the middle of your breakfast?'

Ted sighed once more, although he was now no longer hungry after listening to her list. Once again, he asked her to continue.

'Yew contains taxoids, which are used medicinally for their anti-cancer properties. But in the case of an overdose, the taxoids taxine A and taxine B cause symptoms including nausea, vomiting and abdominal pain.

'After these initial symptoms, there may be bradycardia then ventricular tachycardia, possibly followed by severe ventricular arrhythmia and ventricular fibrillation. All of which means, put simply, that the heart first slows down, then speeds up, then its rhythm is seriously, potentially fatally, disturbed.

'Even if the medical team had known or suspected the ingestion of toxins and knew which one was involved, there is no known, proven antidote readily available. In an elderly patient with an already weakened system, the result was, I would say, a foregone conclusion.'

'Bizzie, this really is very helpful, thanks for simplifying it for me. I probably wouldn't have made head nor tail of the report as clearly as this,' Ted said gratefully. 'But right now, I need to be heading in to the office. May I call you from there in, say, half an hour, for the details of the other one? If that's not disturbing you?'

'Not at all. I will be doing another post-mortem about then, but I am quite capable of chopping and chatting at the same time,' she said breezily.

Ted grabbed a Danish pastry from a nearby shop on his way to work. He wasn't keen on starting the day with a sugar rush, but at least it was quick and easy to eat on the go.

Bizzie had already emailed her reports. He had a quick glance through but decided to call her back for her explanation of the second one. She was better at explaining the main principles than he was at picking them out for himself.

'Yes, as I was saying, utterly fascinating,' Bizzie spoke as if their break in conversation had been less than a minute, instead of more than half an hour. Ted didn't risk asking her what she was doing as she spoke. 'Now this fourth victim, your Mrs Protheroe, the exhumation. So unusual that I had to do quite a bit of research.

'The culprit this time was oleander. Such a pretty flower, but so very deadly. It's a hard call as to which one is the most toxic, oleander or the aconite which said poisoner has used before. For me, the oleander wins hands down, as even smoke from burning it contains the toxic cardiac glycosides, oleandrin and neriine. Their effects are similar to those of foxglove toxins. It's probably because of the robust nature of these toxins that we were still able to detect traces so long post-mortem.

'As with the other plants, there is a beneficial side, in that cardiac glycosides are used in the treatment of congestive heart failure and cardiac arrhythmia. But in toxic doses, the symptoms manifest as vomiting and light-headedness, often some hours after ingestion, followed possibly by cardiac abnormalities, including ventricular dysrhythmia, tachycardia, bradycardia, and heart block.

'In other words, Mrs Protheroe would in all likelihood have presented with symptoms similar to gastroenteritis, then her heart rhythms would have varied wildly, leading to her heart failing, as in the other cases.'

'So the death would appear to be similar to the others, just yet another different toxin?'

'Correct,' the Professor confirmed. 'And in this particular case, it would appear that this lady had ingested enough to kill more than just one frail elderly person. All of which leads me to a somewhat wild theory. May I suggest it to you?'

'Please do,' Ted said. 'Theories are something we're a bit short of at the moment.'

'Entirely speculative, of course, but if Mrs Protheroe was the first victim, the poisoner may have been playing about to see what dosage was sufficient to do the dastardly deed. Now they are refining their art somewhat, I would brace yourself for the possibility of more victims to come.'

Ted thanked her and rang off, hoping she was wrong.

The team members were all in now, so Ted went into the main office to join them. Jezza was the last to arrive but she was only just late, which Ted hoped was an encouraging sign.

He brought the team up to speed on the latest findings,

while Mike wrote up what he said on the white board, with Steve on the computer to check spellings for him. Ted had to get him to double check the various heart rhythm terms as he was losing track of what was fast, slow or irregular.

When he'd finished, Mike spoke up.

'Boss, I had a sudden theory for a possible motive.'

Ted nodded at him to go on.

'Bed-blocking,' he said, then, as there were blank looks all round, he continued, 'You remember, boss, the ward manager was saying how they get a lot of old people in from homes when all they basically need is more water to drink.

'What if there is a nurse or a carer somewhere thinking there are just too many old people on the planet? That when they finish up in hospital, they're stopping anyone younger, with a better chance of survival, from getting a bed?'

'The ward manager we saw couldn't be our Angela though, she was far too tall,' Ted said. 'Height is one part of the appearance it simply isn't possible to alter significantly, as I know to my cost.'

There were a few chuckles. Even in the smart new brogues with a bit of a heel which Trev had made him buy to go with his new suits, Ted was well below average height. Not that he minded; he was comfortable in his own skin. But the descriptions of Angela which they had so far, suggested she was shorter and more well-built than the tall, slim ward manager he and Mike had spoken to.

'Which home did this Mrs Protheroe come from, before she was taken to hospital?' Jezza asked.

She still looked very tired. She was leaning back in her chair, arms folded, legs stuck out in front of her, in ripped jeans. She was wearing pink Doc Martens boots. Ted envied her their comfort. They had always been his footwear of choice, though not in pink, before the reign of the Ice Queen had begun.

Ted and Mike exchanged guilty looks. Ted suddenly

realised they had not yet got that information, nor visited the home in question.

'Right, that's one for your list today, Jezza,' Ted told her. 'We'll get you the information, you get round there, same questions as before. Then please come in and report back in person.'

Ted also took it as encouraging that there was no back-chat and she made no comment on the fact that both he and Mike had slipped up on a detail.

'How are we getting on with checking staff names?'

'Virgil and I are in charge of that, boss,' Sal told him. 'Still cross-checking between homes, and against the hospital staff records we have so far, too. No duplicates as yet.'

'Keep checking. Whoever our poisoner is, there's a strong chance they're not using their own name at all, and if they do change jobs, they probably change their name.'

'Keep asking about Angela, wherever you go,' Mike told them. 'We still need to find out if she's one person or several. And whenever anyone's in that area, don't forget to call in to see Inspector Turner's father, even if it's only for five minutes.'

True to his word to Kevin, Ted had asked the team to drop in on Mr Turner Senior, whenever they had a few minutes to spare and were in the area. There was always a chance they would get lucky and spot Angela while they were there.

'Keep your eyes and ears peeled while you're visiting. And I don't just mean for a kick by kick account of the 1966 World Cup match,' Mike added.

'I popped in myself yesterday, while I was over that way,' Ted told them. 'I know absolutely nothing about football so I couldn't contribute much to the conversation. Not that it seemed to matter.'

Jezza was gathering up her things, ready to head out by herself, following up her leads.

'Geoff Hurst scored the winning goal in the one hundred and twentieth minute, the third of a hat trick, although computer simulation later showed that his second goal had not, in fact, crossed the line,' she tossed over her shoulder as she walked out of the door, leaving the rest of the team looking at each other, surprised.

# Chapter Eighteen

Ted answered the land-line when it rang. Trev was in the kitchen preparing their evening meal. The home phone seldom rang. They both tended to give out their mobile numbers in preference.

A coldly formal voice said, 'I wish to speak to Trevor Armstrong.'

'Who's calling, please?' Ted asked guardedly, some sixth sense telling him it may not be a call which Trev would wish to take.

There was a pause, then, 'It's a personal matter. It is extremely important that I speak to him. Please ask him to come to the telephone.'

'One moment, please,' Ted said, taking the cordless phone with him to the kitchen, his hand over the mouthpiece. 'It's for you. A woman. She won't say who it is,' he explained.

He handed the phone to Trev and made himself scarce, in case it was something his partner didn't want him to overhear.

The call was not a long one. Trev came into the sitting room where Ted was watching the news, the cats vying for position to sit on him, kneading with their paws. Trev opted to sit in the armchair, unusually for him. He was a tactile person who normally liked to sit close to his partner. He looked suddenly pale under his lingering suntan.

'Don't speak of the devil or he might appear,' he said, with a note of bitterness in his voice. 'Remember me saying that? Or in this case, she might. That was my mother.'

Ted looked at him in surprise.

'Really? What did she want?'

'I am summoned to her presence. Tomorrow. In Manchester. She won't tell me what it's about, just that it's a vitally important personal matter which she has to tell me in person. Initially, I refused point blank. I don't want to go. I don't want to have anything to do with her. She insisted and said it's in my own interests to do so.'

He looked beseechingly at Ted and asked, 'Will you come with me? Please?'

'Of course I will,' Ted said immediately. 'But won't that just be like a red rag to a bull?'

'I don't care,' Trev replied. 'I want you there. I need you with me. I can't do this on my own. Unlike your mother, mine really did abandon me. There will be no sentimental reunion, no hugs and tears. This will be some sort of formal business meeting. Pure and simple.'

'How did she get hold of the land-line number?' Ted couldn't resist asking.

Trev snorted.

'Certainly not from me,' he said. 'No, my father can get any information he wants about anything or anybody, through his contacts. He probably knows all about us. I can't imagine why she wants to see me, but I know it won't be good news for me.'

Trev had been given the address of the hotel where his mother would be staying, briefly, and told to report there the following afternoon, a Saturday, at three o'clock. The hotel was the best and most expensive in the city, or for miles around. Trev supervised what Ted was to wear, knowing they would be refused admission, let alone service, if they turned up in the sort of casual attire they both preferred for weekends.

When he saw the impressive Edwardian façade and stepped into the plush opulence of the hotel interior, for once Ted was glad he had been persuaded to wear a suit and tie, even though it was the weekend. He would have felt hopelessly out of place here otherwise.

Trev was more comfortable and at ease in such surroundings as a rule. But this time he was clearly on edge at the prospect of meeting his mother, the woman who had thrown him out when he was barely sixteen, the day that he told his parents he was gay.

He strode across the impressively appointed lobby, heading towards an incredibly elegant woman, sitting alone near the window, Ted following in his wake. She looked up as she saw her son approaching, then frowned. She had the same jet black hair and piercing blue eyes as Trev, but there was a coldness about the eyes which he did not usually show.

'This is a private family matter, Trevor,' she said coldly, her only form of greeting.

'Hello to you too, Mother,' Trev said sarcastically. 'This is my partner, Ted. Either he stays or I don't.'

'Please do not be facetious, Trevor, it does not suit you,' she said, eyeing Ted up and down and clearly finding him wanting. 'Very well, since this is important, your friend may stay. Sit down, both of you.'

Ted had never encountered anyone quite like her, with such commanding presence. She could even have outdone the Ice Queen at her coldest. She raised an imperious hand and made a silent clicking motion with her fingers, without looking round. A waiter appeared as if by magic. Had he not seen it for himself, Ted would not have believed it.

'Tea. China. For three,' she said without either looking at the man or consulting Trev and Ted.

'May I possibly have green tea, please?' Ted asked, addressing the waiter directly. 'With honey, if you have some available?'

'Certainly, sir,' the man replied. 'Organic tea and Manuka honey?'

Ted nodded, aware that Trev's mother was now regarding him as if he should not have been admitted. He imagined she was not used to anyone who would dream of saying please to a waiter.

She sat back down, gesturing to them to do the same, which Trev did with evident reluctance.

'What did you want, Mother?' Trev asked impatiently, clearly keen to be gone.

Ted had never seen him so ill at ease.

'Your father is in hospital, Trevor. He has suffered a serious heart attack and is undergoing surgery,' she said.

'Am I supposed to care?' Trev asked harshly. 'Is he in hospital in Manchester? Is that why you've come up here?'

'Don't be ridiculous,' she said dismissively. 'He's in the Royal Brompton. I've come in person because I need to tell you that the reason for his heart attack was a previously undiagnosed illness, an underlying condition, which has the potential to be hereditary.'

Trev went ashen. Ted wanted to reach out a hand to him, but sensed the moment might not be right.

'It is vital that you get yourself tested for it as soon as possible. There is a chance that you could have the same condition,' his mother continued, her tone still coldly clinical.

The waiter appeared quietly with their tea and set the tray down on the low table in between the sumptuous leather club chairs they were sitting in. None of them made a move towards the drinks.

'We've had Siobhan tested and fortunately she is clear.'

'Who is Siobhan?' Trev asked, his voice brittle.

'Our daughter,' his mother replied, as if it were obvious.

'I have a sister?' Trev queried incredulously. 'How old is she?'

'Nearly fourteen.'

'Fourteen? How does that work, then?' Trev demanded, his voice rising. 'You throw out your sixteen-year-old son because he's a total disappointment to you when he announces he's gay. Then what? You rush upstairs and start shagging to see if you can make a better one? One that isn't quite so disgusting, as you told me I was?'

His voice was so loud now that people in other nearby seats were looking across at them. An officious-looking man, presumably a manager of some sort, came over and addressed Trev's mother.

'Is everything all right, Lady Armstrong?' he asked. 'Are these two gentlemen bothering you?'

His tone was scornful. He made it clear that he considered neither Trev nor Ted to be gentlemen.

Trev had got to his feet and looked as if he was preparing to storm out. Ted rose too and went quietly over to him.

'Everything's fine,' he said to the manager. 'Sorry for the disturbance. It won't be repeated.'

Trev's mother waved the man away and after a lingering look at the two men, he moved off and left them to it.

'Trev, calm down,' Ted told him quietly. 'I know it's a shock, a lot to take in. But you need to sit down and listen to what else she has to say. We need to know what we're dealing with here, then we can get you the right sort of help. Come on. Sit down. Please.'

He had his hands on his partner's arms and could feel that Trev was trembling violently, though whether it was from shock or anger or both, he couldn't tell. He had never seen Trev so angry.

'Please,' he said again.

Reluctantly, Trev sat down again. His mother was unconcernedly pouring tea. Trev made no attempt to touch it. Ted took a quick gulp of the green tea, after adding a liberal dollop of honey. He needed something to help him stay calm enough to manage the situation. He could see that Trev was still on the point of exploding.

'The tests are relatively straightforward, although you will need several,' she continued, barely looking at Trev. 'You will require a blood test, then usually an ECG, a stress test and a CT scan. I've taken the precaution of writing the details down for you, as I appreciate that it's a lot to take in. I've also noted the name of your father's heart consultant, should your doctor here require any further detail.'

She put a sheet of paper on the table, with notes on it in neat handwriting. Trev made no move towards it. She then took a dainty sip of her tea, to which she added neither milk nor sugar. Trev was still sitting stiffly, ignoring his cup.

Ted had another quick swallow of his tea. He reached out to take the piece of paper Trev's mother was now pushing across the table, as Trev was still making no move to do so. She looked as if the idea of her hand being so close to that of her son's gay lover was repellent to her.

'Obviously, you will get the results through much more quickly if you go privately,' she said. 'In the circumstances, I would be prepared to pay for you to do so, if you need me to. I cannot stress how important it is for you to get these tests done as soon as possible.

'This is an illness which can strike at any time, without any prior symptoms at all. Your father was as fit as he has always been, still regularly playing tennis, squash and badminton at every opportunity. In fact, he collapsed during a squash match at his club.

'Please be good enough to keep me informed of your test results. Here's my card.'

Once again, she held it out towards Trev who ignored it, his blue eyes flashing angrily. Ted could see that he was still trembling, so he took the card and made to put it in his pocket. Trev sprang to his feet.

'Leave it, I won't be getting in touch,' he almost spat, heading for the door.

'If you care for him at all, make sure he gets those tests,' Trev's mother said to Ted, as he turned to follow his partner.

He caught up with Trev almost back at the car. Without a word, he put his arms round him and hugged him. Trev was shaking from head to toe.

'The bitch! The ice cold bitch,' he said through gritted teeth. 'You think your parents treated you badly? Now you've seen what my mother is like. Let's get out of here, as soon as possible. I don't even want to be in the same city as that woman.'

They drove in silence for a short while, then Ted put a hand on Trev's arm and squeezed it gently.

'We'll get this sorted. As soon as possible. I've got that health insurance, that will cover something like this. It'll be all right, Trev, I promise.'

As they got nearer to Stockport, Trev suddenly said, 'Can you drop me off near the town centre, please? I just need to be on my own for a bit. I'll go and have a beer somewhere. Would you mind? I won't be late back.'

'Let me park up somewhere and I'll come with you,' Ted suggested.

'No, really, I know it's not your thing and I just feel as if I need a bit of space. I'll be fine, honestly, please don't worry.'

Ted was reluctant to agree, but as they neared Mersey Square, the lights were on red so Trev slipped out of the car. Before he walked away, he turned back and mouthed 'Love you' through the window.

Ted felt a sudden cold panic. Trev never had trouble expressing himself and often said the same thing. This time, however, it suddenly had a ring of finality about it. Ted wanted to jump out of the car and run after him.

At that precise moment, the lights changed. Already cars behind were impatiently sounding their horns when Ted did not immediately pull away. He crashed into first gear and almost stalled. When he looked again, Trev had disappeared.

# Chapter Nineteen

Ted had no idea what time Trev would get back, nor if either of them would feel like eating when he did. He stopped to pick up an Indian takeaway on his way home. There was plenty of it and it would keep for another day if it didn't get eaten that evening.

As soon as he got in, the cats started swarming round his legs, purring loudly and demanding food. It was usually Trev who fed them, when he got home from work and at weekends, but they were faithless and clearly only interested in food. Who gave it to them appeared not to concern them.

Ted's head was still reeling with the news. He could not begin to imagine how Trev must be feeling and wished he was with him to offer him some sort of comfort. He put the television on, tried to concentrate on the news, but could not.

Instead he got his laptop out, put it on the table and booted it up. He was not brilliant with a computer but he was determined to find out all he could. He took the notes Trev's mother had written out of his pocket, consulted them, and started searching Google for answers. He was shocked by what his searches found.

He had somehow hoped that, despite what Lady Armstrong had said, Trev being in such peak physical form would protect him from the illness. Instead he read with mounting horror of top rugby and football players collapsing on the pitch with the same condition. Some, but not all, had survived.

There was a teenage boy, a regional long-distance running

champion, hotly tipped for Olympic potential, who had collapsed and died on a run, with no prior warning. A top swimmer, mid-twenties, who had suffered a heart attack in the pool and paramedics had not succeeded in reviving her.

The more Ted read, the more worried he became. He decided it would be more productive to try to find out about the tests which Trev would need and where he would have to go to get them. He was surprised and pleased to find that nearby Wythenshawe Hospital had one of the best heart units in the country.

It was now past the time he and Trev would usually eat in the evenings, but he was still not hungry, much too anxious to want to eat anything. He took out his mobile phone and dialled Trev's number. It went straight to voicemail.

'Hi, I hope you're having fun. I forgot to say, if you want me to come and pick you up from somewhere, just give me a call.'

He hesitated for a moment then added, 'Love you,' as Trev had said earlier. He did, deeply. He just had difficulty expressing it and vowed to say it much more in the future.

He had still heard nothing by eleven o'clock and was starting to get worried. He knew Trev could look after himself in normal circumstances. Ted had first met him when he'd coached him towards black belts in judo and karate. But these were far from normal circumstances and he had no idea how he was coping.

He left another message on Trev's phone a bit later on.

'Just getting a bit anxious now. Can you let me know you're ok? Sorry to fuss.'

Still nothing.

When his mobile rang shortly after midnight, he pounced on it, hoping it was Trev. Instead the caller display showed it was Dave, landlord of The Grapes, the favourite watering hole of Ted and his team, near to the police station.

'Hello, Ted, sorry to bother you late on,' Dave said. 'It's

your Trev. He's had a few too many, won't go home and he's getting a bit punchy. Someone's called your lot. I wondered if you could come and sort it, before things get nasty.'

Ted could hear the sound of raised voices and breaking glass in the background.

'On my way,' he said shortly, grabbing his jacket and his car keys.

He broke several sections of the Road Traffic Act on his way to the pub. When he arrived, there was a police car outside the front door, its blue lights flashing. He screeched to a halt behind it, two wheels on the kerb, and raced inside.

Two Uniform officers he knew by name were standing warily inside, batons drawn. He had worked with PC Susan Heap on occasion. The other was PC Jack Hargreaves. Ted knew the name of every officer in the station.

Trev was over near the bar, in a karate posture. There was an overturned table in front of him, broken glass strewn around the floor. Ted could see that he was very drunk, swaying on his feet, but still dangerous to tackle.

'I didn't want to spray him, sir,' PC Heap told him, 'but we can't get near him any other way.'

'I'll sort it, don't worry,' Ted told her, more calmly than he felt.

'We've got to be seen to arrest him, sir,' PC Hargreaves said, apologetically.

Ted nodded.

'I know, I understand. Just let me speak to him first. I'll get him to go quietly. That way no one will get hurt.'

'Trev,' Ted said, stepping forward.

Trev was drunk enough to take a high karate kick at him. It never found its target. Ted simply moved too fast.

There were still a few late drinkers in the bar, keeping well out of the way. Ted looked across at Dave, behind the bar, still keeping half an eye on Trev, and asked, 'Has anyone been hurt?'

Dave shook his head.

'Not yet,' he said meaningfully. 'What's got into him? I've never seen Trev the worse for drink before, and certainly not punchy.'

'I'm sorry for the disruption, Dave. He's had a bit of bad news today. I'll sort it,' he said again.

Even sober, Trev was no match for the superior technical skills of Ted. Drunk, he stood no chance. On his next attacking move, Ted had him pinned in an arm-lock, face down on the bar and totally immobilised, in a matter of seconds.

Susan Heap moved forward, holding out her handcuffs and putting her baton away.

Ted shook his head and said quietly to Trev, his mouth close to his ear, 'Don't make me cuff you, Trev. Just calm down and go quietly.'

Trev was crying and just kept repeating, 'I'm sorry, I'm so sorry,' over and over again.

All sign of resistance was now gone. The two PCs stepped up on either side of him and took hold of an arm each. Trev went meekly with them, taller and more powerfully-built than either of them but not showing any further signs of fight.

'Please be gentle with him,' Ted said as they walked away. 'I'll be there right behind you.'

He turned back to Dave behind the bar and took out his wallet.

'I'm so very sorry about this, Dave. Please see that everyone who's been affected gets a drink on me. Then add up the damage and I'll make sure that Trev comes in and pays you, and apologises. And thanks for phoning me.'

Before he drove off after the area car, Ted made a quick phone call.

'Bloody hell, Ted, do you know what time it is?' Kevin Turner's voice growled down the phone at him.

'Sorry, Kev, but you know that big favour you owe me? I'm calling it in, now,' Ted told him. 'Can you meet me down at the nick as soon as possible, please?'

There was more swearing but then Kevin said, 'This better be important. I'm on my way.'

When Ted got to the station, the two officers had taken Trev through and put him in a cell. Bill was on duty yet again as custody sergeant. PCs Heap and Hargreaves were standing talking to him. Ted went over to speak to them.

'I haven't started any paperwork yet, Inspector. I can't find a pen,' Bill told him shamelessly, despite the fact that there was one on the counter in front of him. He was being formal in front of the two constables.

'I appreciate that, Sergeant, but I don't want Trevor treated any differently to anyone else arrested for a disorder offence,' Ted told him. 'I would just like to arrange to take him home with me, on bail, if necessary. I've asked Inspector Turner to come in. I don't want anyone to be compromised.'

'Behave yourself.' Bill told him. 'The officers only had to bring him in for form's sake. It can all be sorted out without the need for bail or charges, I'm sure.'

'Resisting arrest?' Ted said pointedly.

'He didn't resist, sir, we were just having a little discussion when you arrived,' PC Heap told him.

'Criminal damage?' he suggested.

'Nothing deliberate, sir,' PC Hargreaves joined in. 'He just lost his balance and knocked the table over.'

Kevin Turner must have broken a few traffic laws himself, as he came into the station at that point and, with a nod at his officers, he invited Ted to follow him to his office, where they both sat down.

'Now what's all this about Trev?' he asked Ted. 'I phoned Bill on the way and he filled me in. It's not like Trev to get stinking drunk. What's going on?'

'He's had some bad news today and it's knocked him for six,' Ted told him. 'Both of us, really, just Trev hasn't handled it very well. I don't want any special treatment, I just want to be able to take him home. I don't want him spending the night in a police cell.'

'You didn't need me here for that. You know Bill would have been happy to sort it for you,' Kevin said. 'My officers think a lot of you, and of Trev. I don't think there need be any charges.'

Ted started to protest but Kevin interrupted, 'Shut up, Ted. If it went to court he'd get a slapped wrist and a fine, which you'd probably pay. What's the point? Take him home, dry him out and make sure it doesn't happen again.'

Ted tried to thank him but Kevin waved it aside.

'The home staff tell me my dad's had a few visitors these last few days. I really appreciate that. This is the least I can do.'

The two men shook hands warmly and Ted went off to the cells to collect Trev. He was sitting on the cot, knees drawn up, arms wrapped round them. He had clearly been sick on the drive to the station. There was vomit on his normally immaculate clothes and he smelled strongly.

'Come on, you, let's get you home and cleaned up,' Ted told him gently.

Trev was in tears again, his voice thick with them.

I'm dying, Ted,' he wailed forlornly.

Ted smiled.

'You're not dying. You're just very drunk. Come on.'

'I am. I'm going to die young and I don't want to. I want to grow old, with you.'

Ted took his arm, helped him to his feet and took him home. He had to stop a couple of times for him to be sick again. When he got him home, he had to practically undress and shower him as Trev was beyond doing much to help himself.

He got him into bed, carefully positioning him so that if he vomited again he would not inhale it. Then he left him to sleep, checking on him frequently to make sure he was all right.

He knew he wouldn't sleep much himself but he tried to

catch whatever he could downstairs on the sofa. The cats, who doted on Trev, refused his company on this occasion, smelling as he did, even after the shower.

As he sat on the edge of the bed on one of his trips upstairs, Ted looked at Trev's perfectly toned and fit body. He wondered how it could be that the generous heart beating inside that muscular chest could possibly be so treacherous.

In the morning, he took him up a cup of tea and a large glass of water. He was worried that the stimulant effect of coffee might not be a good idea.

'Right, let me tell you how it's going to be,' he said quietly. 'When you've had your tea, you're going to get a shower. You still stink of booze. Then put your walking gear on. We're going to the Dark Peak. We're going to walk and talk, and I'm going to tell you everything I've found out about this condition and what we can do about it. It's going to be all right.'

'I'm scared though, Ted,' Trev said in a small voice. 'Scared and feeling dreadfully betrayed. They were so disappointed with me that they had to make another child immediately. And I never even knew I had a sister.'

'I know. I understand. But first we have to make things right. So tomorrow, after work, you're going to call in at the nick, grovel to Kevin and then apologise to the two PCs, if they're on duty. Then you're going to go and see Dave to pay him for the damages.

'In the meantime, I'm going to see about getting you an early appointment for these tests. The sooner we know what we're dealing with, the easier it will be to handle. And none of this is negotiable.'

He gave Trev a brief hug then pushed him away to arm's length.

'But you really do still stink. Go and get in the shower.'

# Chapter Twenty

Monday morning. Traditionally the worst day of the week for absenteeism and unpunctuality. Ted was pleased to see that Jezza was almost on time. Perhaps there was hope for her yet.

Sal was not in. He was taking a lieu day after working the weekend. Virgil had also worked the weekend but he was saving his day off until Friday. He was constantly in the doghouse with his wife as she didn't like his chosen profession and kept trying to persuade him to change. He had booked a surprise long weekend in Paris, hoping it might at least get her off his back for a while longer.

Ted gestured to Mike that he would be joining them shortly. He had been glued to his mobile phone since first thing, trying to get through to the surgery to make an appointment for Trev. The number seemed to be permanently engaged. Even normally mild-mannered Ted was getting close to losing his temper with sheer frustration.

Eventually, he managed to get through and secure an appointment for early evening the following day. Once that was done, he went through to the main office to start the briefing.

'Sorry about that, just something important I needed to take care of. Right, where are we up to?'

Jezza spoke up first. She never seemed to show any reticence in doing so, even as the newest member of the team. A shrinking violet she was not.

'Jane Applegate. Limekiln House elderly care home. Small,

friendly but clearly the same problem as in the others. Even if they had enough staff to keep giving the residents enough drinks, then taking them to let it all out again, they clearly don't do it. It seems she wasn't the only one to have to be carted off to hospital with dehydration and UTIs on occasion.

'The manager and staff confirmed she used to have visits from her former cleaner, from when she lived at home. The manager told me her name was Annie, described her as short, plain, grey hair and glasses, local accent, late forties, wearing what she called cheap clothes which she said stank of cigarette smoke. And yes, she always used to take in some home-baked cakes and treats for Mrs Applegate.'

'But Annie this time, not Angie or Angela?' Mike asked.

'I'm just coming to that, hold your horses,' Jezza told him, but it was more a joking tone than her usual sarcastic one. 'I had a long chat with the manager, Margaret. Nice woman, clearly kind-hearted and does her best for the old folk. But she's under constraints from the higher management in the group, which is why she doesn't have enough staff to do the job as she'd like it to be done.

'I noticed something else, too. She's really quite deaf and she doesn't appear to use a hearing aid, so she often gets words wrong. I asked some of the staff about Annie and they were all convinced she's called Angie. Another positive sighting, I think.

'It looks like, for some reason, Angie hadn't yet dished up a fatal dose to Mrs Applegate in the home before she was carted off to hospital with the UTI. So she's clearly gone there to finish the job off while she had the chance.'

She looked round expectantly, clearly hoping for some praise, or at least acknowledgement, of her work. It was not Mike's style. Ted would normally have said something encouraging but he was too distracted.

'We have to find this Angie,' Ted said. 'Jezza, I want to get you in undercover in one of the homes, see if you can spot her.

At the very least, get an address and preferably a real name so we can check her out.'

'Which home, though, boss? There are a lot and she's already hit four of them, in all probability,' Mike said.

'I favour the fondant fancy home, whatever that's called,' Ted replied.

'Cottage Row,' Jezza said.

She had clearly been doing her homework on the case and had the details off pat.

'Our Angie seems to have been getting ready to strike there but has probably had to bide her time if they're implementing the food ban rigorously.'

'I don't want any heroic stuff, trying to apprehend her or anything at this stage,' Ted said warningly. 'We haven't a whisker of a case against her. All we want at the moment is an address, but how do we go about getting that without arousing her suspicion?'

'I had an idea,' Jezza responded. 'What about a customer satisfaction survey? Get the home to fill one out, tick-boxes on how visitors viewed the home, that sort of thing, and asking for contact details?'

'You really think an intelligent poisoner is going to fall for a trick like that?' Steve asked, to everyone's surprise.

'Have you got a better idea, genius?' Jezza snapped back.

'All right, settle down,' Ted said levelly. 'No need for in-fighting. It achieves nothing and it's not how we work.'

'Why not just watch initially? Make sure the food ban is in place so the risks are minimal. Then if this so-called Angie person comes in, try to get a car registration number? That way we can at least run a PNC check on it?' Rob suggested reasonably.

'And if she clocks me looking at her number plate, then does a runner?' Jezza asked, her tone now taking its familiar sharp edge.

'Don't let her, then,' Steve retorted. 'You're in undercover, you need to keep a low profile. If she clocks you she'll just go underground.'

'At least that would stop the killings,' Jezza spat.

'But it wouldn't get justice for the families of the victims.'

Steve was looking red in the face and surprisingly angry now.

'That's enough, you two!' Ted said sharply.

All of the team members looked at him in amazement. It was so unusual for him to raise his voice at all that they were shocked. Maurice spoke first.

'Are you all right, boss?' he asked anxiously.

'Perfectly fine, thank you, Maurice,' Ted replied more calmly. 'I just don't want bickering in the team. You're professional police officers. Please behave as if you are.'

He took himself off to his office. He needed time to regain control. He was so worried about Trev that he had passed another nearly sleepless night. It had left him feeling scratchy and on edge.

Mike followed him in, again with the briefest of knocks before he came in.

'Seriously, boss, are you all right?' he asked. 'You're not yourself.'

Ted sighed.

'Sorry, Mike. I shouldn't have snapped, but it was getting like the playground out there. What's got into Steve?'

Mike chuckled.

'He certainly doesn't like the newcomer daring to criticise, that's for sure. Give them time, they'll settle down together. And we will crack this case, boss, like we usually do.'

'Can you make arrangements with the home to get Jezza in there, posing as a care worker, please, Mike? What was the name of the home again?'

'Cottage Row, boss,' Mike said, with a frown.

It was not like DI to forget a detail, either. He knew there was no point in pressing him about it, though. The boss could make a clam look open and talkative when it came to his private life.

Ted sighed again and rubbed his hands over his face, as if he could rub away the tiredness and anxiety he felt. Then he looked at Mike and said again, 'Sorry, Mike, I'm not totally on top of it at the moment. Trev and I had some bad news at the weekend. It's a bit knocked the wind out of us both.'

The DS looked concerned. 'Anything I can help with?'

Ted shook his head.

'The advantage of not sleeping much, though, is that I had an idea about your bed-blockers theory. One for Steve.'

He got up and went to the door, opened it and called across the room to Steve.

'Can you come in here a minute, Steve?'

The TDC got to his feet looking stricken. He could see that the DS was also in the boss's office and was worried about what might be in store for him. Neither Ted nor the DS had ever had to reprimand him before. His behaviour was normally exemplary.

There didn't seem to be a spare chair. The DS was sitting in the only one he could see so he stood stiffly, looking anxiously from one man to another.

'I'm sorry about before,' he began.

Ted waved his apology away.

'Just don't let it happen again. I have enough on my plate without breaking up playground fights in the incident room.

'Now, the DS's idea about bed-blockers. I think there could be something to it. I'm going on the assumption that Mrs Protheroe was the first victim. She's certainly the first one we know about. I want you to go through the local papers, weekly and evening, starting at least three months ago, possibly six to be on the safe side.

'You're looking for anything about a relative of someone who died complaining of lack of beds. Particularly anything with a suggestion that old people were blocking beds. You know the sort of thing, and you've got the computer skills to find it. Anything at all, no matter how tenuous.

'Mike, get someone on to the hospital. I want to know if there have been any complaints over the same time-frame from anyone saying the same thing. I suspect they might not be all that unusual, but they will all need checking, even any which were later withdrawn.

'Right, Steve, get on with it, and let's have no more aggro, please.'

The TDC scuttled out of the door, clearly relieved, and headed straight back to the comfort of his computer.

'Mike, you'll need, of course, to send Jezza in at whatever time this Angela has been going to this home. Is it afternoons again? And you'll need to impress on her she must be there for those hours, no sloping off. If necessary, she can come in a bit later to even out her shift, as long as she puts the hours in.

'Let's hope she can get us a lead. I don't like being four victims into a murder enquiry without a single reliable name for a suspect.'

Ted headed for his kettle as Mike was leaving the office. Through the open door, he saw the Ice Queen stride into the main office, looking formidable, as she always did. All of the team members leapt to their feet at the sight of her. Jezza reacted just sufficiently more slowly than anyone else for it to be noticeable.

'Good morning. Please sit down everyone. I don't wish to disturb you in the middle of a trying case,' the Ice Queen said. 'DC Vine, I'm sorry I have not had the time before now to welcome you to the station. I hope you are settling in well?'

'Yeah. Fine. Super.'

The way Jezza replied was ambiguous. She could conceivably have been using the abbreviation for Superintendent, though Ted highly doubted it. She certainly did not call her ma'am as everyone else in the station did, including Ted and Kevin. It was borderline insolence, which she seemed good at, and Ted could see the Ice Queen bristle. But she said nothing. Instead, she headed for Ted's office, went in and closed the door behind her.

'Tea, ma'am?' Ted asked.

'Thank you. Why not?' she replied, taking a seat. 'Although this is not a social call, I'm afraid. But first, how are you getting on with your newest recruit? I can see already why there are so many references to her attitude on her file. She clearly missed her rotation at charm school.'

'I'll have a word,' Ted promised, 'although I've not yet succeeded in getting her to stop calling me guv and DS Hallam, skip.'

He made the tea, put a mug in front of each of them and sat down opposite the Ice Queen. She was looking at him keenly.

'Are you quite well, Inspector?' she asked. 'You look very tired.'

'I'm fine, ma'am, but I do have to leave a little early tomorrow, for a medical appointment. Not for me. It's for my partner, Trev.'

'I see. I do hope it's nothing serious?' she took a sip of the green tea. 'I've met him, you know, your Trevor,' she continued, to Ted's surprise.

'Really?' he said. 'He never mentioned it.'

'He wouldn't have known who I was. It was when I was looking at bikes, before I bought the Ducati. He was delightful, and so persuasive. He could have sold me any bike in the shop. But I was set on my little joke, the 999.'

Ted had been astonished to discover that his ultra-formal boss spent her spare time roaring round on a Ducati 999. It somehow made her seem more human.

'I do hope all goes well, and please let me know if you need to take any time off.'

She switched back into formal mode. 'For now, as you can imagine, I am coming under a lot of pressure from higher up to see some results in this current case, which is already provoking anxiety.

'These days, almost everyone has a family member with, or knows of someone affected by, dementia and living in a home. They need to feel their loved ones are safe there. That's how they deal with the guilt of having them admitted. We need some results.

'I know you're a diligent officer and I'm sure you're doing your best. But you need to be doing more than your best, and you need to be doing it faster. If the full extent of this case were to leak out to the wider press and media, we would all be in hot water. Do I make myself clear?'

'Ma'am,' Ted replied tersely.

He knew she was right. He knew he needed to deliver. Just at the moment, he wasn't quite sure how.

# Chapter Twenty-one

Incandescent with rage was the phrase which immediately popped into Ted's head when Mike Hallam caught up to him on the stairs a couple of mornings later. Mike was usually fairly mild and easy-going but Ted could see that he was seething.

Both men were in early, ahead of the team. Ted invited the DS to join him in his office and went straight for the kettle while Mike sat down. By the look of things, they were both going to need something fortifying with which to start the day.

'What's up, Mike?' he asked, brewing up.

He didn't even bother offering the DS green tea. This was clearly going to be a strong coffee conversation for him.

'I got a phone call shortly after you left yesterday, boss,' Mike began, taking a big swallow of the hot coffee which Ted put in front of him, then wincing at the heat of it. 'It was Cottage Row, the home where Jezza was supposed to be keeping an eye out for Angela.'

Ted groaned inwardly, noting his use of the words 'supposed to be'. He really did not need any more hassle this morning. Trev's appointment with the doctor had not been all plain sailing and both of them were still worried.

'What's she done now?' he asked resignedly.

'It's more what she hasn't done, boss. The phone call was to tell me that Angela had turned up at the home but they weren't sure what to do because Jezza wasn't there.'

'Not there?' Ted echoed in surprise. 'What, not there as in never turned up?'

'Turned up, took a phone call, then left,' Mike told him. 'Boss, we can't go on like this, it's not fair to the rest of the team. Not to mention that it's not getting us anywhere nearer to solving the case. And I imagine you're under pressure to do that. I can't believe the Ice ...' he caught himself just in time. 'I can't believe the Super would really come up here just to welcome Jezza to the team.'

Ted nodded.

'You're right, she didn't. So, we've missed a chance at this Angela. With any luck, there will be other opportunities, and soon.'

'But what are you going to do about Jezza, boss?' Mike persisted. 'She's just taking the piss, and I mean seriously.'

'Do me a favour, Mike, and don't say anything about this in public,' Ted said. 'I imagine she'll be in at some time this morning. Then I think you and I should perhaps have a gentle word with her, find out what's going on.'

'Gentle word? Boss, I really do feel like slapping her,' Mike said angrily. 'This is the nearest we've got so far to an ID on our only possible suspect and she blows it because she decides to swan off early somewhere, without even letting me know.

'I asked the home not to do or say anything at all while Angela was there. I didn't want them raising her suspicions when they're not trained for this sort of thing. But then, Jezza is trained and she just pissed off without a word.'

'All right, Mike, calm down,' Ted said evenly. 'There may be a valid reason why she had to leave. With any luck, no damage has been done. We'll just send her back again to wait for next time Angela comes calling.'

'I used to think I was patient before I met you, boss,' Mike said incredulously. 'If she's got problems stopping her doing her work, why doesn't she just say so, instead of messing us about like this?'

Ted gave him a long look. The DS had the grace to look guilty.

'We all of us have problems from time to time, which we don't find it easy to talk about,' Ted reminded him. 'My early doors every Wednesday? I'm going for counselling.'

Mike gaped at him.

'Bloody hell, boss. I had no idea.'

Ted shrugged.

'Not something I talk about. It's not common knowledge and I'd like to keep it that way. I don't want the team thinking I'm cracking up. There's just some stuff from the past I should have dealt with ages ago and didn't. So I'm trying to deal with it now.

'Maybe there's something similar going on with Jezza. That's why I'd rather not judge, until I know what the reason behind her behaviour is. Let me know when she shows up, then we'll have her in here and talk to her, but calmly and reasonably.'

He looked round his office.

'Where's the second spare chair gone? Honestly, things even get nicked in the nick. Never mind, she can stand, you sit down. I don't want you looming over her. It could be interpreted as intimidating. I imagine our Jezza would be the first to report us if we don't handle her carefully.'

Mike managed a short chuckle.

'At least if she's standing up, she'll find it harder to slouch back with her arms folded and reply with 'whatevs' to anything we ask her.'

Ted had to laugh at that. It summed up their new DC fairly accurately.

Mike rose to go.

'And you leaving early yesterday? Was that …?' he hesitated awkwardly.

'Nothing to worry about, but nothing I want to talk about,' Ted told him. 'A medical appointment for someone other than me, so I wouldn't be at liberty to talk about it, even if I wanted to. Get the team started. You don't need me for that. Just let me know when Jezza arrives.'

Trev's appointment with the GP the evening before had not been easy. Neither he nor Ted were ever ill, so they were unaccustomed to the long wait, the crowded waiting room, the cluster of people coughing and sneezing. Even without the stress of what brought them there, neither of them had greatly enjoyed the experience.

Ted felt old when he thought that the doctor looked too young to be out working without a note from her mother. She was clearly under pressure. She had her prescription pad open and pen poised almost before the two of them had gone in and sat down.

'Mr Armstrong?' she asked, looking expectantly from one to the other.

Trev introduced himself and outlined briefly his father's recent diagnosis and the need for him to have tests as soon as possible, to check to see if he could be affected by the same condition.

'If there's a long delay for an appointment, we're prepared to go privately. I have insurance,' Ted told her.

'And you are?' the doctor asked, giving him the sort of look which Ted might reserve for a kerb-crawler.

'His partner,' Ted replied, as evenly as he could manage.

'Well, that shouldn't be necessary,' the doctor continued briskly. 'With a potentially life-threatening condition like this, the waiting time to see a consultant is usually very short. A matter of weeks at the most. I'll do you a letter for an appointment. Come by the surgery tomorrow some time to pick it up. I'll also find you some leaflets about the condition, although I imagine you've already Googled it? Was there anything else?'

'Well, that was reassuring – not,' Trev smiled ironically when they found themselves outside on the pavement in short order. 'Let's hope the consultant at least gets his stethoscope out.'

Ted looked at him anxiously. 'Are you all right?'

'I will be, when I know a bit more. I stupidly hoped I might get some answers there. Would you mind if I asked a woman out on a date this weekend?' he asked, with a twinkle in his eye.

'Don't forget we're going to my mum's for lunch on Saturday,' Ted reminded him.

His mother had asked them both for dinner. Ted had got used to calling the midday meal lunch and the evening meal dinner, living with Trevor. He had confirmed the time with his mother, to avoid confusion. 'Who did you have in mind?'

'Bizzie,' Trev responded promptly, as they walked the short distance back to their house. 'If anyone knows the workings of the human ticker, she does. If I bribe her with a bike ride, she might talk me through it. I just need to know the worst possible scenario.'

Ted had not been thrilled with the idea. He preferred to focus on the positive. But he accepted that Trev had to deal with the news in the best way for him. If that meant talking to the Professor, then he was happy to agree.

Mike's brief knock on the door jerked Ted out of his thoughts. The DS stuck his head round the opening and said, 'Jezza just got in, boss.'

'Thanks, Mike. Come in and sit down. I'll ask her to join us.'

He went to the door and said, his voice quiet but still carrying across the office, 'DC Vine, could you join us for a minute, please?'

The team members who were still in the main office looked up. They seldom heard their boss raise his voice, but they all knew only too well what that particular formal, measured tone meant. If Jezza knew or guessed, she didn't seem to care. She slouched across to the office with her usual attitude, then looked expectantly about for a seat. The DS was already sitting in the only spare one and Ted was sitting in his own chair, so she was forced to stand.

'How did it go at Cottage Row yesterday?' Ted asked her evenly. 'Any signs of Angela?'

Jezza gave her customary shrug.

'I didn't see her,' she replied.

'That was because she actually turned up, after you had left, very shortly after you arrived,' Ted told her evenly. 'Would you like to tell me and DS Hallam why you left early?'

There was not a flicker of reaction.

'I got a phone call. It could have been something important. I had to go and deal with it.'

'Something to do with the case?' Ted asked, in the same even tone.

She could so easily have lied to him. The fact that she chose not to gave Ted a glimmer of hope.

'Not really, no,' she admitted. 'I just had something to sort. It's sorted. I'll stay longer today.'

'That's big of you,' the DS cut in sarcastically. 'You were late in this morning. The reason the boss said you could come in later was to even your hours out a bit. If you leave early, you certainly don't come in late.'

'Thank you, DS Hallam,' Ted said mildly. 'That is absolutely correct, DC Vine. I expect all of the team to put the hours in, all of the time. Especially when we're working a difficult case like this and making very little headway.

'Mike, I'm sure you have plenty to do. Thanks for your input. DC Vine, you can wait a minute. Please sit down.'

The DS left the office and Jezza sat down. Ted was not surprised that she immediately sat back in the chair and folded her arms defensively across her body.

Ted was quiet for a moment, looking at her. She returned his look with a hard and defiant stare of her own.

'Jezza, I have to say, I'm disappointed in you. I had hoped for better things.'

She still sat in tense silence. Ted was at a loss. He had

never before encountered such dumb insolence.

'I've never yet put one of my team on a disciplinary,' he continued. 'It's a lot of unnecessary paperwork and quite frankly, I would see it as failure on my part, that I hadn't managed the situation better. If there is some reason why you can't do the job you're paid to do, then you need to tell me. Now.'

'I told you. Something needed sorting. I sorted it,' she said, then, after a long pause, she added, 'boss.'

At least it was an improvement on guv, which he disliked intensely, Ted thought.

'Right, let's see a change in attitude and performance from now on, please,' he said. 'Go and talk to DS Hallam, ask him what he wants you to do this morning. And this is really not a good time to be calling him skip. Try Sergeant, or Sarge at least.

'This is the last time we'll talk informally about your conduct. The next time you aren't doing the job you have been assigned to do, it will have to be official. And I don't imagine either of us wants that. That will be all, DC Vine.'

He was not entirely sure that the 'Sir,' she flung at him as she headed out of the office was said in sarcasm. But at least she didn't slam the door this time.

# Chapter Twenty-two

Another Wednesday afternoon of carpet-watching for Ted. This time he had so much he wanted to talk about. As usual, he was finding it hard to get the words out, or even to know how to begin.

He wanted to talk about Trevor. About his fear, his stomach-churning, gut-wrenching fear, of a future without him. As usual, waves of self-loathing flooded him when his first selfish thought was of how he would be affected by the possibility of losing Trev.

He still needed to make sense of the betrayal he felt about his mother. The fact that the father he had loved unreservedly had prevented him from having any kind of relationship with her. Then again, he instantly hated himself for fixating on that when he had now seen Trev's mother at first hand.

Trev had told him about his mother. How he had been constantly juggled between a succession of nannies and au pairs as a child. How, when he came out at nearly sixteen, she and his father had simply disowned him and thrown him out in the street. None of it had quite prepared him for the clinical coldness he had now experienced at first hand.

He needed to find a way to deal with the turmoil he was feeling with the return of his mother into his own life. Especially now that Trev seemed to be developing a bond with her. Ted could understand why his partner had been delighted to find her such an obviously warm and loving person. He just had to deal with the feelings almost of resentment and exclusion that their growing closeness had surprisingly triggered within him.

He needed to talk. The clock was ticking away. Carol was, as usual, not putting any pressure on him. Just waiting for him to begin in his own time. He felt a hypocrite for expecting Jezza, whom he had only just met, to talk to him about her private life when he found it so excruciatingly difficult to talk about his own to a trained professional.

He decided that sometimes the only way was to take a deep breath and plunge straight in. He instantly tried to bury the memories which the swimming analogy brought flooding, suffocatingly, into his consciousness. Then he began to talk. Finally.

He talked for so long that his appointment overran, but Carol didn't seem to be worried. She told him there was no one else following his appointment. When he had finally finished, she smiled warmly as she shook his hand, clearly pleased with the progress he had made.

Ted fired off a quick text to Trev to let him know he was on his way home, slightly later than usual. He really needed the intense activity of their judo club to follow what had been a draining experience. But finally, he felt he was making some progress. All he needed now was to start to feel the same about the case.

Because he was running late, they took the car to the gym instead of walking as they usually did. The evening started as always with the self-defence club which he and Trev ran for school-children, followed by their own judo training and practice session. Ted and Trev were often paired off to spar after training. No one could match Ted for timing and technique, not even their coach, Bernard. Which was why, even with his superior speed, height and reach, Trev could never entirely get the better of him.

Trev's style was always to be on the attack, fast, furious, and never giving his partner quarter. This time, Ted was surprised that Trev was constantly on the defensive, backing away, moving out of reach.

When Ted finally got hold of his jacket sufficiently to position for a throw, he saw something in Trev's eyes which he had never seen before. Fear. A raw emotion he had never associated with his partner. As if Trev was suddenly staring his own mortality in the face and being terrified by what he saw.

Ted held up a hand for a pause and backed away, doubling over, a thumb in the side of his abdomen.

'Sorry, got a stitch, I need to take a break,' he said, bowing before he left the mat. He was fooling no one and he knew it, especially not Trev, who came over to join him.

'Shall we go home?' Ted asked quietly, not wishing to disturb the others, who were practising hard. Trev nodded, looking more subdued than Ted had ever seen him before, even after his drinking binge.

On the drive home, Trev said very little. Then he suddenly blurted out, 'It just suddenly hit me. I could drop dead, at any moment, just like that. Any exertion, and that could be it.'

Ted put a gentle hand on his arm as he drove and said reassuringly, 'You might not even be affected, though, don't forget that. Hold on to that thought. We won't really know anything until the test results. Try to stay positive.'

'But I might, Ted. I might. And that terrifies me.'


Ted seemed to be on auto-pilot all week. He was so worried about Trev that he couldn't concentrate and he knew he was not much use to the team at the moment. Luckily, Jezza seemed to have knuckled down for the time being, which was one less problem for him. She had not yet seen Angela at the home but she had at least been turning up there regularly to keep an eye out.

Mike sensed there was something serious worrying the boss, so he tried to rally the team and field any minor issues himself until the DI was back on form.

Ted was surprised at how much he was looking forward to lunch at his mother's. He thought it might do Trev some good and he would have done anything to put the sparkle back into his partner's eyes. He hoped, too, that Trev's date with the Professor on the Sunday would at least give him some of the answers he was looking for.

If there was one thing they could both be sure of with Bizzie, it was that she would do some straight talking and call a spade a spade. Ted just hoped she might find a bit of tact from somewhere, to temper what she had to say.

His mother had clearly gone to a lot of trouble, and expense, with her cooking. From the moment she opened the door, she kept apologising to Trev, saying the meal she had prepared could never match up to the one he had made when she visited. He silenced her by engulfing her in one of his big, warm, bear hugs, which made her beam with delight.

'Anything you make will be delicious, Annie, I'm sure,' he told her.

He offered to help her bring things to the table but she wouldn't hear of it. Ted was worried when he saw the size of beef joint she proudly produced, knowing how far such a cut would have bitten into a care worker's wages.

'I didn't know if you would remember, Teddy, but you always liked my Yorkshire puddings, so I made those,' she said, producing a plateful of perfectly risen golden brown puddings.

'Oh, wow, I can never get mine to rise as well as those. What's your secret?' Trev asked shamelessly, although his were every bit as good.

Ted's mother smiled with pride as she disappeared in search of the roast potatoes and vegetables.

'You should hug your mum, Ted,' Trev said softly, putting a hand on his arm. 'While you can. While you have the chance.'

Ted took something of a back seat, enjoying watching Trev clearly having such a good time. Trev was tall and well-built and rather dwarfed the small room whenever he stood up to help. He looked so vibrant, so full of life, that Ted struggled to swallow his food past the lump which rose in his throat whenever he looked at him.

When they were leaving, Trev looked pointedly at his partner as he gave Annie another big hug and a kiss on both cheeks. Ted managed a brief peck on the cheek and a clumsy gesture, almost like a pat on her shoulder.

The next day, with Trev potentially tied up for much of the time with the Professor, Ted decided to drop in at the station. He could not settle to much until he knew about Trev. His mother had asked him if he would mind picking up some of his grandmother's things which were still at the home, as she couldn't face doing so herself. He decided that he would also do a tour round some of the other homes, to see if he could pick up on anything his team had missed so far.

He found Maurice and Steve on duty in the main office, still plodding methodically through lists of staff and looking for any crossover.

'I can't believe how high the turnover is for care workers, boss,' Maurice grumbled when he saw Ted.

'I'm not surprised to hear it. Not everyone's dream job, I imagine, and I know the pay is very low,' Ted replied. 'I'm planning on taking a quick trip round some of the homes, just on the off-chance I have a sudden blinding flash of inspiration. I might just get lucky and bump into Angela. I've got to go to Snowdon Lodge anyway, to pick up the last of my gran's things.'

Ted found it a depressing way to spend the day. Some of the homes were clearly well-run and compassionate. Others had more of an air of factory farming about them. He was recognised and greeted warmly by Stacy at The Poppies. He asked about developments, then had to dash off once more in pursuit of the same elderly lady as before, intent on making her escape yet again.

Ted was interested to check security at the homes he visited, to see how easy it was for someone unknown to walk in off the street and visit a resident. He found it disconcertingly simple at many of them. He was beginning to realise how their Angela had managed to insinuate herself into the homes and befriend the nearest elderly person she spotted, sitting by themselves.

He saved Snowdon Lodge for his last visit of the day. That way, he could pick up his grandmother's few remaining things and drop them round to his mother's, before going home to see how Trev had got on with the Professor.

Once again, he simply tagged along behind other visitors going in, this time a couple in their fifties, who held the door open for him when they were admitted. They didn't stop to sign the register. Ted didn't, either.

'Sid! Sid! Where are you, Sid? Sid, I need you. Where are you?'

The same elderly woman, in the same chair, still smelling strongly of urine. Ted wondered if anybody ever attended to her. He looked around optimistically for a staff member. There was no sign of anyone. The one who had opened the door had quickly disappeared back down a corridor.

He doubted that the manager would be at her desk on a Sunday but he walked along the hallway to her office, just in case. The door was firmly shut. He headed back in the opposite direction, towards what had been his grandmother's room. Off duty and out of sight of the Ice Queen, he had adopted his favourite casual clothes and Doc Martens boots, so he made no sound.

There was an elderly woman he did not know in the room which had been his grandmother's. The door was open and she was sitting in an armchair beside the bed, staring blankly out of the window, ignoring one of the endless repeat episodes of Inspector Morse which was playing on her small television. Ted wondered how Morse would have fared with this case.

He continued along the corridor and came to another room with a door standing open. It was clearly the rest room for the carers. Two of them were sitting there drinking tea. As Ted neared the room, a third carer came up the corridor and stuck her head round the door.

'Where the bloody hell is Danni?' she asked angrily, taking no notice at all of Ted. 'She's supposed to be helping me, lazy bitch. The old woman in room twenty-seven is throwing up all over everywhere and I'm not cleaning it up by myself.'

'Danni keeps going off to the bogs. She's puking too,' one of the other carers told her.

Ted stepped forward, a feeling of dread and déjà-vu hitting him.

'Who's in charge here today?' he asked.

The first carer, who was twice his size in all directions, looked him up and down. Her name badge said she was called Mandy.

'Are you a relative?' she asked.

Ted pulled out his warrant card.

'I'm a police officer. I'm investigating the sudden death in this home of Mrs Gwen Jones. Tell me about this current situation.'

The woman shrugged, unconcernedly.

'It's not a situation,' she said dismissively. 'We've got an old dear throwing up. It happens a lot in a place like this. She probably ate too much cake, or she's got a bug. Danni was most likely out on the lash.'

'Is anyone else in the home sick? How long has the resident been like this?' Ted persisted.

'She had cake after her dinner, earlier this afternoon. She's been poorly since, but she's greedy, she always eats too much and too quickly,' the carer told him.

'Was the cake something baked here in the home?' Ted asked, starting to get worried now.

'No, a visitor brought it in for her, I think, but I didn't see who. It's been busy today, a lot of visitors. She'd already had a big dinner. It was just too much for her, making a pig of herself like that.'

'Call an ambulance,' Ted ordered. 'Now. I'll take full responsibility if I'm over-reacting.'

His tone left no room for argument.

Whilst the first carer was doing that, Ted asked the others, 'Could this Danni have had any of the cake? Has anyone else had any?'

They looked at one another, then one of them said, 'Danni took it off Betty as she could see she was gobbling it too fast. She told me she ate some of it herself but said she didn't eat a lot as she didn't like the taste of it.'

'Go and see to the resident who's ill. I've no idea what care you need to give her, but give her whatever you can. Make her comfortable, at least. When the ambulance arrives, make sure they also check out this Danni. And you better call the manager in, she might be needed.

'Why are the residents still being allowed to have food brought in from outside? Why is the ban not still in place?' he asked.

'Ambulance is on its way,' the first carer told him. 'I'm sure it's nothing, she's probably just eaten too much. And what food ban? I've never heard there was one.'

Ted hadn't thought the way this case was going could get much worse. He had a horrible feeling it was just about to.

# Chapter Twenty-three

It was immediately obvious to Ted that he was going to have to take charge of the situation. He was desperate to get home to Trev, to find out how he had got on with Bizzie. But the carers didn't seem to know what they were doing, and there was a possibility he would need to preserve a crime scene, if it turned out to be another poisoning.

'Do you have any nursing staff on duty?' he asked the first, formidable, carer.

She shook her head.

'Not in this wing. We're a care home, not a nursing home. Not many staff on at the weekend, either.'

She was heading back to room twenty-seven, Ted falling into step beside her.

'Who's the duty first aider?' Ted asked. 'I assume you at least have one of those?'

'Danni. The one who's also throwing up,' she said as they reached the room.

The elderly woman in the bed looked in a bad way. She had vomited all over herself and the bedclothes and was now clearly struggling for breath.

'Come on now, Betty, let's get you cleaned up a bit and settled for the night,' the carer said, with enforced jollity.

'You need to try to turn her on to her side,' Ted told her. 'Vomiting like that, she risks choking on it. I would say cleaning her up is the least important thing at the moment. You need to try to maintain a clear airway. Do you need a hand?'

She threw him a look of barely concealed contempt.

'I could probably pick up the both of you together, one in each arm.'

'But do it gently,' Ted told her, his voice authoritative. 'Make her as comfortable and safe as possible until the ambulance gets here.'

'What are the police worried about if another old biddy just eats too much, too quickly?' the carer grumbled to herself.

She effortlessly turned the frail figure onto her side and moved pillows and a spare blanket to maintain her position.

'Because there's a strong possibility this may be more than that,' Ted told her coldly, not impressed by her attitude. 'You could wipe her face a bit, make sure her mouth is kept clear. And try to reassure her. What's her pulse like?'

'I've got other residents to see to, you know, we don't have enough staff for one to one, especially with Danni sick.'

'Stay with her,' Ted ordered, once again his tone allowing no room for argument.

He went in search of the other two carers. One of them was just finishing a telephone call. The other was nowhere to be seen.

'I've called the manager in. I've also phoned through to our other wing, the secure unit. They have a nurse on duty and he's on his way. What else can I do to help?' she asked.

Her badge said she was Katya. She spoke with an accent but her English was extremely good.

'That's brilliant, thank you,' Ted said, relieved to find someone with a bit of gumption. 'Now, where is this Danni and how is she?'

'I sent the other carer to go and find her and make sure she's all right. The trouble is, we really need to be getting on and seeing to the other residents. There's never enough staff on to cope with a real emergency,' she told him.

Ted nodded his thanks and understanding. At that moment, a man came walking purposefully down the corridor. He was stocky and shaven-headed, with tattooed arms, wearing a white tunic with a badge which said 'Derek'. Ted's immediate thought from the way he carried himself was that he may have been an Army medical orderly at one time.

He stepped forward with his warrant card in hand.

'I was here on a routine visit,' he told the man. 'The circumstances of this sickness are very similar to what happened recently with Mrs Jones, so an ambulance has been called on my instructions. If I have over-reacted then I take full responsibility, but I don't think so.'

Ted led the way towards room twenty-seven. They could both hear Mandy grumbling away in the room. Ted wondered if she was like that with all the residents or just those who made a mess when she was on duty.

'I'll take over now, Mandy, you go and get on with the others,' the nurse, Derek, told her.

He seemed competent and his bedside manner was better than Mandy's. At least he spoke kindly to the elderly lady, who was clearly now in considerable distress. Her toothless mouth was opening and closing like a fish, as if searching for air. She was still retching, but there was nothing left to bring up.

Derek took her pulse and gave Ted a worried look.

'Her heart rate is all over the place,' he said quietly. 'How long for the ambulance?'

'Not sure,' Ted replied. 'I'll see if I can speed it up. You have a carer with the same symptoms, though not as severe, I don't think. I'll go and find out more.'

He made a quick call to the ambulance service, identified himself, stressed the urgency and was told that paramedics were on their way. Next he phoned Trev briefly.

'Sorry, I'm going to be late back,' he told him. 'I'm at Snowdon Lodge and we have another potential victim. How did it go with Bizzie? Are you all right?'

'I'm fine, don't worry,' Trev told him. 'I'll tell you all about it when you get back. Go do your policeman stuff.'

He found Katya first, bringing a resident in a wheelchair down the corridor.

'Danni doesn't seem too bad. She's stopped being sick now, at least. We've got her lying down in one of the rooms, one where the resident stays up a bit later. Jane, the other carer, and I are just going to start getting the others to bed,' she said, then asked, 'How's poor Betty?'

'Not looking good,' Ted told her frankly. 'Hopefully the ambulance will be here in time to do something. And I may even be wrong about the possible cause. Let's hope so. If it would free you up, I could wait near the door to let the ambulance crew in when they arrive?'

She flashed him a grateful smile. She had an attractive, open face, but there was a sadness in her eyes which made Ted think of one of his mother's sayings. An old soul, been here before.

As Ted headed for the door, he phoned Maurice.

'Are you and Steve still at the nick, Maurice? I'm at Snowdon Lodge. Looks like we might have another poisoning,' Ted told him. 'No fatality as yet, but I would say it isn't looking good. Can the two of you get down here, please, and start taking statements from everyone. I'm just waiting for the ambulance. There's a carer sick as well; apparently she had some of the same cake.'

Ted had now reached the vestibule and was immediately greeted by the same plaintive, insistent voice.

'Sid! Sid! I want a cup of tea, Sid.'

He went across to the elderly woman and crouched down near to her, but just outside grabbing range. He instinctively knew that if he let her get hold of his arm, he would have a difficult time disengaging himself.

He made eye contact with her and smiled.

'I'll get someone to bring you one soon,' he promised. 'How are you feeling today?'

Her tired old eyes immediately filled with tears.

'You never come and see me any more,' she said sadly. 'I'm all on my own.'

'I'm sorry,' Ted told her. 'I've been busy, but I'll try to come again soon.'

He had no idea if he was being helpful or not. He just couldn't bear to see her loneliness, confusion and distress.

At that moment, he saw blue lights through the window and the ambulance pulled into the car park, stopping close to the door. With a reassuring smile at the old woman, Ted stood up, got out his warrant card and went to let the paramedics in.

'I'm DI Darling, I just happened to be here on another matter,' he told the team of two, a man and a woman, dressed in green. He quickly filled them in on the previous case at the same home and mentioned there had been others. 'But that's to be kept confidential at this stage, please,' he stressed.

They both threw him a look of contempt, but Ted knew he had to try to cover all bases. He led them down the corridor.

'Any idea of what poison we're looking at?' the man asked.

'There have been several,' Ted told them. 'Foxglove, aconite, oleander.'

'Cardiac glycosides,' the woman said, nodding knowingly.

'Have you had experience of plant poisoning cases before?' Ted asked her, surprised.

She grinned sheepishly at him.

'No, but I love reading crime thrillers and watching them on the telly,' she confessed.

Ted showed them to the room and left them with Derek. The woman in the bed was looking more distressed than before. Ted hoped they had been quick enough to save her. He went back into the corridor to leave them to their work. He needed to make another phone call.

'Bizzie? It's Ted. Thanks for helping Trev today. I hope it went ok?'

'Ah, Edwin,' came the familiar breezy voice. 'I think I've been able to reassure him a little. I've also put him in touch with a friend of mine, a cardiac consultant. Douglas owes me a few favours. I've phoned him to call them in, so if you or Trevor call him tomorrow, I'm sure he can arrange these tests soon. It's an anxious time for you both, I know.'

'Thank you. I'm actually calling from one of the homes. I only came in to collect the rest of my grandmother's things and one of the residents, and a carer, were both being violently sick,' he told her, and briefly outlined the circumstances. 'The old lady is still alive, but doesn't look good to me. The paramedics have just arrived and they're trying to stabilise her before they take her to hospital.'

'Do you want me to come over?' Bizzie asked.

Ted had to smile at that.

'It might be seen as a bit grisly, the pathologist in attendance before there's even been a death. I just wanted to know what I need to do to give you the most help, just in case the poor lady dies. I have to say, she really wasn't looking good.'

'Get the cake,' Bizzie said promptly. 'If there's any left, bag it and tag it for me. It could help enormously in determining the poison and the dosage. A sample of vomit, too, could be useful, if that's possible.'

Ted mentally kicked himself that recovering the cake had not been his immediate thought. He realised how much his mind was off its game in his anxiety over Trev.

'Anything else?' he asked.

'Detailed timings help a great deal,' she said. 'When you're taking statements, try to pin the times down as accurately as possible. The problem with a poisoner is that they are usually long gone before you or I begin our work. Good luck with it. And try not to worry about young Trevor, although I know that is easy for me to say and hard for you to do.'

Ted thanked her and rang off. He was feeling surprisingly emotional.

The doorbell rang and Ted went to answer it, knowing

everyone else was busy elsewhere. This time he had to resolutely ignore the plaintive cries of, 'Sid! Sid!' as soon as he appeared. Maurice and Steve were standing outside the inner door. He let them in and briefed them on what he knew so far.

'As yet there is no death, but there's still the strong suspicion that this may have been a deliberate poisoning,' he told them. 'The staff are busy. You may have to follow them round as they work so you can interview them, but we need information, while it's still fresh in their minds.

'One of the residents, Betty, ate some cake just after lunch. We need to know if she had any visitors today, who they were, what they looked like. Timings are important, make sure you get them as accurately as possible. Find out if any of the residents are *compos mentis* enough to tell you anything useful.

'The carer who is ill also ate some of the cake. And we need that cake, if there is any left. Find it, bag it, and whatever you do, Maurice, don't be tempted to try it.'

Maurice chuckled at the boss's attempt at humour.

'Don't worry, boss, even I'm not that desperate for cake these days,' he replied.

'Now, can I safely leave you to it on this one? There's somewhere I need to be. Keep me in the loop with any new developments, any at all. I'll be on the mobile.'

He only realised that he'd forgotten to pick up his grandmother's possessions once he'd put the car in the garage and let himself into the house.

Trev was sprawling on a steamer chair on the patio, with a glass of red wine. He raised the glass in Ted's direction as he said ironically, 'Red wine. It's good for the heart.'

Ted perched on the edge of the chair and gave him a hug.

'Don't even joke about it,' he said. 'Are you ok? Did Bizzie help? I bet she enjoyed the bike ride.'

'I like Bizzie. She certainly doesn't pull her punches, and she's a total speed freak on the back of the bike,' Trev chuckled. 'She told me possibly slightly more than I wanted to know about this stupid heart condition I may have. She did at least assure me that it's not a racing certainty that I will have inherited it. She also gave me the number of a heart specialist friend of hers to get the tests done.'

They were interrupted by Ted's mobile ringtone, Freddie Mercury singing Barcelona. Ted glanced at the screen.

'Sorry, I have to take this, it's Maurice.'

Trev shook his head in mock despair. 'I've told you, you can have different ringtones for different people.'

'Maurice? What's the latest?' Ted asked as he took the call.

'Sorry, boss, it just became a suspicious death,' Maurice told him. 'Poor old Betty didn't even make it as far as the ambulance before she popped her clogs.'

# Chapter Twenty-four

Unusually, Virgil Tibbs was the last to arrive for the morning briefing on Monday. Even Jezza beat him in. His weekend in Paris had clearly gone well as he was beaming from ear to ear when he came into the main office.

Ted, already in position in front of the white board, noticed and said, 'If you have some good news, Virgil, let's hear it. I have bad, so we could do with something for us all to smile about.'

Virgil took his seat, still grinning and said, 'Me and the wife had an amazing time in Paris. And she told me she's pregnant.'

There was a chorus of congratulations, then Maurice added, 'How'd you manage that? I thought you weren't getting any, as you're always falling out about your hours?'

'Yeah, but come on, what woman could resist me for long?' Virgil asked jokingly.

'Right, quick drink on me in The Grapes this evening after work. This is certainly something to brighten the day. Jezza, I hope you'll join us?'

'I'm washing my hair,' she replied curtly.

'That's a shame,' Ted said evenly. 'It would be nice if you could join us, even for half an hour, after you leave Cottage Row. You're part of this team.'

'Can't do it,' she said with a firm shake of her head.

Ted decided to let it go and continue with the briefing.

'Right, bad news. We have a fifth death. Elizabeth Hibbert,

known as Betty, at Snowdon Lodge once more. It happened yesterday when I was there on a different matter. Same symptoms as before. One of the care workers was also taken ill but she's younger, stronger, and may well have ingested less poison, or got rid of it more effectively. She's now fortunately making a good recovery.

'Yet again, there was cake involved, brought in from someone outside. Maurice, can you you fill us in on what the witnesses said about who brought it? I take it Steve's taking a lieu day today?'

Maurice nodded, then Jezza chipped in.

'Why the hell weren't they implementing the ban on food from outside, for God's sake? You'd think with one dead already, they would have been more careful.'

Maurice looked acutely uncomfortable.

'I think that might be my fault, boss,' he said guiltily. 'When we did the tour of the homes checking details and asking them to stop letting food in, I went to that one but I forgot to tell them. Well, I sort of thought they would do it automatically, as they knew how the first victim died. I should have made sure. I'm really sorry, boss.'

Ted sighed to himself. He felt like karate-kicking Maurice right round the room and out of the window. But he made it a point not to blame members of his team, and certainly not in an open meeting. And it was a reasonable mistake to have made. He, too, would have thought that the home would have realised for themselves, after the first death.

'Don't sweat it, Maurice, it was a reasonable assumption to make. Just please don't assume anything next time,' he looked round at the team, 'any of you. But now we know that lightning can strike twice in the same place, we need to be extra vigilant. Do a ring-round of the homes again, remind them all how important it is.

'So, what about the bearer of the cake? Is it the same Angie as in the death of Mrs Jones? Maurice, did you get a description?'

'I did, boss, but the carer I spoke to had never met the first Angie. She only works weekends there, so she wouldn't have been there on the day your gran got poisoned,' Maurice told him. 'But according to her, the woman who brought the cake was called Ann, a neighbour of Betty's. She said she was about forty, medium height, short, curly, brown hair and green eyes. That's all she knows.'

'Could easily be the same person,' Jezza said with a shrug. 'The height is about constant through all the descriptions. Hair can be changed with a wig. Eye colour can be altered with coloured contact lenses. It could even be a bloke in drag.'

Ted was scribbling the description up on the white board with the others as Maurice spoke.

'We're missing something in all of this,' he said, standing back and looking at it. 'This can't surely be just a random killer? There's got to be something linking all our victims. But what the hell is it?'

'They're a bunch of parasitic old grunters taking up valuable oxygen?' Jezza said, then as Ted and the rest of the team glared at her, she shrugged and spread her hands. 'What? I'm just trying to get inside the killer's head. Look for their motivation. Maybe it's time to think of bringing in a profiler?'

This time, the other members of the team chuckled and even Ted smiled. Seeing her puzzled look, Mike told her, 'The boss is rather allergic to the whole idea of profilers.'

'It works wonderfully well on the telly,' Ted explained. 'You know, someone like Fitz or that Geordie bloke start talking to themselves and come up with exactly what the killer is thinking and where they're going to strike next. Unfortunately, in real life, there's not much concrete evidence that it does any good. But I promise to consider it, if we don't get a breakthrough soon.

'But Jezza is definitely right on one thing. We need to keep coming back to Motive, Means, Opportunity,' he reminded the team. 'The waste of oxygen and the bed-blocking idea both seem reasonable to me as possible motives. Where's Steve up to on tracing press cuttings of relatives with an axe to grind, Maurice?'

'He's done us a printout, boss, some names we can start checking up on today,' Maurice replied, producing a sheaf of papers, which he handed round. 'The trouble is, there's a fair bit of 'a relative who asked not to be identified' in most of the articles, so we may not have all the information.'

Ted nodded.

'Right. Means. Just about anyone would have, I would say. Jezza, from what you found out, anybody could buy any of the plants involved from their local garden centre, is that right?'

Jezza nodded.

'They'd need to know in advance which were poisonous but that's a piece of piss to find out from Google.' She saw Ted's disapproving look at her turn of phrase and protested, 'Well, I was going to say a piece of cake but I thought you'd say I was being flippant.'

Even Ted had to smile at that.

'What about opportunity. Well, I can say, from personal experience at Snowdon Lodge that Jack the Ripper could get in there and do whatever he wanted to, without anyone noticing. Can one of you compile a list of security or the lack of it at all the other homes, just so we know where we're at? Also find out which of our victims had ever had to be hospitalised, just in case the bed-blocking idea is the real motive.'

Ted headed for his office while the rest of the team got on with their appointed tasks. He had yet another mountain of paperwork awaiting his attention. But first he needed to make a phone call to sort out Trev's appointment for heart tests. He had undertaken to do it, so he could be sure it was sorted as soon as possible.

He grabbed a quick sandwich at lunch time, intending to work through at his desk. He was just about to tuck into it when his mobile rang. The caller display showed it was Steve.

'Hi, Steve, I thought you were on a day off today?' Ted said in greeting.

'I am, sir, but I thought you'd better take a look at the local rag's website.'

Dreading what he was about to see, Ted reached for his computer. It did not sound good. Trev had patiently shown him how to bookmark pages for easy retrieval, as Ted was not a natural with technology. He found the one he needed.

'And I thought you might like to see it before the Super does, sir,' Steve added.

Ted's eyes fell on the page in question and went straight to a headline asking, 'How safe are your parents?'

He swore under his breath as he quickly scanned the text which began, 'Parents are used to worrying about their children in the modern world. But here in Stockport, it's the turn of children to worry about their parents and grandparents, after a succession of sudden deaths in care homes, which the police are treating as suspicious.'

'Thanks, Steve, for the heads-up,' he said gratefully. 'The Super's been out all morning so I'll try and catch her before she sees this for herself. Forewarned is forearmed and all that. Now go and have a day off that actually consists of not doing any work.'

He phoned down to the front desk to ask them to let him know the minute the Ice Queen put in an appearance. He did not have long to wait. He went hurriedly downstairs to her office the minute he got the call, knocked, and waited for her summons to go in.

She gave him a shrewd look, then went to switch on her coffee machine.

'I'm sensing from your expression that this is not a social call?' she asked.

Ted shook his head and filled her in on everything, from the fifth victim to the newspaper article online.

'I don't understand how this latest death happened,' she said. 'Did you not tell me that you had asked the homes to stop allowing food from outside to be consumed by the residents?

'I did, ma'am, but there was a breakdown in communication somewhere along the line,' Ted told her evasively.

'Are you saying one of your team slipped up, Inspector? Which one?'

'I accept full responsibility, ma'am, so I would prefer not to say. If something went wrong, I clearly didn't brief the team correctly.'

'As ever, your loyalty to your team is commendable,' she said dryly. 'Now, this débâcle with the local newspaper, yet again …'

She was interrupted by the ring of her mobile phone. She checked the caller display and said tersely, 'Chief Constable,' then took the call.

She was clearly getting an ear-bashing as she barely managed to say two words. Finally, she said, 'Yes, sir, he's here with me now,' and wordlessly handed the phone to Ted.

Instinctively, Ted stood up to take the phone from her, then remained standing, almost to attention, as he received the biggest bollocking he'd ever taken in his entire career.

The top brass usually approved of Ted. He had an excellent clean-up rate, he generally did things by the book, his personnel management skills were good and his paperwork was always on time. They were always disappointed by his refusal to accept commendations and honours, and his PR skills were definitely lacking. He had a habit of scowling at the press during conferences as if secretly plotting painful martial arts deaths for all of them. But he was normally flavour of the month.

Not today, however, as he stood in silence in the face of an almost non-stop tirade. Matters were made worse by the fact that he felt himself that he merited most of it. He had had his eye well and truly off the ball with this case. Basic, sloppy mistakes had been made. It was not like him and he knew the comments directed at him were largely justified.

The newspaper article was bad enough as it stood. But it had been written before news of the fifth death had leaked out. He hardly dared to think what would happen once that news became public.

He did not get the chance to say a single word, even in goodbye. At the end of the call, it was disconnected so abruptly that he had a mental image of the Chief Constable hurling his mobile phone across his office in fury.

The Ice Queen was just putting bone china mugs of coffee in front of each of them and sitting back down.

'That's me thoroughly told, then,' Ted said ruefully, also taking a seat.

'I do hope you don't find this situation amusing, Inspector?'

'No ma'am, not at all. I apologise for the flippant remark.'

The Ice Queen was studying him keenly.

'I have to say, Inspector, that you are not up to your usual performance. Is there something I should be aware of? Is the presence of DC Vine putting too much of a strain on the team during an already difficult enquiry?'

It would have been so easy to latch on to the excuse she was offering him. But it was not Ted's style. He always took full responsibility for his team and any mistakes they made, without making a scapegoat of any of them. It was one of the reasons he was universally popular, throughout the division.

'No, ma'am.'

'Then I have to ask, and I do so without any wish to pry into your personal life. Is there something worrying you at present? Is it perhaps connected to the medical appointment you told me about?'

She was certainly astute, Ted gave her that. He was, as ever, loath to talk about himself and his personal life, but he clearly owed her an explanation.

'My partner, Trev, recently found out that he may possibly

have inherited a life-threatening heart condition,' he said, trying to keep his voice steady. 'We're arranging tests but we won't know for some time whether or not he is clear.'

'I see,' she said. 'Then can you give me a straight answer to a simple question? Are you up to heading this enquiry, or do I need to look at replacing you?'

Ted held her gaze steadily as he replied, 'Can I just say, ma'am, that I believe I am. But that if or when that changes, I promise to let you know immediately.'

She nodded in apparent satisfaction.

# Chapter Twenty-five

The team had seldom seen Ted quite so down. When they made the short walk together for a swift drink in The Grapes, he looked like exactly what he was. A man who had just taken a serious verbal kicking, made worse by the fact that he believed he deserved it.

Maurice was mortified, blaming himself for his mistake. He kept apologising over and again to the boss he felt he had badly let down. In typical Ted fashion, he kept assuring him that nothing was his fault and that he took full responsibility himself for the direction the case had gone in.

When they went into the pub, Dave was all smiles to see them and asked Ted, 'How's your Trev now?'

Ted shook his head imperceptibly and Dave understood the message. The team knew nothing about Trev's unfortunate behaviour and it would stay that way. As a landlord, Dave was nothing if not discreet about what his customers got up to in the sanctity of his bar.

'I look forward to seeing him again soon,' he said, already pouring Ted's customary Gunner drink. 'Tell him not to be a stranger.'

Once the drinks were served and a toast drunk to Virgil's good news, Maurice sidled over to Ted once more.

'Maurice, if you're going to apologise again I may have to use Krav Maga on you,' Ted said with a weak smile. 'It's fine, really. We're all at a low ebb as we're not winning this one at the moment. But we will. We just need to knuckle down a bit harder and cover the routine stuff.'

Ted didn't feel like staying long, so he left the price of a second round behind the bar and headed home. He felt a pressing need to spend as much time as he could with Trev, never easy in the middle of a difficult case.

Trev was in the kitchen, cooking. As soon as he saw Ted, he stopped what he was doing and wrapped him in a hug.

'You look like you had a very bad day,' he said. 'Do you need a brew?'

Ted slumped in a chair and nodded.

'I got a right roasting from the Chief Constable. I'm definitely not on his Christmas card list any more,' he said wearily. 'Did you see the piece on the local rag's website? And that was before they knew there'd been another death. If ever they find out I was in the home when it happened, I might be reduced to issuing fixed penalties for parking.'

Trev finished what he was doing and sat down next to him.

'Do you want to talk about it?' he asked.

Ted shook his head emphatically.

'Not remotely.'

His mobile phone started to ring. As he took it out of his pocket, he saw the name on the screen and said, 'Jim.'

'Have you told him about me, yet?' Trev asked. 'You can, if you want to.'

'Jim, it's nice to hear a friendly voice,' Ted said, as he took the call. 'At least, I hope it's going to be friendly. I've had enough of a kicking for one day, thanks.'

The gruff voice of his former boss, Jim Baker, greeted him jovially enough.

'I saw the article. I imagine you're not having an easy time of it. How's the Ice Queen taking it?'

'She's being surprisingly supportive at the moment. The Chief Constable, on the other hand, chewed me up and spat out the pieces.'

He made an apologetic face and mouthed 'sorry' at Trev.

He hated bringing work home at the best of times, and this was currently not the best of times. Trev shrugged and made a waving gesture of hello towards the phone.

'Trev says hi, by the way.'

'I'm hoping he can say that in person soon,' Jim replied. 'I was phoning to ask if you're both free on Saturday night. There's someone I want you to meet.'

Ted sat up a bit straighter and smiled into the phone.

'That sounds interesting. I think we're free Saturday night,' he looked at Trev, who nodded in response. 'This is someone special, I take it?'

Jim sounded almost embarrassed as he said, 'Well, I think she is. That's why I'd like you to meet her, if you're free. Say, around seven-thirty for eight?'

'Seven-thirty is perfect. Are you expecting us to dress up? Trev made me buy new clothes, ready for Willow's wedding,' he said, as if it had been a real trial.

'I think I've known you long enough not to expect you to dress up off-duty,' Jim chuckled. 'Come in whatever you feel comfortable in. And good luck with the case. I know you, you'll crack it, eventually. You always do.'

Ted felt his spirits lifted somewhat by Jim's words. He had served under his friend for several years when Jim had been a DCI. He'd been sorry when Jim's promotion to Superintendent had seen him transferred to another division. Ted's relationship with the Ice Queen was not remotely on the same footing and he highly doubted if it ever would be.

Trev had made him tea and put it down in front of him.

'How hungry are you? Food won't be ready for a while. You've got time to forget about work and chill a bit first. Shall we sit in the garden? I think it's still warm enough, and it's not raining for the moment. Might as well take advantage.'

They went out and sat down in the steamer chairs.

'You didn't tell him, then?'

'It didn't seem quite the moment, really,' Ted told him.

'We'd love to come to dinner on Saturday evening. Oh, by the way, Trev may have inherited a serious heart condition. I did tell the Ice Queen, though. I hope you don't mind. I had to tell her something. She was giving me a look which made Vlad the Impaler look like quite a reasonable chap.'

Trev threw his head back and laughed at the image, but his laughter only served to make Ted look contrite.

'I'm sorry, here's me, as usual, banging on about my problems at work and you have enough on your mind right now,' he said.

'What's a life-threatening heart condition compared to what you go through on a daily basis?' Trev smiled. 'How are you getting along with the feisty Jezza these days, or is she still one of the problems?'

'She certainly doesn't help,' Ted admitted. 'She has the potential to be a good officer, I can sense that. But she doesn't do herself any favours at all with her attitude and I still have no clue as to why she's like that. The team clearly think I'm going soft, keeping her on. But for this case, working undercover, she really is the best bet I have at the moment.'

'Could you not borrow an officer from uniform? That PC Heap seems like a very nice type,' Trev said with an ironic wink. He had found her to be kindness itself when he'd gone into the station to apologise for his drunken behaviour in the pub.

'I could, but it still wouldn't be enough. There's a lot of these homes on the patch. It's clearly a lucrative business to be in, judging by how many there are. Even if Kevin would lend me Susan for long enough, and I keep Jezza in a home, that still leaves a lot them with no one in undercover. And frankly, I wouldn't know which home to put her in, without a lead.

'And can you really imagine the likes of Maurice or Virgil blending into the background and not looking suspicious enough to put our Angela off showing her face? We have no leads on her at all at the moment, even assuming she is one and the same person every time, and is involved in the case.

'But at least we've got your appointments sorted out now, and not too long to wait.'

'You will be able to come with me, won't you?' Trev asked anxiously. 'With all that you've got going on, I know it's hard for you to get away from work. But I really would like you to be there.'

Ted reached across and laid a reassuring hand on his arm.

'I'll be there. If I have to work some twenty-four hour shifts to make up the time, I will be there.'

Trev took a drink of his red wine, then said thoughtfully, 'You know what you should try with Jezza?'

'Sacking her? Too much paperwork,' Ted said firmly.

'No, I'm being serious now. Try using a bit of psychology. What have the two of you got in common, apart from both being coppers?'

'I hope you're not saying I have the same attitude as she does?'

'Martial arts,' Trev said. 'Why don't you reach out to her a bit? Tell her about our self-defence club for kids. Ask her if she'd come along and give a demonstration. The kids would love to see her kickboxing. You could even spar with her. Kickboxing versus Krav Maga. Show the kids how that goes.'

This time Ted laughed at the mere suggestion.

'I'd be afraid to. She might beat me. And besides, it would probably be breaking all sorts of rules of professional conduct.'

'But why? In the dojo, dojo rules and etiquette, Bernard to referee. Kids like Flip would absolutely go wild to see that.'

'I'll think about it,' was all Ted would say. 'Now tell me a bit more about what Bizzie told you. How are you feeling about it? Did you find out anything about her? I feel I still hardly know her at all.'

'She's great. She really did help. I think our Bizzie might have been a bit of a tinker in her day,' Trev said, smiling fondly. 'I also think someone broke her heart very badly, so badly that it can't be put back together again.'

'Do you think it was a man or a woman?' Ted asked.

'Oh, Ted, please,' Trev said reproachfully. 'Surely you, of all people, are not going for the cliché of Bizzie must be a lezzie because she lives alone with a farting dog and she wears tweeds and brogues? My guess is that it was a man, and not a very nice one, at that.

'I suspect her life is full of regrets because she kept telling me to carry on living my life to the full. She told me that if I didn't and there turned out to be nothing wrong with me, I'd regret bitterly the lost opportunities along the way, even if it's only a matter of weeks before I know. And that if the worst did happen, I would probably know nothing at all about it and at least I would have enjoyed myself in the meantime.

'She also told me,' he said with a suggestive wink, 'that I shouldn't let it interfere with my sex life.'

'She said that?' Ted gaped at him.

'Oh, yes. Like I said, I think Bizzie might have been a rare old gal in her day and she is now deeply regretting that she didn't carry on as she started. That she let one person, whoever it was, ruin her life for her.'

Ted looked at him thoughtfully.

'And you say the supper won't be ready for a while yet?'

Trev stretched languorously in his steamer chair, looking like one of the cats who surrounded him, as always.

'It can happily stay in the oven for as long as it needs to.'

Ted stood up.

'In that case ...'

# Chapter Twenty-six

Finally, there was the first sniff of a lead, the possibility of at least bringing someone in for questioning. Meticulous checking of personnel records had revealed two carers who had worked in more than one of the homes where there had been deaths. There was also one who had worked in one home and the hospital. It was not much to go on, but it was their first real break of the case.

It did at least mean that Ted could report to the Ice Queen that they were bringing people in for questioning, and she in turn could inform the Chief Constable. Ted had decided to make the questioning formal from the start, partly to show they were making progress, of sorts.

Sal filled the team in on what had been revealed by cross-checking staff records at all of the homes on their patch, as well as the hospital.

'Gillian Shaw, works at Limekiln House now, home of Jane Applegate, before she went into hospital, where she died. Before that, Shaw also worked at Snowdon Lodge. They seem to have the highest turnover of any of the homes. So far, they're the one constant between the three possible suspects.

'Mandy Griffiths, now at Snowdon Lodge, was previously a Health Care Assistant at the hospital. Two deaths to date at Snowdon Lodge, Gwen Jones and Betty Hibbert.

'Finally Stacy Bancroft. He works at The Poppies now, where Maggie Tyler died, and before that he was at Snowdon Lodge.'

Maurice gave a snort.

'I thought there was something suspicious about him, the moment I saw him.'

Ted smiled and said mildly, 'Just because he has eye-liner and a pony tail doesn't make him a murderer, Maurice. Any more than it means that he's gay.

'Right, I'd like all of these people brought in at some point for questioning. Stress that it's just routine at this point. We have nothing more than circumstantial evidence to point to any of them at the moment, but let's at least check them out.'

'Surely none of them can be Angela though, boss?' Sal asked. 'If they're already working in a home where there's been a death, they can't be going in posing as someone else. They'd be recognised, surely? And one of them's a bloke, anyway.'

Maurice was about to say something, saw Ted's face and thought better of it.

Jezza scoffed.

'Like I said before, it's easy enough to change appearance, even for a man, as long as the height is right.' She glared challengingly round at them and said, 'I bet I could fool the lot of you into not recognising me, if I wanted to.'

'Put your money where your mouth is, bonny lass,' Maurice replied. 'Tenner says you can't.'

'All right, settle down, this is serious,' Ted said. 'You can have your playtime once we crack this case, not before, please.

'I don't think we have anything to lose if Jezza carries on going to Cottage Row for now. That's still the best lead we have to Angela. The sooner we find her, the sooner we can eliminate her from our enquiries or identify her as a prime suspect. And we should also not overlook the possibility that if Angela is our killer, she could be working with an accomplice inside the homes. Someone who tells her which are likely targets, and if and when any of them go into hospital.

'Now, I can't get involved in any of the questioning of potential suspects, because of my grandmother. If I were to question someone who later turned out to be our killer, any defence lawyer worth his salt would have a field day tearing our case apart.

'So, Mike, it's up to you to sort out who questions which suspect, but keep me in the loop at all stages, please. And this needs to be done meticulously. I don't think we should get fixated on appearance. Even if it's someone who doesn't fit the physical description of our Angela, be thorough and check alibis.

'Let's not have any more slip-ups. My future police pension might depend on you,' he added with a smile.

He was feeling a bit more optimistic as he went downstairs to brief the Ice Queen. It made a pleasant change to be able to report any kind of progress, especially in the shape of their first possible suspects. Even if they all turned out to have perfect alibis, it was a start. She listened in silence while he told her of the latest turn in the enquiry.

'Well, that is promising,' she said. 'I can at least pass that on to the Chief Constable. He is, of course, bracing himself for the next side-swipe from the press when they learn of the fifth death, as are we all. Now, there is something I wanted to talk to you about. Would you like coffee?'

It always worried Ted when she offered him coffee. It immediately made him suspicious of her motives. He thanked her and accepted. The jug was already full of fresh, hot coffee, which smelled  good and was probably expensive. Ted wondered what brand she used. He was not a coffee connoisseur but even he appreciated it.

She sat down opposite him and began.

'Now, let me say at the outset that I am in no way telling you how to do your job. That would be presumptuous of me in the extreme as I have never worked in CID. But there is one area of your work in which I feel there is clearly room for improvement.'

Ted was tempted to ask, 'Only one?' but fought the urge.

Instead he prompted, 'Yes, ma'am?'

'Your relations with the press, Inspector,' she said dryly.

'Ah,' Ted replied, with a guilty smile. He knew it was true and made no secret of it.

'Ah, indeed. But remember, your sins will always find you out,' she said, with the air of a headmistress dealing with a particularly troublesome pupil. 'This latest press article could, perhaps, have been less damaging if you had a better relationship with the local reporter, don't you think?'

Ted thought it might be wise not to voice what he actually thought. He simply waited expectantly to see where the conversation was going.

'I wonder if it might be prudent to start building some bridges with the local press. Hold out an olive branch. Meet him halfway.'

She appeared to have run out of metaphors for now.

'With respect, ma'am,' Ted said, largely because he knew how much the phrase irritated her. 'I'm not sure what it would achieve. Is it not a case of shutting the stable door after the horse has bolted?'

'Let's just look at the logistics of it for a moment, shall we?' she asked in a reasonable tone. 'You have young TDC Ellis spending hours on his computer, checking newspaper articles, looking for relatives with an axe to grind about bed-blockers. If you had a good working relationship with the press, could you not have easily obtained that information in a half hour conversation with the reporter over a glass of beer in The Grapes?'

'Are you telling me that's what I should be doing? Cosying up to the local reporter for help to solve the case? He's going to want something in return if I do. What are you proposing that I offer him, ma'am? Isn't it safer if I just keep referring him to the Press Office, which is what I always do?'

'That approach, although orthodox, is not really bringing the desired results, though, is it?' she asked. 'You can be charming when you try. Good company. I've seen it for myself. Why not just try to improve things a bit? Think of it as a campaign of hearts and minds rather than your preferred combative shock and awe approach to the press. Promise him that as soon as you have a name to release, he will get it before anyone else. In exchange for which, you'd like some help tracing any relatives whom he may have interviewed.'

'He's definitely going to want payment up front, so to speak. How will I know what information to give him, without compromising the case in any way?'

'The Press Office has already prepared a crib sheet for you.' She slid a sheet of paper across her immaculate desk as she spoke. 'Make yourself familiar with what is on there. Go through it with him, make sure he has all the information it contains.'

'So this was already drawn up, before you talked to me?' Ted queried. 'In other words, this is a done deal?'

'You're an intelligent man. I'll leave you to join up the dots. You really need to be seen to be making an effort at improving your relations with the press, which are certainly not helping with this enquiry. The Chief Constable was very clear to me, as I suspect he was to you, that he wants this case wound up. To use the jargon, he is looking for early closure.'

'But surely, if too much leaks out in the press at this stage, we risk driving Angela underground for good? That would stop the deaths, but what about justice for the five victims and their families?'

'The Chief Constable's orders were unequivocal. He wants this case wrapped up, whatever it takes. I would venture to suggest that if we could begin by stopping the killings, that would give you and your team the breathing space to try to track down this Angela, if indeed she is the killer.

'We're not in the Mounties, Inspector. Sometimes you don't always get your man. But at least you might be able to spare other families the grief of losing an elderly relative. Isn't it worth a shot?'

Ted suspected 'No' might not be an appropriate answer, but it was what he was tempted to say. He also had to suppress a smile at the unfortunate pun from the Superintendent who was, like he was himself, a former Firearms officer and a crack shot, at that. Instead, he asked formally, 'Is that a direct order, ma'am?'

She looked at him for a long moment, then said, 'It is a suggestion, with a very strong recommendation that you act on it. Does that make it clear enough?'

He only just stopped himself from doing a Jezza-style sigh. Instead, he nodded his understanding, then went back to his own office. Then he kicked the waste-paper basket right round his room a couple of times. After that, he picked up the phone.

'Alastair,' he said, with all the joviality he could muster. 'Ted Darling here.'

There was a pause, then the oily, nasal voice which always made Ted cringe said, 'This is a joke, right? You're someone from local radio, pulling my plonker? That would be about as likely as the real Ted Darling phoning me.'

Ted forced a laugh he did not feel like giving.

'Fair point,' he conceded. 'But this is a genuine olive branch.' He decided to be blunt and continued, 'As you can imagine, I got my backside well and truly kicked after your latest article. But that's not what this call is about.'

'Go on,' Pocket Billiards sounded suspicious.

'I haven't always been fair to you,' Ted continued, his toes curling up with the effort. 'There is more information that I could give you. Are you free to meet for a drink? Today, perhaps?'

There was a pause, then the journalist said, 'I'll be going for my dinner in about an hour. I could meet you at The Grapes?'

'Looking forward to it,' Ted said, through gritted teeth.

Ted strolled to the pub ahead of time. He wanted to catch a few words with Dave, the landlord, before his meeting. Trev had been in and paid his dues. He had not told Dave much and was not keen to share his news with everyone, but Ted wanted to make sure there was no lasting damage done, and no hard feelings.

He was still chatting amicably with Dave when the journalist came in. When he walked up to the bar and said, 'Hello, Ted,' as if they were best friends, Dave's eyebrows shot up.

'Alastair. Nice to see you,' Ted said, trying to sound as if he meant it. 'Go and find us a table and I'll bring the drinks over. What are you having?'

'Pint of lager top. And bring the menu with you,' he said ungraciously.

'Lager top?' Dave queried derisively, once the journalist moved away. 'I didn't think grown-ups still drank that. What sees you schmoozing the gutter press, Ted? Not usually your style,' he said, making up Ted's Gunner as he spoke.

'Basically, the top brass's jackboots up my backside,' Ted said with a wry grin. 'They are not happy with the way the current case is going and they think me supping with the devil is the answer to it all.'

'Well, if he's the answer,' Dave nodded contemptuously towards the reporter, pushing the lager top across the counter to Ted, 'then it must have been a bloody silly question.'

Ted took the drinks and a menu across to the table and said expansively, 'Whatever you want to eat, Alastair. It's on me.'

'I suppose you're going to ask me not to reveal the fifth death,' he said with a sneer. 'I'll have the steak, well done.'

'I wouldn't dream of it. I'm here to make sure you have all the information you need,' Ted assured him. 'I'll just go and order our food.'

Ted did not feel like eating anything himself, especially not in present company, so he just ordered a cheese and tomato panini.

'If you notice my hands creeping round his throat, Dave, make sure you call the boys in blue,' Ted said, before heading back to the table.

'The thing is, Alastair, I should have been a bit more helpful to you, instead of always palming you off with the Press Office,' Ted began, picking his words carefully and hating every minute of it. 'At the moment, I could do with a bit of help from you. In exchange, I promise that you and your paper will be the first to get a name in this case, once any arrests are made.

'I've got some more detail here for you,' he pulled his crib sheet out of his inner pocket. 'I can't give you the whole sheet, you understand, but I can make sure you have more detail than anyone else.'

He could see that the journalist was interested. He was eagerly craning his neck, trying to see what was on the sheet of paper which Ted kept tantalisingly just out of his clear view.

'First, I'm going to give you some information which we don't, at this stage, want publishing. Can I trust you on that?'

The reporter nodded briefly so Ted continued.

'Up to now, these are officially all just unconnected suspicious deaths. Off the record, and I really mean that, we are looking into a possible link between them, which is where you come in. In particular, I'm interested in various articles which you've written about grieving relatives complaining over lack of available hospital beds when someone has died.'

Dave brought their food over and put it in front of them. Both men waited until he had gone before they continued.

'Is that what you think the link is? Bed-blockers? You don't need me for that,' the reporter said, sounding suspicious again. 'You can read the articles yourself.'

'True, but that takes a lot of valuable time. Plus you have a number of unnamed sources who might be of interest to us.'

'A journalist never reveals their sources,' he said sanctimoniously, beginning to eat.

Ted didn't have much of an appetite to start with. The sight of Pocket Billiards shovelling food past his rotten teeth and chewing with his mouth partly open robbed him of any that he did have. He managed two bites of his sandwich, then put it back down and ignored it.

'Of course not, I understand completely and I'm not asking you to,' Ted said, feeling as if he was crawling. 'But if you did remember anyone who stood out in your mind that you could steer us towards, without naming them? Maybe a date? Or details of the death in question? Something we could check with the hospital and find out names for ourselves? I would see that your paper got the credit for helping us solve the case.'

He had never seen anyone dispose of a meal so quickly. In no time at all, Pocket Billiards was looking up expectantly, grease round his mouth and a dribble of ketchup down his chin.

Ted sighed. 'I'll get you the dessert menu,' he said and stood up.

'A brandy wouldn't go amiss at the end of the meal, either,' the journalist said. 'It might just help to jog my memory. As it goes, I do vaguely remember one or two relatives I interviewed who might be of interest to you. But I'd have to go back through my notes for names and addresses. Then we could do this again, when I give you the details.'

'Give me a large brandy for my new best friend, Dave, will you, and what puddings have you got today?' Ted asked, when he went to the bar. 'Oh, and if you have any toxic substances at all behind the bar, can you put a good dollop in his drink, before I really do strangle him with my bare hands.'

# Chapter Twenty-seven

Ted had heard nothing yet from the local reporter. He did not expect to. He rather thought that the Ice Queen was barking up the wrong tree with her attempts to forge a better relationship there. The bad feeling on both sides was too long-established.

The article on the deaths had now appeared in the weekly paper, as well as online, both updated to include a mention of the latest death. The best that Ted could say about it was that it was no worse than the original piece.

Jezza was still going to Cottage Row every afternoon. She seemed, for the time being, to be keeping her head down and trying to do her job. Whether because of the press coverage or not, Angela had not put in an appearance since the last time, when Jezza had missed her. In fact, things had gone quiet on all fronts.

Professor Nelson had phoned Ted with the latest toxicology results as soon as she had them. Mike had drawn the short straw of attending the post-mortem this time.

'Aconite again, Edwin,' she announced, once again not bothering with much of a greeting. 'So that's two in the same home with the same toxin, unless I am very much mistaken? Is that significant, do you think, or just coincidence?'

'I honestly have no idea with this killer, Bizzie,' Ted replied. 'I'm having difficulty coming up with much of a theory at all, to be honest. What about dosage, this time? The same quantities as before?'

'I would say he, or she, is honing their skills. Significantly less this time, although still more than enough to kill, especially an elderly person. You still have no suspects?'

'Not really, although we are at least now finding a few tentative links,' Ted told her candidly. 'Thanks for hurrying this through for us once again, Bizzie. I really appreciate it.'

'How is young Trevor bearing up? Have you got his appointments sorted out?'

'Next Monday,' Ted told her. 'And thanks for all you've done to help him. He really appreciated your advice. All your advice. And so did I.

Bizzie gave a throaty chuckle.

'I'm glad,' she said. 'Perhaps when he gets the all-clear, as I hope he will, you'll let him take me out on the motorbike again. I don't think I've ever had so much fun.'

'I'm sure he'd be thrilled to. I hear you're a bad influence on him when it comes to mundane matters like the speed limit.'

She was still laughing delightedly when she hung up.

Mike had begun interviewing the three care workers. Disappointingly, it had not yet thrown up anything much to advance the enquiry.

'That Stacy is interesting, boss, and not just because of the eye-liner,' Mike told him when they had a quick catch-up. 'I asked him why he left Snowdon Lodge to go to The Poppies. He said Snowdon was like factory farming, more money-driven than about caring for the residents. He likes The Poppies because he says they all genuinely seem to care about the old folk they look after. He certainly sounds as if he does. An unlikely suspect, I would say.'

'Do his alibis stack up though, Mike? We can't go off hunches, especially when we're getting nowhere fast.'

'He'd left Snowdon Lodge before either of the deaths there and he was working at The Poppies, actually on duty, at the likely times the victims there were poisoned. With Mrs Tyler, at The Poppies, he wasn't on duty when she was probably poisoned, and other staff corroborated what he said about this neighbour having been in with a picnic for her.'

'When are you interviewing the others?' Ted asked him.

'They're both working all this week and they do long shifts. I thought I'd risk leaving it till the weekend, when they're off-duty. I'm working over the weekend so that would work, if you think that's all right, boss?'

Ted scratched his head, considering.

'It's a calculated risk, I suppose,' he said. 'We don't really have enough on either of them to make them definite suspects. On the other hand, if we delay and either of them is the killer and goes on to kill again … It doesn't really bear thinking about.'

'I could do a bit more checking on both of them and make an informed decision based on that?' Mike suggested. 'If anything sets the warning bells off, I'll pull them in, long shifts or no long shifts.'

'I'd quite like to have a quiet weekend, if that's possible. Trev and I are invited to Jim Baker's for dinner on Saturday night,' Ted told him.

'No sweat, boss, if the worst happens, I'll cover for you,' Mike promised him. 'I'll be looking for a return favour soon. The missus and I have promised to take the kids to Blackpool, now she's doing so much better. Be nice to have a family outing again.'

'And I won't be in on Monday morning,' Ted told him. 'In fact, I'm not sure if I'll get in at all that day, certainly not until late on. There's somewhere I need to be. The Super knows, she's cleared it. I'll have my mobile off for most of the time so it's dire emergencies only, please, and even then I can't guarantee to respond immediately.'

Ted hoped that Mike could hold the fort on Saturday evening, as he and Trev drove over to Jim Baker's house in Didsbury. Just in case, Ted kept his mobile phone switched on, but set to vibrate-only mode.

Jim opened the door to them, smiling expansively. He was clearly keen for them to meet the new woman in his life. He led the way into the front room.

'This is Bella,' he said proudly, putting an arm round her shoulders. 'And this is Ted, and his partner, Trevor.'

She was quite short, no bigger than Ted, shapely, and with a pleasantly smiling face. Ash blonde hair was pulled back from a high brow, and her eyes were a striking shade of violet. Remembering what Jezza had said, Ted wondered if she was wearing tinted contact lenses.

Introductions made, Jim left his guests to sit down with their drinks and went to busy himself in the kitchen. Ted could tell that he was on edge, anxious that the evening should go well. He thought he must be serious about Bella and hoped she would bring some happiness into his life. He noticed, too, that all photos of Jim's previous wife had disappeared from the room.

'James has made the starter and the main course,' Bella told Ted and Trev. 'He's quite a good cook. I prefer baking, so I've made the dessert. I do hope you'll like it.'

Ted was curious to know more about the potential future woman in Jim's life. He was amused that she called him James. He noticed that Jim had shed a few pounds since they'd worked together in Stockport. He wondered if that was from choice, or whether Bella was trying to change him. Jim had always been a big man. He dwarfed Bella.

As they ate, Ted started to ask Bella a series of searching questions about herself. Trev was watching curiously. It was not like Ted, when he was not in policeman mode.

'Do you work at all, Bella?' was one of the things he asked her.

'Only part-time,' she said. 'I do book-keeping for various companies and small businesses. I work mornings. Mostly I go out to see the clients, as they tend to be busy and it's easier for them to do it that way.'

'What sort of businesses?'

'Oh, all sorts, it's very varied. Let's see, this week, I've been to a garage, a website designer, a hairdresser and a care home,' she replied.

'This is a lovely meal, Jim,' Trev put in, trying to lighten the conversation, which was beginning to sound a bit like a police interview.

'Care homes seem to be springing up all over the place at the moment,' Ted said, ignoring him. 'Turning into big business, it seems. Do you have many on your books?'

'Oh, yes,' she said. 'I have some which are part of a big chain, and also a few of the private ones.'

'Do you visit them all, or do some of them send their books in to you?'

'No, all my work is done going to see the clients. I work from home, I don't have an office, as such,' she replied, trying to find time to eat as well as to answer his questions.

'And do you share Jim's love of gardening? The same green fingers?' Ted persisted.

Jim pushed his chair back and dropped his knife and fork with a clatter.

'Talking of gardens, Ted, why don't you come and see the latest improvements I've made to mine,' Jim said, with a loaded glance at Ted.

Bella put a hand on Jim's arm.

'Surely that will keep until we've finished the meal, James?'

'We won't be long. Just a bit of a leg stretch before the next course. Trevor will keep you company.'

Ted could see the anger in him by the set of his heavy shoulders as he strode off down the lawn to the furthest part of the garden. Jim knew perfectly well that Ted was not interested in gardens. He stopped and whirled round, his face dark.

'What the bloody hell are you playing at?' he demanded. 'I bring you to meet the woman I'm thinking of marrying and you start interrogating her like a prime suspect. I feel like punching your lights out, Ted, I really do. Except I know that I wouldn't stand a chance.'

Ted looked contrite. 'Sorry, Jim. Really, I'm sorry. It's just this case. I'm getting obsessed. Bella fits the profile in many ways. I suddenly got this mad idea that she might be, you know, Belladonna ...'

'For God's sake, Ted, what the hell is the matter with you? It's not that long since you suspected me of being a serial killer in another case. Now you've turned your sights on Bella in this one. Is the therapy not working? Her name's Isabelle.'

Jim was one of the few who knew that Ted was receiving counselling, and the reason for it. It had been Jim who had pushed him to take the first step to get the help he needed.

'And what's all this crap about profiles? I remember trying to get you to use a profiler in the past and you refusing point blank. What the hell is wrong with you, man?'

Ted was looking about him, feigning an interest in the garden to buy himself time before answering. He couldn't actually see any improvements, but he didn't like to say so.

'Apart from being five murders into a case I can't solve? Apart from the Chief Constable threatening to put me on point duty?' Ted asked ironically, after a pause. 'Then I meet someone who looks as if they change their appearance with tinted lenses, who likes baking and who goes round a lot of the care homes. You can't blame me for clutching at straws.'

'Life's full of coincidences,' Jim growled. 'You know that as well as I do. The sort of thing that, if you put it in a book or a TV crime series, the readers and viewers would claim it could never happen.'

Ted made a small noise which could have been a laugh.

'Like Trev's delightful mother turning up out of the blue, not long after mine did, you mean?'

He had told Jim about the return of his own mother into his life. They were close friends and kept in touch, although they no longer worked in the same station.

'Really?' Jim look astonished. 'I thought he had no contact at all with his family?'

'Now I've met the lovely Lady Armstrong, I can understand why he's pleased he doesn't. She makes the Ice Queen look like a warm, motherly, caring sort of person.'

'Lady Armstrong? Blimey, I knew Trev came from a posh background but I didn't realise they were titled.'

'His father's a senior diplomat, with a knighthood. It doesn't give Trev a title.'

Jim was still looking searchingly at Ted, who was sniffing randomly at plants, trying to look interested, while hoping none of them was toxic.

'Stop pissing about, Ted. I know you. I can read you like a book. What's really bothering you?'

Once again, Ted looked wildly about him for something else to talk about, feeling Jim's intense gaze burning into him as he did so.

Eventually, he said quietly, 'Trev has hospital appointments on Monday. It's possible he has inherited a life-threatening heart condition. That was the reason for her Ladyship's visit, to drop that bombshell on him. His father has had a serious heart attack. He's going to be all right, but it was touch and go for a while. We won't know, until all the tests have been done, whether or not Trev has inherited the same condition. So I apologise for my behaviour. I'm a little distracted right now.'

Jim stared at him, stunned.

'Bloody hell, Ted. Bloody hell,' was all he could manage to say to begin with. Then, 'But he's so fit. Not a spare ounce on him.'

'It's the way it goes with this condition. No advance warning. We just have to wait and see.'

Bella appeared on the patio, just outside the French doors.

'James, the meal is going cold. Are you two coming in?'

There was an unmistakable note of reproach in her voice.

As they moved off up the garden, Jim put an awkward hand

on Ted's shoulder and gave it a clumsy pat.

The rest of the meal went well. Ted had a moment's anxiety at the prospect of eating the Black Forest gateau which Bella had made, obsessed as he was with the case. But he did eat it and it was delicious.

Ted was quiet for the rest of the evening, leaving Trev to turn on the full charm, which clearly already had Bella under his spell.

When they were leaving, Jim walked them to the car.

'I'm really sorry, Jim, once again,' Ted said contritely. 'Please make my excuses to Bella. Tell her I'm under stress at work. Or certifiable, or something. She's very nice, and no, I don't think she's a serial killer.'

# Chapter Twenty-eight

'Try to sit down,' Ted said quietly, as Trev paced the small room like a caged animal. There were other people waiting and from the looks on their faces, Trev was making them nervous with his prowling.

Trev flung himself back in his seat and said tersely, 'What, in case I drop dead of a heart attack in the waiting room?' Then he immediately looked apologetic. He reached for Ted's hand and squeezed it hard.

An older man, sitting alone opposite them, frowned and looked disapproving. Trev responded by putting his other arm round Ted's shoulders, leaning closer and giving him a lingering kiss on the cheek. Despite the seriousness of the situation, Ted couldn't suppress a smile at the man's shocked reaction.

'Behave,' he said fondly, in a quiet voice, to Trev.

He was so anxious himself he could not begin to imagine how Trev was feeling. He kept hold of his hand and squeezed it back in what he hoped was a reassuring gesture.

A woman in a white tunic put her head round the inner door of the waiting room and asked, 'Mr Armstrong?'

Trev jumped to his feet, keeping hold of Ted's hand. Ted got up to go with him.

'Just you for now, I'm afraid, Mr Armstrong,' the woman said firmly. 'Your friend can wait here. Then when all the tests are finished and you're having a chat with the consultant, he can come with you.'

She gave Ted a friendly smile and said, 'We'll take good care of him, I promise. It's all pretty straightforward. Don't worry, I'll bring him back in one piece as soon as I can.'

It was Ted's turn to pace the waiting room, in the face of more disapproving looks from the man opposite. Eventually he went out into the corridor and got his mobile phone out to call Mike, asking to be brought up to speed. At least it would take his mind off what was happening to Trev.

'The carer Gillian Shaw checks out perfectly, boss,' Mike told him. 'Tight alibis, nothing in her behaviour to suggest anything to worry us. She's the same as Stacy. Started out at Snowdon Lodge, didn't like it, didn't get on with the management, so moved to Limekiln and is much happier. So far I'm not convinced about the other one, Mandy Griffiths. I think she's one you saw when Mrs Hibbert was first taken ill?'

Ted remembered her. Large, lacking in sympathy, clearly not in the low-paid work for the love of looking after elderly people.

'She's the one who's also worked at the hospital?' he asked. 'So she would know her way around there well enough. Alibis?'

'Day off when Jane Applegate died at the hospital and no alibi. Says she was at home all day, alone, doing housework. On duty the day Betty Hibbert died, as you know. She could easily have been in a position to give her the cake, or to let in an accomplice. Although I still have no idea what the motive would be. Also on duty the day your gran died, so the same things applies.'

'Hang on a second, Mike,' Ted asked and put his head hopefully back into the waiting room. There was no sign of Trev. Logically, he knew he would not be back yet, but he wanted to make sure he was there when he did return. A couple came walking down the corridor towards him and went into the waiting room, looking anxious. Once they were out of earshot, Ted spoke again.

'Listen, Mike, I made a bit of a prat of myself at Jim

Baker's on Saturday night. I was practically interrogating his
new lady-friend at the dinner table because she wears coloured
contact lenses and likes to bake. But it did make me think of a
different angle we need to check on, soon, as it opens up
another possibility for a motive.

'Do we know if all the residents in all the homes pay the
same rate for their rooms? Is the price fixed or does it go up?
I'm just wondering if some, who may have been residents for
some time, are tied in to a lower rate. Is it more lucrative for
the homes to lose a resident, then bring one in at a higher fee?'

Mike let out a low whistle.

'Now that would be a seriously cynical motive,' he said. 'I'll
get some of the team onto checking that. Rates, length of stay,
variable contracts, that sort of thing. So where does that leave
us with the lovely Angela? Is she connected to the financial
side of it?'

'I really have no idea about Angela. I'm starting to wonder
if she is just a coincidence, maybe not always the same person.
The Big Boss reminded me that such things do happen in life,'
Ted said, using Jim Baker's old nickname from when he was in
the same station.

'Oh, by the way, when was it you needed me to cover for
you, Mike, for your theme park outing?'

'It's on Saturday, boss,' Mike replied and Ted groaned
inwardly. He had had a bad feeling it would be. Saturday was
Rupert and Willow's wedding. Trev was going to kill him if he
had to interrupt that for work.

'Who's on duty?'

'It's Sal and Jezza,' Mike told him.

'Fine,' Ted said, even more disconcerted, but trying not to
show it. He hoped this was not going to be another occasion
when Jezza let the team down. It would be the first weekend
she had been on the rota to work. 'I'll be at a wedding, so tell
them my phone will be switched on, but on silent. Ask them to
keep it to real emergencies only to call me, please.

'I'll hopefully be in later today, but I have no idea when. Oh, and get someone digging a bit deeper into the background of this Mandy Griffiths. I didn't much take to her when I met her. I'd like to know more about her. I may drop in on Snowdon Lodge again myself later today, if I get time. I still need to pick up my gran's things. I'll see what else I can sniff out while I'm there.'

Ted went back into the waiting room and sat down. The disapproving man had disappeared, presumably having gone for his appointment. Ted picked up an old copy of National Geographic and started to flick through it, although he couldn't really settle to much.

After what seemed like an eternity, Trev reappeared. He had a small piece of cotton wool, held in place with a strip of surgical dressing, in the crook of his elbow, where he had clearly had bloods taken. Ted got up and went to him, anxiously scanning his face.

'How was it? What now?'

Trev nodded to the door and Ted followed him out.

'Now I have to trot down the corridor and wait outside the consultant's room,' he said, leading the way. 'No one has told me anything so far, but apparently he will tell me all he can for now. They were very thorough. They've scanned every mortal bit of me and taken an armful of blood.

'I was wired up to a machine and had to run on a treadmill, stripped off to my grundies. The technician in charge of that was flirting with me and he couldn't take his eyes off my pecs,' he added with a small teasing smile.

The consultant didn't keep them waiting for long before he opened the door. He had thinning, light sandy hair, and his face and the arms which protruded from his short-sleeved shirt were liberally sprinkled with freckles. He had the same outdoorsy air as Bizzie and looked to be of a similar age.

'Mr Armstrong? Please come in and take a seat. I'm Douglas Campbell, your consultant.'

'This is my partner,' Trev indicated Ted. 'Can he come in as well?'

'But of course,' the man beamed expansively.

He turned and led the way into his office, inviting them to sit down. Then he sat at his desk opposite them and opened a large folder, which contained various X-rays, ECG traces and other results.

'Now let me say from the start, so as not to raise your hopes too high,' he began, looking at Trev over the top of half-moon glasses, 'that I don't yet have all the information to hand. So I'm afraid at this stage, I can't give you a definitive answer. I need to wait for the blood test results to be absolutely sure. What I can tell you, from the results so far, Mr Armstrong, is that you are currently in very good physical shape, with no signs of anything sinister. Do you work out to keep as fit as that?'

'Martial arts,' Trev said shortly. He was too nervous to be his usual polite and charming self.

'Excellent. I just wish more of my patients took such good care of themselves. It would make my life a lot easier. Now, I am going to do my best to get you the test results as soon as I can. The moment I have them, I will contact you again to come in to hear the findings.

'Bizzie Nelson is an old and dear friend. We've known each other since childhood, did med school together. Believe me, when she tells me to jump, my only question ever is how high,' he chuckled at his own joke.

'I'm sorry I can't tell you more at this stage but it would be wrong of me to do so. I imagine that in your profession,' he looked at Ted as he spoke, 'you cannot go on guesswork alone and it's the same for me.

'Now, I know this is easy for me to say, but not for you to hear. Please don't worry. It serves no purpose at all and could do you more harm than good. Carry on living your life as normal for now, and above all, continue to take such excellent care of yourself.'

He stood up and shook hands with both of them.

They walked in silence out of the hospital and back to Ted's car.

'What do you want to do now?' he asked Trev. 'Go home? Get something to eat?'

Trev shook his head.

'You need to get back to work, catch your killer,' he said, and cut across as Ted opened his mouth to speak. 'I think I'd quite like to go into work, too. It would take my mind off things. I might as well be doing something I like, rather than fretting about stuff. Can you drop me off there and I'll get a bus home afterwards?'

He saw Ted's worried expression and smiled reassuringly.

'Honestly, I'm not going on another bender. I learned my lesson last time. I'd just rather be doing something, and I know you probably would, too. Thanks for coming with me.'

'I'll try not to be late tonight. Do you want me to pick up a takeaway on the way back?' Ted asked, when they pulled up outside the motorcycle dealership where Trev worked.

'Perfect, thanks. Love you,' he said as he got out of the car.

'Love you, too,' Ted said and was rewarded by seeing the smile on Trev's face as he headed in to work.

Ted was determined to be more demonstrative in the future. On a whim, he took out his mobile phone and called his mother's number. It went straight to voicemail. She was probably on her way to work.

'Hi, it's Ted. Sorry I haven't picked up Mamgu's things yet. I hope to go today after work. Then perhaps I could fix a time when Trev and I could come round to deliver them?'

He hesitated, then continued, 'It would be nice to see you again.'

He dropped in to see the Ice Queen when he got to the station, as a courtesy. She was surprisingly supportive, expressing her concern and again asking if he needed to take time off, which

Ted refused.

He spent much of the afternoon at his desk, going through the statements which Mike had taken from the possible suspects, and trying to clear the ever-present paperwork mountain before it became overwhelming. He kept having the feeling that there was something he was missing, something glaringly obvious.

Although he knew Trev was not yet in the clear, he felt more optimistic now that the tests had been done, at least. He and Trev both preferred action to waiting. He felt he might be able to concentrate a bit better now. He made a mental note to speak to Bizzie as soon as possible, to thank her again for her help. Then he set off for Snowdon Lodge once more.

The carer called Katya opened the door to him with a friendly smile.

'How's the carer who was ill?' Ted asked, as she let him in.

'A lot better. She'll need a few more days off work but she should make a full recovery.'

Ted could see that she was busy, as usual, so he asked for his grandmother's things. He followed her down a corridor to a store cupboard at the end, which she unlocked with a key from her belt. She lifted out two small holdalls and handed them to him. It didn't seem much to show for his grandmother's life.

'Can I ask you a question?' Ted asked her.

She laughed.

'Isn't that what policemen always do? Ask questions?'

He smiled in acknowledgement.

'Why do you work in this home? I mean this one in particular, rather than any other one? It doesn't seem quite as caring as some of the ones I've visited.'

'Can we walk and talk?' she asked him. 'I'm doing the rounds of the rooms, making sure they're ready for the old dears at bedtime.'

She headed off to do her appointed tasks, Ted following her from room to room.

'I looked at more or less all the homes in the area before I took this job. It wasn't the one I liked the most but it was easy to get to and they promised to help me with my continued training. There's been no sign of that so far, though. I was a nurse in my own country, but although I'm told my qualifications should be recognised here, somehow I never get the nursing jobs I go after. So, here I am, wiping bums and cleaning up sick.'

She laughed again. Ted tried to work out if there was any hint of bitterness in her voice.

'Do you not enjoy looking after the elderly?'

She shrugged.

'It's a job. I try to be kind to them, because that's what I'm trained for. Even on the low wages I get here, it's more than I would earn at home. So I have to say nothing and keep working.'

She looked at him across the bed which she had just turned down and was now smoothing flat and wrinkle-free with practised hands.

'I finish at six,' she said, smiling. 'If you wanted to go for a drink, or a coffee, maybe?'

To his alarm, Ted realised she was actually flirting with him.

'Ah, no, it's very kind, it's just that ...'

'I know, you're on duty,' she smiled.

'Erm, not just that. I'm gay. I have a partner,' he said, a little awkwardly.

It was her turn to look flustered.

'Oh, I'm so sorry,' she said hastily, going red. 'You don't ...'

' ... look gay?' Ted interrupted, with a smile. 'We're just people. We don't all look the same or sound the same.'

'Your partner is a very lucky man,' she said, with apparent sincerity.

'No, I'm the lucky one. You should see him. He's stunning,' he smiled with pride.

They chatted for a few more moments, trying to put the incident behind them. Then Ted picked up the holdalls, gave her a smile and went back to his car. He took out his mobile phone.

'Mike?' he asked. 'Can you make a note to check out in more detail another member of staff at Snowdon Lodge, as soon as possible? Her first name's Katya, I don't know her surname. It'll be on the records. She has a very good motive to be resentful of the old people she looks after. And she's visited most of the homes on our patch, when she was first looking for work.'

# Chapter Twenty-nine

Ted felt full of a new resolve the next day. Even though the rational part of him knew there could still be devastating news ahead for Trev, his optimistic side was doing its best to convince him that there would not be. He started the morning briefing with an apology.

'I've been a bit off my game lately,' he began. 'I had the feeling there was something blindingly obvious that I'd been missing, and I've finally come up with a few things. I've already asked the DS to start looking into the financial side of this case, from the point of view of the homes. Could they make more money if beds were freed up and new residents came in on higher rates, for example?

'But now for what I've missed so far. Have we looked fully into who benefits from these deaths, directly or indirectly? Who inherits? I know we have with Mrs Jones and there's no evident financial motive there, but what about any of the others?'

There was a deafening silence. The team members looked at one another, clearly embarrassed. It seemed no one else had thought of it, either. Or if they had thought of it, no one had yet taken any action.

'We need to look into the wills of all the victims, and we need to do it soon. Mike, please also check who drew the wills up. We haven't found a solicitor called Angela Mortice, and that's probably a false name. But I was speaking to an accountant at the weekend who goes round to visit clients, including care homes, which got me thinking.

'If our Angela exists, and if she really does have a connection to all our victims, could she perhaps be a solicitor, or a legal executive, under another name? Could she be the person who drew up their wills, and is she coercing our victims into making her a beneficiary?'

'Shit, boss,' Mike said apologetically, 'you're not the only one off your game. I should have been on top of that from the start.'

'We're on it now, that's the main thing,' Ted said reassuringly.

'But boss, what about witnesses?' Rob O'Connell asked. 'You need two witnesses to a signature on a will, people who aren't beneficiaries, surely? Would they not spot when signing it that all was not as it should be?'

'Depends on who they were,' Ted told him. 'And that's another thing we need to check out. Just suppose that Angela asked carers in the homes she visited to witness a signature. Would they even have the time to scrutinise a document or would they just scribble their names?'

Jezza gave one of her characteristic snorts of scorn.

'From what I've seen of some of them, even signing their name would be a challenge. And bear in mind I'm in one of the better homes, with some genuinely nice and caring people. But honestly, the level of writing in the day book, where staff note things, is pretty shocking. I'm sure some of them would never dream of questioning anything someone official-looking asked them to sign, even if they're not supposed to sign anything.'

'Glad you mentioned Cottage Row,' Ted said, looking directly at her. 'What do we know about the potential victim there, the one Angela may be targeting? I don't even know her name,' he added, looking pointedly at the white board. 'Have we checked into her background? Looked for any links between her and the victims?'

More blank looks and some shuffling in seats. Jezza got up,

went to the white board and picked up the marker pen.

'Sorry, my fault, I should have filled it in,' she said, much to the surprise of some of the team. 'Lucy Lee, eighty-two, has dementia and failing eyesight. Widowed, no surviving children, just a grandson who works in London and only visits her once every Preston Guild. Well, maybe a bit more often than every twenty years, but not much.

'She's a nice old dear, no trouble, most of the carers genuinely seem to like her. Most of the time she just sits in her chair not far from the door. She keeps trying to stab any shafts of sunlight she sees with the end of her walking stick. Because her eyes are so bad, goodness knows what she thinks they are.'

Ted thought he detected a slight note of affection in her voice as she spoke, which rather surprised him.

'So would a carer just sign a document without looking at it carefully, based on what you've learned so far?' Ted asked her.

'With respect, boss,' a phrase which Ted disliked as much as the Ice Queen did, 'you should try a shift in a care home some time. I'm only there to keep an eye on Lucy, but I occasionally lend a hand in passing the tea round, that sort of thing. Most of the carers are so busy they've no time for anything. Not all of them have English as a first language, and those who do are not all very articulate.

'I would say it would be the easiest thing in the world for anyone who looked like a solicitor or someone official to get a passing carer to add a signature to a document, without giving it so much as a second glance.'

'And there's been no sign at all of Angela at Cottage Row recently? Any theories as to why not?' Ted asked.

Jezza headed back to her seat and sat down, her arms as usual folded defiantly across her slouching body.

'Maybe she's just gone on holiday? People do, even murderers, and it is that time of year,' she suggested, with a shrug.

Ted nodded.

'Fair point. Well, I think we have nothing to lose by keeping you in there a bit longer, to see if she shows. She might just have gone to ground because of the publicity, but at least if she has, there should be no more deaths for the time being.

'Right, Mike, there's plenty more we can be getting on with for now. Let's see if we can have a definite suspect by the end of the week. If we do, the drinks are on me after work on Friday. And don't forget to cross-check everything with the hospital. It's easy to overlook that that was the scene of crime for Jane Applegate, not the home she was in.

'So let's have this Mandy Griffiths in again. Mike, you and Maurice see what you can get out of her. If you think there's enough to go on, we'll get a warrant, give her place a turning over, see what that throws up. And whoever does that, make sure they have a look in the garden, if there is one, for any signs of poisonous plants. Get print-outs from Steve, so you know what you're looking for.'

'If anyone's rummaging round looking for aconite, they need to be gloved up. There have been a couple of recent poisonings in the news, thought to be accidental, just from handling their leaves,' Jezza threw in.

'Thank you. Good point. I hope you'll manage to join us for drinks this time, Jezza?'

'Can't,' she said bluntly. 'Painting my toe nails.'

Ted was disappointed that she showed no inclination to want to join in with the social side of being part of a team. He understood and respected when his officers wanted to keep their private lives to themselves, as he often did. But he found the occasional get-together was a great exercise in team-building. He wished he could get Jezza to see that and to participate.

He nodded to Mike to follow him to his office when he'd finished.

'I know this is all very tenuous, Mike, but at least it's

something. Get the rest of the team on to the other stuff while you and Maurice have a crack at Griffiths. I'll just be glad I can tell the Super we're bringing someone in for further questioning. It looks so much better than me constantly scratching my head and admitting I haven't a clue.'

The Ice Queen did seem encouraged by the news, though she certainly wasn't turning cartwheels, with still no signs of a charge.

'And where are you up to with the local reporter?' she asked. 'Have you heard anything further from him?'

'Ah,' Ted said, which she knew by now was his shorthand for having done nothing.

She made a tutting sound.

'Too much 'ah' and not enough action, Inspector,' she said, in her usual acerbic tone. 'Why not tell him you're interviewing a suspect?'

'But I can't give him any more detail yet, so is there any point?'

'Of course there's a point,' she said firmly. 'You have to show him you meant what you said about a new spirit of cooperation. He will find out anyway that you're questioning someone, as he always seems to. At least if you tell him first he may see that as a sign you're sticking to your side of the bargain. And he may just offer something in return.'

Ted went back to his office to phone Pocket Billiards. He felt as if he were bargaining for his soul with the devil.

'Alastair,' he said, as brightly as he could manage, in greeting. 'Look, I can't give you any detail at all yet but I just wanted to give you the heads up that we have started questioning a possible suspect.'

The journalist immediately launched into a barrage of questions, which Ted cut short.

'Sorry, you know the rules. That is absolutely all I can tell you for now. I just wanted you to be the first to know, in good faith, to show I'm keeping my side of the bargain. So I wondered if you had anything for me in exchange?'

'There was one woman I remember, as it goes,' the oily voice mused. 'I know grief does strange things to people but I had the feeling she'd probably always been as mad as a box of frogs. I talked to her a bit but she didn't want to be named, didn't want to be quoted, even anonymously, so I haven't got much for you to go on.'

'Can you at least tell me where and when this happened?' Ted asked.

'It was at the hospital. I was there on another lead entirely and I just happened on this woman, ranting like a mad thing in the corridor. The staff were trying to whisk her away somewhere quiet. It seemed her husband had just died on a trolley, waiting for a bed, and she was not a happy bunny.'

Ted winced at his crassness but asked, 'Any idea at all of when it was? Or anything else you can remember?'

'I honestly can't remember, Ted,' he said, making Ted cringe even more at the familiarity. 'I would have said maybe six, seven months ago. If I remember anything else, I will let you know. As I know you're going to let me know as soon as you have anything I can publish.'

'Count on it, Alastair. We'll talk soon,' Ted said and rang off, feeling slightly tainted.

Further questioning of Mandy Griffiths did not reveal anything to take the enquiry further forward in respect of the deaths. There had been no need for a search warrant, in the end. Once it had come out in questioning that her real name was not Mandy Griffiths and she did not actually hold any of the care qualifications she claimed to, she started being cooperative.

She was happy for officers to look through her small ground-floor flat and the attached garden which went with it. She claimed to have no knowledge of the foxglove plants growing there. But as Virgil, who searched the property, said, there were a lot of them in the neighbouring gardens, too. It seemed to bear out her explanation that they must have self-seeded there.

It was not quite the result Ted had been hoping for before the weekend, but it was something, at least. They still had to check all the paperwork recovered in the search of the house for a financial motive, but at the moment, the woman remained no more than a possible suspect.

Ted decided the team all deserved a drink at the end of the shift regardless and once again told Jezza she was welcome to join them. Once again, she declined the offer.

It did the team good to get together over a pint, or in Ted's case, a Gunner, in The Grapes. There were not many people in early in the evening but Ted knew from experience that it would liven up somewhat, later on a Friday night.

They were all sitting round a table with a clear line of sight to the door, some on bench seats, Maurice perched at the end on a low stool. As a young woman walked into the bar on her own, the others grinned as Maurice almost fell off his stool through craning to look at her.

She had shoulder length black hair. Smoky eye-liner brought out the sultry tones of her eyes. She was wearing the shortest pair of tailored shorts imaginable, below an exquisitely cut jacket, both in black. Her creamy camisole was as fine and insubstantial as a cobweb and left nothing to the imagination. Her legs looked impossibly long in strappy sandals, with the highest heels Ted could ever remember seeing anyone walk on successfully.

In a beautifully modulated, slightly husky voice, she ordered a glass of white wine as she carefully eased herself up onto a tall bar stool, crossing her legs so that her shorts rode up even higher. Then she placed what was clearly an expensive designer bag on the floor at the foot of her stool.

Ted chuckled.

'Put your tongue away, Maurice,' he said. 'It's getting embarrassing.'

'Yes, but, bloody hell, boss, you would, wouldn't you?' he

replied, then grinned and said, 'Well no, you wouldn't, but most blokes would.'

Ted smiled indulgently. For all his total lack of political correctness, Maurice had a heart of gold. He may not have been the brightest copper in the division but he was without doubt one of the kindest men he had ever met, who would do anything for anyone.

Well, I would,' Virgil admitted. 'But first I'd snatch that handbag she's got. The missus has been after me to buy her one of those for ages, but on a copper's wages? No chance!'

The woman was taking absolutely no notice of them, which was just as well. With the exception of Ted, the rest of the team were all gazing at her in unconcealed admiration. The fact that young Steve was going visibly pink in the face as he looked made Ted wonder what his thoughts were.

Ted got no more sense out of any of them until the woman finished her drink, slid elegantly from the stool, picked up her bag and headed towards the door. She made a small detour, taking her nearer to their table, and bent down, her mouth close to Maurice's ear. Her voice was quiet, but they could all hear what she said.

'You can pay me the tenner you owe me on Monday, Maurice, bonny lad,' Jezza said, before she sashayed her way out of the pub.

# Chapter Thirty

When Ted saw the venue for Willow and Rupert's wedding, he was relieved that Trev had insisted on taking him clothes shopping. The stunning long, low country house hotel was surrounded by beautifully manicured lawns and rose gardens, with a large lake, fed by a stream tumbling down a small waterfall, as the focal point.

Ted's old Renault was put to shame by the expensive collection of cars pulling up to deposit the beautiful people from Cheshire's Golden Triangle. It was not just the scent of expensive perfume in the air. The smell of money, both old and new, was almost tangible.

Trev would be in his element in such company, Ted knew. With his background, his charm and his good looks, he would fit in perfectly. Ted would feel like a spare part, trailing in his wake. But he was fond of both Willow and Rupert and wanted to be there for their special day. He was just praying that there would be no phone call from work to spoil it for him.

The wedding was at eleven and the reception would follow on, in a different part of the hotel. Ted and Trev arrived in good time to take their seats in the magnificent reception room which was to host the marriage ceremony. They were greeted by an usher in morning dress who handed them the order of service and asked if they were friends of the bride or groom.

'Both,' Trev told him, 'but Willow longest, so perhaps we'd better sit on that side.'

They were shown to seats on the left-hand side, about

halfway down. Ted took the aisle seat and Trev gave him a reproachful look.

'I hope that doesn't mean you're poised for a quick getaway?'

Ted looked apologetic.

'I do, too, but you know I will have to go if I get a call. Fingers crossed, eh?'

The room was simply but beautifully decorated with white floral arrangements. They could see Rupert sitting in the front row on the right, glancing anxiously from time to time towards the doorway.

Before long, they heard the strains of Pachelbel's Canon and all eyes turned to watch Willow start to float her way up the aisle on the arm of a tall and distinguished-looking man, her father, Ted presumed. Both Willow and Rupert were professional models and she looked sensational in a simple creation of ivory silk and lace, with a posy of wild flowers.

As she walked, she stopped from time to time to smile at special guests. When she got to where Trev and Ted were standing, she beamed in evident delight and gave Ted's arm a small squeeze in passing.

Just as the ceremony began, Ted felt the muted phone in his pocket vibrate. He mouthed 'Sorry,' to Trev as he slipped as quietly as he could out of the room. The screen showed him it was Sal calling. He accepted the call, said a very quiet, 'Hang on,' then waited until he got outside to speak.

Sal's voice was full of apology. 'Sir, I'm really sorry to spoil the wedding. I'd have managed without calling if I hadn't been on my own.'

'No Jezza?' Ted asked, feeling himself getting angry at being let down.

'Nothing, boss, she hasn't turned up and there's been no message. I tried her phone but it goes straight to voicemail. It wouldn't matter ordinarily but there's been a serious assault and rape and I've also had a call from the hospital, just now.'

Ted felt his stomach sink into his boots as he asked, 'Another death?'

'Not yet, boss, but it sounds very much like the same thing, and it was on the same ward as last time. The victim's in intensive care and is critical, but still alive. I can't cover both on my own, and I know the sarge is away. Do you want me to call someone in?'

Ted felt like swearing, but did not. He knew Trev would not be best pleased, though he would understand. But Ted himself was sorry he was going to miss the occasion.

'No, I'll come in. Why don't you take the assault case and I'll go to the hospital? Then we can catch up at some point and see how we're both getting on. Just remind me, the last death at the hospital, that was yew leaves, wasn't it? As our killer repeated poisons at Snowdon Lodge, that might possibly be helpful information for the hospital.

'Keep trying Jezza's phone, whenever you get the chance, just on the off-chance you can get hold of her. It would be good to make sure she's all right, apart from anything.'

He ended the call and went back into the reception room. As soon as he slid into his seat, Trev could see from his face that he was going to have to go. Ted put his face close to Trev's ear to speak.

'I'm sorry. Jezza hasn't turned in and there are two cases that need dealing with. Please can you apologise to Willow and Rupert for me? If it's remotely possible, I'll get back here somehow later on. If not, can you get a taxi home?'

Trev smiled resignedly and said quietly, 'Go, Mr Policeman. At least Willow knows that you came. And she saw you in your nice new suit.'

Ted headed straight for the hospital, feeling overdressed but not wanting to take the time to go home and change. There was always an outside chance he could get back to the hotel for the last part of the reception.

He went straight to the same ward as before. He wondered

if he might spot Oliver Burdon there once more, but there was no sign of him. He made a mental note to talk to him again. He was the sort who noticed things. He might just have seen something which was significant, without realising that it was.

He didn't see anyone he recognised on the ward, and it looked as busy as the last time he had been there. He managed to catch the attention of a passing nurse to show his warrant card and ask who was in charge. She promised to send the duty ward manager in his direction, but said that it might take a while.

Eventually, a man in a blue tunic appeared, walking towards Ted.

'Sorry to keep you waiting,' he said. 'I'm Senior Charge Nurse Chris Ferguson. How can I help you, Inspector …?'

'Detective Inspector Darling,' Ted told him, showing his card again. 'I believe you've had someone on this ward taken suddenly ill, with similar symptoms to a patient who died here recently, a Mrs Applegate?'

'That's right, a Mr John McAlpine. He's seventy-eight, he's in a home but he was admitted with a serious UTI,' the nurse explained. 'Same old, same old. They don't give the old folks enough to drink, they get dehydrated and get infections. Poor old boy's been quite poorly but he was on the mend, doing really well. Then he suddenly started with violent vomiting and a very irregular heartbeat.'

'How's he doing, and where is he now?' Ted asked.

'We managed to get him stable and he's gone up to ICU. He's a really tough old boy, so we're hoping he might pull through. Can you tell us anything which might help identify what's caused this? I know my colleague told me after the last one that you were treating it as a suspected poisoning.'

'We're investigating a series of sudden deaths involving elderly care home residents,' Ted told him guardedly. 'A number of different poisons appear to be involved, but most contain cardiac glycocides, if that helps. The last victim here was poisoned by *taxus baccata*, yew tree. The leaves to be precise. I'd rather this information stayed confidential, on a need to know basis, at this point in the enquiry, though.'

The man nodded and went to a telephone at the ward's main desk.

'Of course. Just let me ring up to ICU and tell them. That information could be very helpful in how they treat Mr McAlpine.'

He made a brief phone call then turned back to Ted.

'Is there anything else at all I can help you with?'

'I don't suppose by any chance you would know if Mr McAlpine had any visitors today, or yesterday? Did he have any food brought in from outside?'

The man spread his hands in apology.

'Sorry, but it can get manic in here. We're often short-staffed, we really don't have the time to monitor that sort of thing. There are notices up requesting visitors not to give food to patients without asking but we simply don't have the staff numbers to enforce it.

'I don't know if he had any regular visitors, although I think someone from the home dropped in to check on him. If it's helpful, I could look in the locker, next to his bed, just in case there's any food in there?'

'That would be brilliant, thank you,' Ted told him. 'I don't suppose by any chance there are any stomach contents available?'

The man laughed.

'We tend to dispose of those fairly promptly,' he smiled. 'Or rather the HCAs do.'

He saw Ted's questioning expression and said, 'Health Care Assistants.'

'Speaking of those, would you happen to remember one who used to work here, by the name of Mandy Griffiths?'

The nurse frowned.

'Gobby? Built like a brick shit-house?' he asked.

'Well, I wouldn't have put it quite like that,' Ted said, 'but now you come to mention it ...'

They had reached a bed, the screens still pulled partially round it, empty and in a state of disarray. The nurse bent over the locker at the bedside and pulled out the drawer first.

'Bingo!' he said, as his hand went to remove the contents.

'Please don't touch,' Ted said hastily. 'Evidence. What is it?'

He pulled the drawer wider open and Ted could see a partly eaten piece of cake on a paper plate inside.

'I'll need to take it with me but funnily enough,' Ted indicated his best suit, 'I don't have any evidence bags with me. I've just come from a wedding. Do you have anything I could use, please?'

The nurse smiled.

'I thought it was a bit formal for your line of work. No worries, I'll sort something out for you. And about that Mandy woman you asked about? We had to let her go. Too many question marks about her and her behaviour. She wasn't good with the patients, especially the elderly ones.'

Ted went next to the police station, clutching the piece of cake in the bag the nurse had supplied for him. He would send that off for immediate forensic testing to see what, if any, poison it contained.

Sal came back into the office not long after him.

'Really sorry to drag you in from a wedding, boss,' he said apologetically. 'There's still no word from Jezza, but this other case has dissolved a bit. It seems to have been something of a drunken episode, with a lot of accusations and fists flying on both sides. The two main parties have changed their stories a bit, so it's looking like one I can easily wrap up on my own.

'Why don't you get off back to the wedding? You look great, boss, I guess Trev took you shopping?' Sal added, with a grin.

Ted made a face at him and asked, 'Are you sure, Sal? I don't like to leave you in the lurch.'

'Honestly, boss, it'll be fine. Virgil's gone off shopping for baby stuff so I don't want to bother him but Rob says he could come in if I need him to. Why not go back to enjoy the rest of your friends' wedding? That's a one-off, it would be a shame if you missed it. Especially all dressed up like that.'

Ted nodded.

'Thanks, Sal, I appreciate that. I might as well get my money's worth from the new suit. Not something I'll be wearing often. Let me know in the morning if Jezza shows up or not. If she doesn't, I'm happy to cover for her, save dragging anyone else in. Just phone me.'

He was pleased he would be able to get back for at least part of the reception. With any luck, he could wish Rupert and Willow well and see them leave for their honeymoon. He imagined it would be somewhere exotic.


He parked the Renault and went back into the hotel. He found his way to the room where the reception was in full swing. The meal was almost over, the speeches had clearly been made, and a few couples were up on the dance floor.

He glanced round but couldn't see Trev anywhere at the moment. Rupert and Willow were both still sitting at the top table. When Willow saw him, she got up immediately and came over to greet him. He thought she looked rather worried, and her kiss on his cheek was perfunctory.

'I'm so sorry, I got a call to go to the hospital,' he began.

'Yes, of course. How is he?' Willow asked anxiously.

Adrenaline suddenly flooded Ted's body as panic hit him. His mouth went dry and his heart started to race alarmingly.

'How's who?' he asked.

'Trev, of course,' Willow sounded puzzled.

'What happened?' Ted said. 'I got called in on a case. What's happened to Trev?'

'He was suddenly taken ill, not long after the meal began. He was vomiting violently and his heart was racing,' she told him. 'One of Rupert's friends took him straight to hospital. We thought that would be quicker than calling an ambulance. I thought someone had called you. Ted, I'm so sorry.'

But Ted was gone, sprinting as fast as he could for the Renault. As he backed out of the parking space and floored the accelerator, gravel flew up from the spinning wheels and pebble-dashed the line of sports cars and Bentleys parked nearby.

# Chapter Thirty-one

Ted slammed the Renault to a halt in the first empty parking place he found, threw his official Police sign on to the dashboard and raced to the entrance of the Accident and Emergency Department. He pulled out his warrant card and thrust it in the face of the first member of staff he saw, demanding, 'Where's Trevor Armstrong?'

The nurse looked him up and down, barely acknowledging the warrant card and said patiently, 'If you'll just take a seat for a minute, I'll find out for you.'

'I need to see him, as soon as possible,' Ted persisted.

This time the nurse did look at his warrant card before saying, 'Inspector, everyone who comes in here is in a hurry to see someone. Please just wait a moment and I promise you, I will find out.'

Ted took a deep breath and tried to calm down. It was not often that his good manners deserted him, but he was panic-stricken.

'Sorry,' he said contritely. 'You're right. I apologise.'

He couldn't contemplate sitting down. He knew he would not be able to keep still long enough. Instead he paced up and down in front of the desk where the nurse was checking information for him.

'Right, Inspector, if you'd like to follow me, I'll take you to him.'

She led him to a curtained cubicle and stood aside so he could go in. Trev was sitting propped up against the pillows, a drip in his arm, his shirt open, a heart monitor connected to his chest. He looked pale and wan and had a kidney dish on the bed in front of him.

'Hey,' he smiled, as soon as he saw Ted. 'I didn't want to bother you.'

Ted went over to him and kissed him on the forehead, which felt damp.

'How are you? What happened? How are you feeling?'

Trev gave a weak laugh.

'Typical policeman. So many questions. I'm fine, now. I've no idea what happened. One minute I was happily munching my way through a delicious meal. Next thing I was in the gents, being as sick as a dog. I went all clammy and my pulse was all over the place. And no, I hadn't been drinking too much.

'One of Rupe's friends, who was on the same table, very kindly came looking for me when I was a long time. He brought me straight here. Luckily, I managed not to puke up inside his brand new Audi, but it was a close thing.'

'What have they said? What caused it?'

'Not a lot, and I have no idea,' Trev said, looking tired.

At that moment, the curtains parted and a doctor came in.

'Sorry, Mr Armstrong, I didn't know you had company.'

'This is my partner, Ted. You can speak in front of him, it's fine.'

'What caused this? Is he going to be all right?' Ted began.

'He's a policeman. He asks a lot of questions,' Trev told the doctor apologetically.

'I see. Well, I'm Dr Hamilton, the registrar who has been looking after Mr Armstrong. I'm pleased to say he is doing very well and his condition is giving no cause for alarm,' the doctor told them.

'Have you told him about the blood tests?' Ted asked Trev.

'Yes, mother,' Trev smiled, with a wink at the registrar. 'He also fusses rather a lot.'

'Yes, Mr Armstrong has explained about the possibility of a genetic heart condition. I'm pleased to say that I don't think this is anything more sinister than a nasty allergic reaction to something.

'Sometimes, violent vomiting can cause dehydration, which can in turn lead to the heart going flippity-flop. That's a technical term,' he added as an ironic aside. He clearly had a sense of humour, despite appearances to the contrary.

'We've treated Mr Armstrong conservatively, with an anti-emetic to control the vomiting, and put him on a drip for the dehydration. Now that both are under control, there is no sign of any heart irregularity. I'm inclined to say that he can probably go home as soon as the drip has finished going

through, which won't be too much longer. As long as there is someone to keep an eye on him.'

'I'll be with him,' Ted assured him. 'What do you think caused this?'

'My first inclination was towards food poisoning, until Mr Armstrong mentioned where he had eaten. I think it would be unlikely in such a venue, unless he had been unlucky enough to get the one bad oyster in a batch.'

'No oysters. No R in the month,' Ted and Trev said, almost in unison. Neither of them really believed the old saying for a moment, but it was a long-standing joke between them.

'In that case, I would suspect a food allergy. Do you have one that you're aware of?' he asked Trev.

Trev shook his head.

'Never been allergic to anything, as far as I know. Except my mother.'

'Well, they can sometimes appear without warning. I would strongly recommend that you see your GP soon and ask for allergy tests. Explain what happened. You're probably aware that a severe allergy can sometimes lead to anaphylaxis, for which you may need to carry adrenaline.

'With an allergy, there is often some swelling of the mouth

and throat, rather than just violent vomiting, as in your case. Perhaps your system is just very efficient at protecting itself, getting rid of whatever it didn't like as quickly as possible.'

Ted produced his warrant card again.

'At the risk of sounding paranoid, I'm currently investigating a series of poisonings of elderly victims, including two in this hospital. One fatal, one not yet so. This information is confidential, at this stage.'

'You don't need to remind a doctor about confidentiality, Inspector,' the registrar replied with a dry smile.

'The poisons used have all been plant extracts. The toxins are mostly cardiac glycosides. Trev's symptoms sound to me as if they were very similar. Could this episode be connected?'

The registrar looked carefully at all the notes he had on Trev's case. He then went across to check the trace on the heart monitor. After that, he put his stethoscope to Trev's chest and listened for a few moments.

'I can see nothing at all which would indicate poisoning of any sort, and certainly not with cardiac glycosides,' he said. 'Mr Armstrong, I can't comment at all on the possibility of any inherited heart condition. What I can tell you is that, at this moment, your heart is as strong as an ox. I would therefore have to stick to my original diagnosis of a food allergy. Or possibly an extreme gastroenteritis.

'Just to be sure, I will check with my consultant. If he is in agreement, and if your vital signs continue to return to normal as they are doing, I think we can consider releasing you shortly.'

He made to leave. Ted followed him, telling Trev he would be back in a few moments.

'While I'm here, I need to check on the elderly patient from this morning. He was in intensive care. Can anyone help me to find out how he's doing, please?'

The registrar nodded towards the main desk.

'Just ask a member of staff to phone ICU for you. Try not

to worry about your partner. He should make a good recovery, at least from today's little episode,' he said. 'And try not to get fixated on the poisoning theory. Sometimes, coincidences happen in real life, as well as in soap operas. This might just be one of them.'

The same nurse he had seen earlier was at the desk, going through some files. Ted felt ashamed of his earlier behaviour, which was so out of character for him.

'Hello again,' he began awkwardly. 'I'm really sorry about before. I panicked a bit. I wondered if you could help me again, please?' He held out his warrant card once more so she could see it more clearly. 'I need to find out how someone on intensive care is doing, in connection with an ongoing enquiry.'

This time she studied his card more closely and looked at him.

'Inspector Darling?' she queried, her eyebrows going up.

Ted grinned. He was used to hearing remarks on his surname, although it was not all that uncommon. He had also heard all the jokes and all the references to the old Blackadder television series. He had a charming grin. The nurse was clearly not immune to it as she smiled back, her expression much more friendly. 'What's his name?'

'John McAlpine.'

She picked up the phone and made a short call, then told Ted, 'Still seriously ill but he is improving steadily. Is Mr Armstrong also connected to the enquiry?'

Ted shook his head.

'No, he's my partner. That's why I was unprofessionally anxious,' he said with another smile.

The nurse sighed audibly.

'There are going to be some disappointed nurses when I tell them,' she smiled. 'Me included. He's gorgeous.'

Trev was already looking brighter when Ted went back into the cubicle. They did not have long to wait for the consultant to come and give him a cursory once-over, before saying he was ready to be discharged, once the drip had been disconnected.

'Why didn't you get someone to call me?' Ted asked him, as they walked out to the car park shortly after. Ted was relieved to find his car was still where he had left it and had not been clamped or towed. He could see now that he had parked badly and it was actually straddling two spaces. 'I only found out because I managed to get away and go back to the reception.'

'I didn't want to worry you,' Trev said lightly, as he got into the car. 'You've got enough on your plate at the moment. I had a bit of panic at the, what did the doctor call it, the flippity-flops. But once that settled down, and my stomach had stopped turning itself inside out, I was fine. Well, almost fine.'

'Well, I'm going to keep a very close eye on you until we get the results of those blood tests. And until we know for sure what caused this,' Ted told him firmly. 'If Jezza is a no-show again tomorrow, I'll tell Sal to bring Rob in. And it's no use arguing,' he said, as Trev opened his mouth to speak.

Ted phoned the hospital first thing the following morning to check on John McAlpine. He was relieved to hear that, although he was still in intensive care, his condition was continuing to improve. A nurse on duty told him that they hoped to be able to send him back to the ward later in the day.

Trev was much better, too. He had eaten nothing on his return but, as instructed by the consultant, Ted had made sure he had drunk plenty of water and had taken it easy.

Ted phoned the office while he made Trev's breakfast, plain wholemeal toast and tea much weaker than he usually drank it. He thought that avoiding too many stimulants would be a good idea until his system had fully recovered.

'Sal? Any news from Jezza today?'

'I had a text first thing, boss,' Sal told him, then added, clearly quoting verbatim. 'Been ill. Still am. Can't come in. Soz.'

'Soz?' Ted asked in disgust. 'What does that even mean?'

'It's text-speak for sorry, boss,' Sal said helpfully.

'I know that,' Ted said sharply, although he only knew because Trev constantly tried to educate him in how to write text-speak. 'What I mean is, what kind of a message is that from a serving police officer, to excuse their absence?'

Then he added hastily, 'Sorry, Sal, I'm being a bit tetchy. I had an anxious day yesterday. Trev had been carted off to hospital when I got back to the reception. He had symptoms not dissimilar to some of our victims. Luckily, it seems to have been a food allergy or an attack of food poisoning or something, and he's much better. I'd still like to keep an eye on him today, if you can manage without me?'

'Sorry to hear that. Poor Trev.' Sal said.

Trev was popular with all the team members, especially Sal, who shared his love of big bikes.

'Give him my best wishes, boss. And yes, unless anything big goes off, I should be fine. Sarge is back from his day out and Rob's free, so there are reinforcements I can call on if I need them.

'You keep an eye on Trev and I promise to call you if there's anything major. How's yesterday's victim, by the way? Have we got another death?'

'Luckily, he seems to be holding his own so far,' Ted told him. 'Seems like a tough old boy and he may not have eaten much of the cake, which is probably what saved his life.

'Right, I'd better feed the invalid. Remember to keep me in the loop at all times. My mobile will be switched on. I'll be in first thing tomorrow as usual, hopefully. I'm anxious to have a few words with Jezza so I can find out for myself exactly how soz she really is.'

# Chapter Thirty-two

Jezza sauntered into work on Monday morning, seemingly without a care in the world. Sal in particular looked daggers at her, after being left in the lurch by her on Saturday. He was clearly about to say something but Ted caught his eye and shook his head. He would deal with it later.

Instead Sal asked, 'How's Trev now, boss?'

'He's a lot better thanks, Sal,' Ted told him. 'In fact, he's gone in to work today.'

He briefly explained to the team about Trev's sudden mystery illness. They all knew Trev, except for Jezza, and made sympathetic noises. Ted was just about to bring them up to date about the latest poison victim, John McAlpine, when Maurice stood up and took out his wallet.

'Fair play to you, bonny lass,' he said, handing a ten pound note to Jezza. 'You really had me fooled on Friday. You said I wouldn't recognise you and I certainly didn't. You're not Angela, are you?' he added with a laugh.

Jezza took the note, folded it and tucked it into her jacket pocket.

'If I brought in a cake I'd made, would you dare to eat it?' she quipped in reply.

To everyone's surprise, Steve piped up, 'Someone get a picture of that on their phone. Maurice, with his wallet open.'

It was the first time anyone had heard him make a joke.

'Right, settle down,' Ted said good naturedly, then briefly outlined the sequence of events on Saturday. He noticed Jezza squirm a little awkwardly in her seat when she heard that the boss himself had had to leave a wedding to come in to cover for her.

'I phoned the hospital first thing. The good news to start the day is that Mr McAlpine is continuing to make a good recovery. He's out of all danger and is back on the ward. I'm waiting on the tox results for the cake which was in his drawer, but this has all the hallmarks of yet another plant poisoning.

'What we don't know at this stage is why he didn't eat all the cake, although that's undoubtedly what saved his life. Or why he was targeted. First port of call needs to be the home where he usually lives,' he checked his notebook and added, 'Apple Orchard Court. Mike, I'll do that one myself.

'I also want to widen the net for people other than relatives who may visit elderly residents in care homes. I still think we're missing something obvious. Accountants, lawyers, but who else? Jezza? Any suggestions? Who have you seen coming and going at Cottage Row?'

'Hairdresser, aromatherapist, chiropodist, for starters,' she said. 'I'll get some names this afternoon when I go in, and ask who else visits.'

'Right, good. Now, the hospital told me that Mandy Griffiths was let go because of concerns over her attitude, so let's dig a little deeper into her background. Even if we can't pin any murders on her, can we at least charge her with something? I'd like a result of some sort. And what about Katya, at Snowdon Lodge? Anything further on her?' Ted asked.

'Comes up squeaky clean on all counts, boss,' Mike told him. 'Alibis for all the deaths. An impressive CV, excellent references, which appear genuine. If she is resentful of having to wipe bums instead of doing real nursing, she doesn't appear to be showing her resentment by bumping off old folk.'

'Another thing,' Ted said. 'Is there something wrong with Honest John? We haven't heard anything from him this time, even after the press coverage. Whose turn is it to check?'

There was a general groan from the older team members. Jezza just looked puzzled. Honest John was their local confessor. Almost every time there was a murder on the patch, he would phone up to confess, punctuating every sentence with, 'Honest, it was me.'

In reality, he was a desperately lonely and clinically obese depressive, who lived in a block of flats. He could never go out, because of his medical condition, so his confessions were a way of obtaining the attention he so desperately craved. Most officers would have ignored him. Ted had a caring side and liked to send someone round for ten minutes from time to time, just to check he was still alive.

'Put someone on it, Mike, please. Even if you have to draw lots. Just a five minute call. It's not like him not to have phoned us. Make sure he's all right.'

Ted's mobile phone rang. When he saw the caller identification, he said hastily, 'I have to take this. Mike, can you carry on, please?'

He accepted the call as he made his way to his office.

'Good morning, Inspector Darling, this is Douglas Campbell, Mr Armstrong's cardio-thoracic consultant. I have your number down to call to make the next appointment. I thought I'd better do it myself, rather than leave it to my secretary. Bizzie Nelson would never forgive me if I gave you anything less than first-class treatment,' he said jovially.

'Now, I have the final results I was waiting for. Would it be possible for you and Mr Armstrong to come in later today, say at about five o'clock, to go through them?'

Ted acquiesced, then asked anxiously, 'Can you give me any indication now?'

The consultant's tone was apologetically professional.

'I think that you know already that I cannot, Inspector. All I can say to you is please try not to worry. I know it's hard, but it truly never does any good.'

When he rang off, Ted phoned Trev at work and arranged to pick him up later to go with him to find out the results. He tried to sound matter-of-fact and reassuring but he could tell from Trev's voice that he was worried sick. They both were.

Mike had finished allocating tasks for the day when Ted went back into the main office. Ted suspected it was a touch of malice on his part that he had put Jezza down to call on Honest John on her way to Cottage Row.

Ted asked Jezza to join him in his office. He had deliberately moved the spare chair so she would have to stand. He was not making a point. He just preferred it when she was not slouching while he spoke to her.

'So, Jezza,' he began. 'Saturday. You didn't let anyone know you were unable to come in. You know that's a requirement.'

'Couldn't,' she said shortly. 'I was too busy talking to God on the big white phone.'

Seeing his look, she corrected herself. 'Projectile vomiting.'

'Is there no one else who could have at least let Sal know what was happening?'

'No,' she said shortly, without even bothering with formality. It was borderline insolence, yet again.

'And this was definitely illness?' Ted asked.

'What, you mean because I was bladdered the first time we met, you assume it's a regular occurrence? Your boyfriend was ill, no one queries that. I was ill so it must be skiving?' she left a long enough pause for it to be insubordinate, before adding sarcastically, 'Sir.'

Ted leaned back in his chair and looked up at her.

'DC Vine, you are treading very close to the line,' he said quietly. 'There is a procedure to follow in the event of absence and you didn't follow it. That's potentially a disciplinary matter. And for the record, Trevor is my partner, not my boyfriend. Please remember that in future.'

He held her gaze. To her credit, she neither flinched nor looked away. Although it was more of an aggressive glare in her case.

'I sent a text as soon I was able to. I don't know what else I could have done,' she replied defiantly. Another long pause, then another, 'Sir.'

Ted considered her for a moment longer, then sighed.

'Very well. There will be no further action this time. Just please try, next time, to make contact somehow, rather than leave a team member in the lurch. Right, go and get on with whatever DS Hallam has assigned you to.'

This time he did add, 'And don't slam the door.'

Not that it did any good.

Ted guessed from her file that countless senior officers before him had tried storming after her, shouting the odds. It had clearly not worked. He decided to save himself the effort. For now.

He wondered, as he had several times since her arrival, if Jezza was some sort of punishment by the Ice Queen for a misdemeanour he could not remember committing. Despite her attitude, he still felt there was something about Jezza which made her worth persevering with. She had certainly fooled all of them in the pub on Friday. She clearly had the makings of a brilliant undercover officer.

Ted was in need of something to occupy his mind, to stop him worrying about the forthcoming meeting with the consultant. He knew he should go and mention his early departure to the Ice Queen, as a courtesy, but he didn't feel much like seeing her yet. He still had nothing tangible to offer her by way of progress.

He decided to try making contact with the hospital, to follow up on patient complaints after relatives' deaths. The team had not yet had the time to fully pursue that angle. That, and having Jezza in one of the homes, remained the best, though still slim, chance of finding Angela, if she existed. Or it might throw up someone else with a grudge.

After being passed from pillar to post on the phone, he

managed to get through to an administration manager, who met him with the usual blanket refusal on the grounds of confidentiality. Even Ted's patience was wearing thin by now.

'Look, I could get a warrant but it really would be so much more helpful if I could just come along later today and talk to someone who might be able to help,' he said. 'After all, one of the deaths I'm investigating happened in your hospital, and there was an apparent attempt on another patient at the weekend.'

Grudgingly, the woman agreed to talk to the CEO and gave Ted an appointment for later that day. At least Ted could now go to see the Ice Queen with a faint glimmer of a lead to hold in front of him like body armour. He also mentioned the appointment and his need to leave early that afternoon to go with Trev.

'So your new relationship with the local paper is paying off?' she asked. 'You said the reporter had pointed you in a helpful direction regarding time-scales?'

Ted shook his head. 'I wouldn't say that exactly, ma'am. But at least there may be the chance of a lead or two to follow up from today's meeting with the hospital administrator.'

'Keep me up to speed at all times. The Chief Constable is still phoning me frequently for news. It would be good to have something, no matter how insignificant, to tell him,' she said.

'He must surely realise how difficult it is to catch a random killer?'

'I'm sure he does. By the same token, we mustn't forget he is under considerable pressure himself for results,' she said, and added, 'I do hope all goes well for your partner this afternoon. You must be worried. I would appreciate knowing the outcome of that meeting, too.'

That was an understatement, but Ted tried to stay professionally detached when he went to meet the hospital administrator.

She was frostily efficient and made it clear that she was

going against her better judgement in giving him any information at all. She did give him details of any deaths where a formal complaint had been made. But, apart from confirming that there had been other incidents with nothing more than a verbal complaint, she refused to give him anything further on those.

She also told him that there was an official enquiry under way to find out how a patient had apparently again been poisoned on one of the hospital wards, with no one knowing anything about how it had happened. She promised to keep him informed of the results of that enquiry. In response to his question, she told him that there was no CCTV on the ward.

It was a start, and it would have to do for now. He thanked her politely for her help and took his leave.

He was in plenty of time to pick Trev up and take him for his appointment. Once again, Trev was fidgeting and prowling the corridor outside the consultant's office, especially as he was running slightly late.

Eventually, he opened his door and showed someone out, pausing to shake their hand. Then he turned his attention to Trev. With his detective's training, Ted was doing his best to read the body language, dreading the prospect of bad news, hoping he would be strong enough to support Trev if it was.

'I'm so sorry to have kept you waiting, Mr Armstrong, Inspector Darling,' he said. 'Do please come in and take a seat.'

It seemed to take him an eternity to walk past them to his own chair and sit down. He had Trev's medical file in front of him. He opened it and scanned it, clearly familiarising himself with the details.

Trev reached across wordlessly and took hold of Ted's hand, gripping it so tightly that Ted was sure he could feel the circulation being cut off. His own mouth was so dry he could barely swallow. Whatever the news was, he just wanted to know it, as soon as possible.

The consultant looked directly at Trev. Only then did he smile.

'Mr Armstrong, I'm so pleased to be able to tell you that your results have come back clear. All of your results,' he said. 'There is no reason at all why you should not live a long and healthy life, based on the condition of your heart. Especially if you continue to take such good care of yourself, as you clearly do.

'I am truly delighted for you, and heartily relieved for myself. I think I may well have become your next murder victim, Inspector Darling, if I had not been able to give good news to someone Bizzie clearly holds in such affection and high esteem.'

Trev was still gripping onto Ted's hand as if his life depended on it. Ted could see that his eyes were sparkling with tears of relief. He was clearly so emotional that he couldn't speak.

'Thank you so much,' Ted said, finally finding his own voice. 'It's a huge weight off both our minds.'

'You're very welcome,' the consultant said, standing up to usher them to the door. 'It makes such a pleasant change for me to be able to deliver good news.'

Trev finally let go of Ted's hand as they both stood up to leave. The consultant held out his hand, which Ted shook warmly. Trev started to do the same then, to the man's surprise, engulfed him in one of his famous hugs.

'Sorry,' he said. 'I know not everyone's into man hugs, but it's such bloody marvellous news.'

The consultant looked a little taken aback, but not too nonplussed. In fact, he smiled indulgently and said, 'Well, I think that is probably the most effusive thanks I have ever received.'

Trev was practically bouncing like Tigger on the way back to the car. Ted found he could not stop grinning with delight.

'Let's go out for a meal tonight, to celebrate,' he suggested.

'If your stomach's feeling up to it?'

'Love to,' Trev beamed. 'I am so hungry I could suddenly eat a scabby donkey. I'm going to ask Bizzie out at the weekend, if you don't mind, to thank her properly. She's always wanted to go to the Lake District and has never been. I said I'd take her on the bike one day. Why don't you take your mother out somewhere nice, too?'

'She might be working,' Ted said evasively.

'And she might not,' Trev replied. 'Carpe diem, Ted. That's my new motto. Go for it!'

Trev went bounding upstairs for a shower when they got in, singing tunelessly at the top of his voice. It may have been a Queen number but it was unrecognisable with what he did to it. Ted marvelled, as he always did, that someone with such a good ear for languages could be so totally tone deaf.

Ted went out of the kitchen door into the back garden, where he would not be overheard. He got out his mobile and took a card from his wallet, dialling the number on it. It was answered on the second ring.

'Lady Armstrong? This is Ted Darling, Trev's partner.'

'Yes?' the cold voice asked.

'I wanted to tell you that all the results have come back clear. Trev has not inherited any heart disease.'

'Thank you for informing me. Was there anything else?'

Ted waited until he was sure he had control of his voice before he replied formally, 'No, ma'am. There is absolutely nothing else to say.'

# Chapter Thirty-three

The following morning, Ted decided to visit Apple Orchard Court, home of John McAlpine, and to take Jezza with him. It would give him a chance to perhaps get to know her a bit better, and also to see her at work, if he let her lead the questioning.

The elderly resident from the home was doing remarkably well in hospital, having made a strong recovery from a suspected poisoning. They were still waiting for tox results but it certainly seemed the likely cause, especially with the cake in his drawer, which had not come from the hospital.

As Ted and Jezza got to his trusty old Renault in the car park, she said ironically, 'Nice wheels, boss. Retro shabby chic is all the rage at the moment.'

Ted could not help smiling. She certainly had some bottle and did not appear to be in the least bit intimidated by him. Nor, judging by her track record, by any of the other senior officers she had served under, some of them very briefly.

'I'd like you to do most of the questioning,' he told her. 'I'll just chip in if I think you may have overlooked something. We're looking for anything and everything which may link Mr McAlpine to any of the other victims, homes, carers or visitors.'

She looked as if she was about to say something, then she clearly thought better of it. Ted would have put money on it being something like, 'No shit, Sherlock.' It was progress, to a degree, that she had resisted the temptation.

'How did you get on with Honest John?' Ted asked, by way of conversation.

Jezza rolled her eyes expressively. Ted noticed that she still had dark circles under them and looked as if a good night's sleep would not do her any harm.

'Is that the office initiation test, for the newest team member?' she asked. 'You know, like sending someone out for a left-handed screwdriver, or a skirting board ladder? I mean, why do we even bother with him? He's clearly just a time-waster.'

'He's a lonely human being, with nothing else in his life but confessing to crimes he didn't commit,' Ted told her mildly. 'I know we're busy, but if someone just takes ten minutes once in a while to go and see him, he's as happy as Larry for months. It's a small kindness. Good PR, showing the caring side of coppers.

'How was he, anyway? Strange he's not been in touch.'

'His phone's out of order,' she told him.

'I'll get on to his social worker when I get back to the office. Can't have him all alone with no means of contacting the outside world.'

Apple Orchard Court turned out to be similar in appearance to Snowdon Lodge, with its functional modern lines and total lack of character. The sign at the gate showed that it was, in fact, owned by the same group, Carlington Healthcare Ltd.

'Hope I never finish up in a place like this,' Jezza said, getting out of the Renault and looking around. 'Factory farming for the elderly. I'd sooner put my head in the oven, if I could afford the gas.'

She was struggling to close the passenger door, which had a mind of its own. Ted came round and shut it for her.

'There's a knack to it,' he said.

'How quaint.'

'What do you drive?' he asked.

She shrugged dismissively. 'A Golf.'

Ted nodded his comprehension.

'This can't compete with German engineering. But the seats are comfortable.'

The home had the same airlock system of doors as Snowdon Lodge. The outer one was open, leading into a medium-sized porch, with a visitors' book. The inner door was locked. Jezza rang the bell then looked through the book while they waited a few moments for anyone to appear. It was a rather harassed-looking woman in a dark blue tabard-style overall.

Ted and Jezza both had their warrant cards out. As instructed, Jezza did the talking.

'DC Vine, DI Darling,' she said brusquely. 'Is it possible to speak to the manager?'

The woman looked immediately anxious. When she spoke, her English was strongly accented.

'She busy. I go find her. Please to wait here.'

The layout was similar to Snowdon Lodge. There were elderly people in armchairs and wheelchairs in various parts of the large vestibule, many of them dozing quietly. An open doorway to one side showed more of them sitting in another room, where a television droned away to itself loudly in one corner. There was no sign of any visitors. It was perhaps early in the day for the visiting to start.

They were kept waiting for several minutes, with no sign of any staff about. Jezza was looking round observantly.

'It looks like no one can just walk in off the street. They would need to ring the bell, if that door is always kept locked.'

'Or wait for a chance when someone was just arriving, or just leaving, as I did the first time at Snowdon Lodge,' Ted told her. 'I must ask Professor Nelson what quantity of cake it would take for these poisonings. We've had enough time already to get someone to eat a fair bit.'

'Has anyone gone through the visitors' books in the different homes, checking them for names that appear more than once?' Jezza asked him.

'Not as far as I know,' Ted replied. 'It would be a very long shot. Certainly in Snowdon Lodge, there was no one signed in at all to visit Mrs Jones on the day she was poisoned. Nor on any other day. Only her daughter ever signed in. I'll get someone on to it, though, it might be worth a go.'

He always referred to his mother and grandmother formally, without any reference to his relationship to them, when talking to the team.

At that moment, a woman came towards them from a side corridor. She was tall and well-built, with a wide moon face, large glasses and the appearance of slightly too many teeth. She headed instinctively towards Ted, clearly the older of the two officers.

'I'm Mrs Watson, the manager. What can I do for you, officers?'

They both produced their warrant cards and Jezza replied, 'We're here to ask you about Mr John McAlpine.'

The woman looked at her, as if doubting she really was a police officer, despite the warrant card. With her ripped jeans and air of having just come back from an all-night rave, she certainly did not look like a typical officer.

'You'd better come to my office,' she said grudgingly. 'We hopefully won't be disturbed there.'

She ushered them in, saw them seated and went to a filing cabinet against the back wall. She found a folder, which she put on the desk in front of her, then sat down.

'We're investigating Mr McAlpine's poisoning as a possible attempted murder,' Jezza told her. 'I'm sure you already know that a resident in one of your group's other homes, Snowdon Lodge, died in similar circumstances recently. We're particularly interested in anyone who may have visited Mr McAlpine while he was in this home.'

The manager was looking through the file.

'There's no mention here of any relatives or frequent

visitors,' she said. 'I wouldn't really know if he did have visitors. This is a big home, lots of residents. I'm not always aware of who comes and goes. They have to sign in when they visit, you could look in the book to see who comes to see him.'

'This person may not necessarily sign themselves in, and certainly not with their own name. Who is his named carer?' Jezza asked.

The manager looked again at the file before replying, 'Sandy Dennison.'

'Is she on duty today?'

Mrs Watson picked up her desk phone and made a quick call.

'She is, she'll be here in a moment.'

There was a brief knock at the door and a woman came in. In her mid-fifties, by the look of it, wearing a dark blue tunic and trousers. She looked worried, glancing from the manager to the visitors, both of whom produced their warrant cards in a reflex gesture.

'We're here about Mr McAlpine,' Jezza told her. 'I presume you heard what happened to him? Can you tell me about any regular visitors he has, or anyone he talks about?'

'There's just his niece, who comes about once every week or two,' the woman said. 'Angelique. She's very kind to him, usually bakes him something nice. She was in early last week. I had to tell her about the food ban, so she took the cake away with her. She said she'd freeze it for next time.'

'Can you describe her, please?' Jezza asked.

'Always smart, well-spoken. In her late thirties, I'd say. It's hard to be sure.'

'Anything more you can remember about her? Height, build, hair colour?'

'About your height, perhaps,' the carer said, looking thoughtfully at Jezza. 'Hard to say, she was usually sitting down with John when I saw her. Medium build, quite smartly dressed. I don't know about hair colour really, she always wears a hat of some sort.'

'Do you have any idea where she lives?'

The woman shook her head.

'None at all, I'm afraid.' She looked pointedly at the manager as she added, 'We're kept very busy. We have no time to chat to visitors or even to the residents.'

The manager was looking through the file again but raised her head to throw a warning glance at the carer.

'There's no mention of a niece on his records,' she frowned.

The carer looked puzzled.

'She said she was his niece. John wouldn't know. He doesn't know who anyone is, bless him. But he always seemed pleased to see her. They'd have a good natter and a laugh together.'

'Was she informed about his hospitalisation?' Jezza asked the manager. 'I'm presuming not, if you don't have her on your records. You won't have any contact details for her, is that right?'

'Yes, she did know,' the carer chipped in. 'She popped back later in the week, to see if he was allowed the cake yet. She said it was his favourite. I told her he'd had a turn and been taken to hospital. She said she'd go and visit him there.'

Ted and Jezza exchanged looks.

'If you think of anything else, anything at all, please contact us at once,' Jezza said, standing up to leave. 'And please do make sure the food ban stays in place until further notice.'

As they walked back to the car, Ted said, 'That was good work. So, we now have an Angelique, who knew that Mr McAlpine had been moved to the hospital. That's one coincidence too many for me. Somehow, we have to hope that she appears soon at Cottage Row and that you can get something, a car number or anything, to point us towards her.'

Ted phoned Honest John's social worker when he got back to his office, just to make sure he got the help he needed to get his phone working again. He knew that meant more phone calls confessing to crimes, but he didn't like to think of the alternative, of him being marooned without contact.

Then he phoned Jim Baker. He wanted to tell him that Trev had got the all-clear, and to invite him and Bella to dinner at the weekend. He felt he owed them both more of an apology, after his behaviour at their dinner party. Trev had been delighted at the suggestion. He loved cooking and entertaining. Ted also wanted to ask Jim something which he was sure would not go down as well as a dinner invitation.

'Bloody marvellous, Ted,' Jim boomed with delight when Ted told him the good news. 'And I'm sure we'd love to come to dinner. I'll have to check with Bella first, obviously, in case she has anything planned. I'll let you know soon as.'

'Just one more thing, Jim,' Ted said warily. 'Now don't go off the deep end ...'

'Why do I know I'm not going to like this?' his former boss growled.

'I need to get one of the team to talk to Bella, so can you give me her contact details?'

He could hear that Jim was about to explode so he went on hurriedly, 'She's not a suspect, Jim, she's a potential witness. You know that. I wouldn't be doing my job if we didn't interview her. We'll be talking to anyone who regularly visited the homes, and she told me she does visit them.

'The Chief Constable already wants to use my hide for a rug on his office floor. Can you imagine what he would say if he found out I hadn't had her questioned, just because of her relationship to you?'

Jim made a low rumbling noise. It sounded like a volcano which had not yet decided whether or not to erupt. Eventually, he said, 'Morgan. Bella Morgan. And she's not a serial killer, Ted. I'm going to ask her to marry me. I'd like you to be my best man. So I don't want you appearing at the wedding with handcuffs.'

Ted chuckled as he took down the telephone number and

address, in Heaton Mersey, which Jim gave him. He took it through and put it on Mike's desk, with a note to get someone to check it out. The main office was empty, all the team out following up leads from the morning briefing. He hoped at least one of them would bring an advance, no matter how small, in the case.

His next phone call was to his mother, to find out if she was free at the weekend. Trev and Bizzie had arranged their day out on the bike up to the Lakes for Sunday, so Ted wanted to ask if his mother was working that day.

She sounded thrilled at his phone call, and even more delighted at his suggestion that he take her out.

'Oh, Teddy, that's so kind of you,' she said emotionally. 'It's my day off. I'd love to go for a little run out, if it's not too much trouble for you.'

'It's no trouble. It would be nice to spend some time together.'

He was surprised to find that he really meant what he was saying.

'We could go to Roman Lakes?'

Oh, Teddy!' she exclaimed again, and he could hear that she was close to tears.

Somehow, now that he knew that Trev was going to be all right, he not only felt better about the case, but was suddenly determined to take some time to get to know his mother. Especially after his contact with Trev's. It made him appreciate her all the more, despite what had happened in the past. He was taking Trev's advice to heart. Carpe diem. Seize the day. Or as Trev had so eloquently put it, 'Go for it!'

# Chapter Thirty-four

From the grins on the faces of some of the team the next morning, Ted knew there was at last going to be some progress to report with the enquiry. He asked Rob O'Connell to kick off the briefing, as he was clearly bursting with some news.

'Well, we don't yet have anything concrete to tie Mandy Griffiths in to any of the poisonings,' he began. 'But now we've finished going through the paperwork we collected from her home, we have a very good paper trail to a pretty nasty fraud and theft.

'With the excuse of supposedly helping an elderly woman in the same road, it seems she's been robbing her of most of her pension and savings. Best of all, we can prove it. Armed with that, I think that if we bring her in and confront her with the physical evidence, she may just start singing about anything else she knows.'

Ted nodded in satisfaction.

'Excellent, good work. Go and bring her in as soon as you can. Ask Inspector Turner if he can spare you an officer to go with you to arrest her, and an area car too, if he can. The sight of a uniform and some blue lights at the home may just rattle a few cages. What else?'

Virgil Tibbs spoke up next.

'I got a lead from talking to relatives who lodged complaints in the past about non-availability of beds. Those where they were convinced that the lack of a bed had led to someone dying.

'One in particular was very sad. The parents of a young lad, just eighteen. He and a mate had been to a party and drunk too much. The driver should never have been at the wheel, but he was. He walked away unhurt from the crash he caused. The other lad was seriously brain injured. He died while they were waiting for a bed to be found for him on intensive care.

'The parents were understandably devastated. More so because they were convinced the lack of a bed was the cause of his death. So they made a formal complaint. I can't imagine how they must have been feeling. But it was just a knee-jerk reaction to grief. Once they came to terms with it, they accepted that he would not have survived, even on life support, and withdrew their complaint.

'But they do remember a woman talking to them at the time. Ranting, they put it. Her husband had just died, too, and she was going on about there not being a bed for him, either. The interesting thing for us is that they remember her saying that a bed had been found for an elderly patient who had come in at the same time as her husband, but not for him. She told them he died on a trolley in a corridor.'

'Angela?' Ted asked.

'It could just be, boss. They couldn't remember anything about her, just her ranting. They were too overcome by their own grief at the time to take much notice. But the man did remember her saying that her husband had died of meningitis.

'Now, we have the dates for when their son died. If we can check hospital records to see if there was a death from meningitis the same day, or maybe even a few days before, we could just have our first lead to who Angela might be.'

There was a general air of anticipation from all the team members at the news. It was the closest they had come so far in the enquiry. Only Jezza was not showing much reaction. The dark smudges under her eyes spoke of yet another night of not enough sleep.

'Mike, that might be one for you and me,' Ted said to the

DS. 'It's not easy getting information from the administrator at the hospital. Perhaps if we go in mob-handed, we might do a bit better. I'll also check with our newly friendly local reporter, to see if that story rings any bells with him.

'Right, let's get to it. Rob, go and bring in the Griffiths woman again. Then you and Sal question her, see what you can get out of her. Keep looking for anything at all that links her to any of the other victims.'

Ted stood up and headed to his office, saying to the DS as he went, 'Mike, have you got a minute, please?'

The DS followed him into the room and closed the door behind him. Ted nodded to him to sit down.

'This is a delicate one, Mike, so I want you to handle it,' Ted told him. 'The Big Boss's newly intended, Bella Morgan. I put the details on your desk but I wanted to explain further. I need her checking out in detail, please, with kid gloves on. I hope she's not our Angela. I don't even really think it any more, after behaving like an idiot when I met her. But I'm between a rock and a hard place. If I check her out, I risk being crossed off Jim's Christmas card list and not being invited to the wedding. If I don't, I'm not doing my job properly. And if by any chance she is connected, then I really can kiss my career goodbye for good.

'Please treat her as a potential witness, not a suspect, initially. Go and see her, don't bring her in. But she has been to some of the homes we're interested in, doing their books. She might just have seen something.

'She works mornings only, like our Angela seems to, so you need to call round in the afternoon. That's one of the things that had me convinced she could be our Angela,' he added ruefully. 'And then I had to sit there and eat some of her cooking.'

'No worries, boss, I can do diplomatic,' Mike smiled. 'I'll get in touch with her after we've been to the hospital.'

'What do you think about Jezza?' Ted asked, changing the

subject. 'She always looks as if she's short on sleep but she doesn't seem to want to talk about the possible cause.'

'She looks like one of the undead to me. Are we sure she should be out in daylight?' Mike joked. 'I can't make her out at all. She's as prickly as a hedgehog. I'm almost afraid to speak to her in case she accuses me of harassment or something. But we can't have someone who's not reliable on the team. And I'm suspicious of her real reasons for being absent at the weekend. Do you want me to rota her on again next weekend?'

'Leave it for now, wait until it's her turn again. I agree with you, let's not be accused of harassment. I still have high hopes that she might be the one to get the first real lead on Angela, through Cottage Row.

'I'll just phone everybody's favourite journalist then we'll get off to the hospital, see what we can find out. I think we might just get more cooperation if we turn up in person.'

As Mike left the room, Ted picked up his phone and braced himself.

'Alastair. Ted Darling here. How are you?' he asked, with enforced joviality.

'I'd be a lot better if you had a little something for me, something to make the front page,' the familiar wheedling voice replied.

'Nothing definite as yet, but I'm just calling you with an early heads-up,' Ted told him, trying to keep his voice neutral. 'We may not be in a position to charge the suspect I mentioned to you in connection with the sudden deaths. But I just wanted to let you know that there may be other charges of a serious nature coming out of our enquiries, on a different matter. One which might make your front page.'

As the journalist started to ask questions, Ted interrupted, 'That's as much as I can give you for now. But if and when there is a remand hearing, I promise you will be the first to know. Now, did you have anything for me in exchange? Anything to do with your articles on relatives complaining of lack of beds?'

'I've honestly been trying to think of anything else on that woman I told you about. I really want to help you, now you're being so helpful to me.'

His smarmy voice made Ted wince. It was precisely the reason he had always avoided any direct contact with him, preferring to refer him instead to the Press Office.

'I did talk to her a bit, but I can't find my notes from then. The only thing that I did remember was that she said she lived up near Dooley Lane somewhere. Well, up that way, anyway, going towards Romiley. I remember thinking at the time it was very apt. She struck me as completely doolally, so Dooley fitted very well.'

'Thank you, Alastair, I appreciate that, really helpful,' Ted said, feeling he should cross his fingers for the lie, then hanging up with relief.

Ted and Mike were met with the same initial wall of non-cooperation at the hospital, the insistence on patient confidentiality which prevented personal details being given out. It meant another frustrating delay while permission was sought from higher up to give them the information they needed. They came away with nothing much, just a promise to contact them as soon as anything was known.

Rob O'Connell had had much better success and had arrived back at the station with Mandy Griffiths safely under arrest and cautioned on suspicion of fraud and theft. He put her into an interview room and left her to cool her heels while he went to report back to Ted and the team.

Sal was the only other one in, waiting to help with questioning the suspect. Ted came out into the main office to hear what Rob had to say.

'Well, she really is a piece of work,' Rob began. 'When we got to Snowdon Lodge and asked for her, the carer who let us in told us which rooms Griffiths was working in and left us to find our own way. We could hear her shouting from halfway up the corridor. Good job there were no visiting relatives about who could have heard her.

'The old lady whose room it was had clearly had a little accident in the bed and Griffiths was calling her all kinds of names. I've never been happier to go in and arrest anyone.'

Ted had been perching on the edge of a desk to listen. He stood up to go and said, 'I know I don't need to remind you, Rob, or Sal either, to keep personal feelings out of this interview. No matter how unpleasant a person she is, you stay professional at all times, please. I don't want anything which could give a smart defence lawyer a get out of jail free card. Has she asked for a solicitor?'

'Doesn't have one of her own, boss, so I've said I'll arrange one for her.'

'See that you do, and don't say anything to her until they get here.'

Ted knew he was teaching his grandmother to suck eggs. Both Rob and Sal were experienced officers who played it by the book. It was just that they had come so far on this case with nothing to show for it that he didn't want to risk anything going wrong now.

# Chapter Thirty-five

Ted was surprised to get a phone call from Pocket Billiards first thing the next day. He forced himself to sound enthusiastic.

'Good morning, Alastair. What can I do for you?'

'It's more what I can do for you, Ted. I thought of something else which might just be helpful to you. Perhaps I could tell you about it over lunch?'

Ted was not sure he could stomach the prospect of eating with him again.

'I've got a pretty hectic day today, Alastair,' he said, trying to sound regretful. 'I won't have time to eat, but perhaps we could meet at The Grapes for a quick drink.'

He heard the expectant pause and added reluctantly, 'And of course your lunch is on me.'

They agreed a time and rang off. There was a light knock at the door and Mike put his head round. Ted told him to come in and sit down.

'I spoke at length to Bella Morgan,' Mike began. 'I also dug as deeply as I could into her background. I sort of got the feeling that's what you wanted me to do, boss.'

'Don't tell Jim Baker, whatever you do,' Ted told him. 'So, does she check out?'

'Clean as a whistle. Watertight alibis for all of the deaths. In fact, she was with the Big Boss for a couple of them, with other people there as well, so those check out,' Mike reported. 'I expect Superintendent Baker will hear I've been asking around for those alibis, so prepare for a rocket.'

Ted smiled ruefully.

'I did tell him we'd have to check her out as a witness. I'm glad we can clear her as a suspect now. Was she able to help in any way?'

Mike shook his head.

'She didn't see much of the daily comings and goings at all. Just straight to the manager's office, head down over the books, then on to the next one. I must say she seems very nice.'

'After the team meeting, you and I need to go back to the hospital, see if they've been true to their word and found anything out for us,' Ted said, as the two of them headed out to the main office. 'I've got a meeting with Pocket Billiards again later. He says he may have something for us, but I suspect he just wants another free lunch.'

The rest of the team members were already in, Jezza yawning widely at her desk and not even bothering to disguise the fact.

Mandy Griffiths had been kept in police custody overnight. They had plenty to hold her on for a few hours longer and were hoping she might be more talkative after a night in the cells, in her eagerness to be released. As the DS was going to the hospital with Ted, and Rob O'Connell was out on another case, he asked Virgil and Sal to carry on interviewing her. He knew he could trust them both and sometimes a change of face brought different results.

The rain was coming down in stair-rods when they went outside, bouncing up off the surface of the car park. It effectively soaked Ted and Mike from below as well as above as they sprinted for Mike's car to head to the hospital. The weather seemed to be stuck in permanent rain mode at the moment.

Ted was pleased Trev had insisted he got himself a trench coat for work on their last shopping trip. It certainly seemed to be keeping more of him dry than Mike's old waxed jacket was doing. His feet were sopping wet, though. He would have much preferred to be in his waterproof walking boots, or even his Docs.

They had another soggy sprint at the hospital, longer this time, as the car park was heaving and they couldn't park near to the main building, not even by relying on a Police sign on the dashboard.

They headed first to the administration manager's office. She greeted them with reserve, once again, then escorted them to the CEO's office, saying he had agreed to talk to them. Ted, who was used to being the smallest man in most circumstances, was surprised to find that the CEO was no taller.

Even when the man stood up from behind his large and elegant antique desk, he looked like someone's schoolboy son who was playing a prank by pretending to be in charge. To compound the look, he had the kind of smooth complexion which looked as if he had not yet started shaving.

Ted always claimed that dressing up in a suit made him look like Wee Jimmy Krankie. From the look of the CEO's suit, he solved the problem by having his clothes expensively made-to-measure.

'Gentlemen,' he said, shaking hands with both Ted and Mike.

When he spoke, Ted got the feeling he had had a lot of voice coaching to get the pitch sufficiently low to help him to appear old enough to be at the helm of a big hospital.

'I'm Nicholas Forbes, the CEO. Our administration manager, Mrs Riley, tells me you need our help in identifying a possible suspect. As I'm sure you're aware, we are bound by confidentiality towards our patients ...'

'Mr Forbes, please excuse me,' Ted cut in smoothly, 'but firstly, the person we are interested in was not a patient here. And secondly, we are investigating a series of killings of elderly people. I'm sure I don't have to remind you that one happened in your hospital, and there was a second attempt here recently.

'I can, if necessary, go and get court orders to authorise me to search your records. But that would be tedious and take time. It's essential that we contact this person as soon as possible, so that we can at least eliminate her from our enquiries, if she's not involved.'

The CEO looked at him thoughtfully, as if weighing up an adversary. Then he turned his attention to a file on his desk and looked through it.

'This was a particularly tragic case, Inspector. All death is tragic, of course, but this one was unexpected. A man barely into his forties, taken suddenly ill with bacterial meningitis, the most serious kind,' the CEO said.

'From the notes here, it seems that his wife initially thought it was nothing to worry about and tried various herbal concoctions, to no avail. By the time she called an ambulance, her husband was very gravely ill. He was taken first to the Acute Admissions Unit. We were waiting for an intensive care bed but unfortunately, he deteriorated very quickly and died before he could be transferred.'

'And how did his wife react, sir?' Ted asked him.

'Well, she was hardly in the mood to celebrate, Inspector,' the CEO said ironically. 'According to the notes here, she wanted to make a formal complaint about the lack of an available bed.'

'But he definitely died on the unit, not on a trolley in a corridor?'

The CEO looked at him searchingly, then looked back at the notes.

'No, he was definitely in a cubicle on the unit, according to these notes. Not on a ward, just a side cubicle. I suppose that could perhaps have led to confusion?

'We carried out a hospital post-mortem examination, at his wife's request, which confirmed our earlier findings. Her husband died from septicaemia as a complication of the bacterial meningitis. It can happen very quickly, as it did in this case. Sadly, the probability is that it was her delay to get him to hospital which was the causal factor, not the lack of a bed. It would seem that even had we been able to transfer him to the ICU, he would not have survived.

'Had his wife called an ambulance sooner, instead of thinking her various herbal and homoeopathic potions were going to make any difference, he may possibly have stood a chance. I suspect that, in her heart of hearts, she knew that. I imagine it may well have been feelings of guilt as much as grief which made her react as she did.

'Mrs Mortensen had a lot of trouble accepting the findings to begin with. She paid many visits to the hospital and caused quite a few problems. She would accost other relatives of patients who had died. It reached the point where we had to get security to escort her off the premises a few times.'

'Mortensen?' Ted queried, with a meaningful glance at Mike.

'Much as it goes against the grain, Inspector, I am prepared to disclose names on this occasion, because of the serious nature of your enquiries,' Forbes told him. 'The deceased was Robert Mortensen. His wife's name was Angela. I've written down the address we had for them at the time. I don't know if it is still current.'

'Thank you, sir,' Ted said, pocketing the details and nodding at Mike to take over.

'Mr Forbes, the other thing we had asked for was information about a Health Care Assistant who

worked here for a short time, a certain Mandy Griffiths. Are you able to tell me anything about her, please?' the DS asked.

Forbes closed the Mortensen file and reached for another, which he opened and looked through. He gave the two men a shrewd look.

'I'm assuming it's no coincidence that you are asking me

about these two women at the same time, in view of the incident?' he asked.

'What incident would that be, sir?' Mike asked.

'Ah, perhaps you were not aware, perhaps your interest was merely coincidence, after all? However, there was an incident involving both Mrs Mortensen and Ms Griffiths which led to us having to, as they say, get without the latter.'

'Ms Griffiths was sacked?'

'Not sacked, no, we simply did not renew her contract after her probationary period,' Forbes clarified. 'She did not have a great deal to commend her, according to these notes. She had already been spoken to on a few occasions about her conduct and attitude.

'Then came the very unfortunate incident with Mrs Mortensen. It was when she was still coming in and haranguing the staff about the loss of her husband. Ms Griffiths was overheard by a member of staff sympathising with her, which was acceptable, but claiming that it was an influx of elderly patients causing bed-blocking which led to his death. Clearly, that was not acceptable. Nor was it true.

Ted and Mike exchanged another look.

'It is sadly accurate that we do often get elderly patients in from homes who should never have finished up here, had they simply received the proper basic care. That applies particularly with regard to maintaining fluid levels to prevent dehydration. But that was absolutely not a factor in Mr Mortensen's death and it was completely improper of Ms Griffiths to have voiced an opinion to that effect.

'There was no elderly patient occupying a bed on the ICU at the time. They were all younger people whose needs were every bit as vital as his. We were doing everything we could do to keep him alive where he was. And it was impossible to transfer him to another hospital as he was too critically ill. The sad and simple truth is, he came in too late for us to save him.'

'Thank you, sir, you have been most helpful,' the DS said,

rising to leave.

'Just one more thing, Mr Forbes,' Ted said, as he also stood up. 'Do you know if Mrs Mortensen still comes to the hospital? What I mean is, would your security staff have been instructed not to allow her entry?'

'We are a hospital, Inspector. We're not really in the business of refusing entry to people,' Forbes told him. 'However, we do have a duty of care to everyone who comes through our doors. Part of that duty is to see that hospital users, especially those recently bereaved, are not further upset by incidents such as we had with Mrs Mortensen.

'The security staff were put on alert to keep an eye out for her and to make sure her behaviour was not causing any distress to anyone else.'

'Can you give me a description of Mrs Mortensen, sir?' Ted asked.

The CEO turned back to the first file.

'I can do better than that, Inspector. I have a photo of her. Not a very brilliant one, admittedly. Taken from CCTV at the hospital entrance, on an occasion when she was being escorted from the premises. That was an unfortunate occasion indeed, as she was causing trouble when a reporter from the local paper was here about another matter.'

Ted put the photo with the piece of paper inside his trench coat pocket. He and Mike headed for the doors. It was still raining hard outside.

'Do you want to wait here and I'll bring the car round, boss?' the DS offered.

Ted shook his head.

'We'll run between the raindrops,' he said, then added, 'My mother used to say that to me when I was little. I'd forgotten about it.

'And it seems it's an old wives' tale,' he added, as they reached the car, hair dripping, feet soaking wet once more. 'You can drop me off near The Grapes, Mike, for my meeting with the lovely Pocket Billiards. Make sure Sal and Virgil are up to speed on the connection between Griffiths and Mortensen, then get someone round to the address we have for Angela and see what you can find.'

He took the piece of paper and photo out of his pocket and put them in Mike's glove compartment.

'So what do you think, boss? The two of them in league?' Mike asked. 'Griffiths spots the likely targets, Angela bumps them off?'

'Let's not get ahead of ourselves with speculation,' Ted cautioned. 'This case is strange enough without that. But the sooner we can speak to Angela, the happier I'll feel. Just drop me here, that's fine. I'll see you back at the station later.'

The reporter was already propping up the bar when Ted squelched his way in, cursing yet again the smart shoes he was obliged to wear for work. His walking boots would have given him dry feet at least. He noticed Alastair was nursing a half, clearly waiting for Ted to arrive and buy him something more expensive.

'Usual for me, Dave, please, and a pint for Alastair. Lager top?'

The reporter nodded.

Once they had their drinks, they made their way over to a quiet table in a corner. Ted took off his wet trench coat before he sat down.

'So, what have you got for me?'

'I remembered afterwards about one of the times I saw the ranting woman at the hospital,' he began. 'She was badgering someone in a corridor. I went to talk to her, see what she had to say. One of those, what do you call them, almost a nurse, came over.'

'Health Care Assistant?' Ted asked.

'Yeah, one of those, I think. Built like a prop forward. Anyway, she started banging on, too. Going on about how too many old wrinklies were taking up beds younger people could have and how it wasn't right.

'It would have made a good story but security came along and frog-marched the woman outside and sent the care woman packing. Then someone quickly whisked me away to where I was supposed to be, so I never got the chance to follow it up. I thought that might be useful for you.'

His tone had turned wheedling now, obviously looking forward to the lunch he thought he had just earned himself.

'Is that it?' Ted asked, draining his glass and standing up. 'I already know that. In fact, we're questioning that Health Care Assistant right now. And we now have an address for the woman from near Dooley Lane. You'll have to do better than that, Alastair. That only merits a bag of crisps, not a lunch.'

He took a two pound coin out of his pocket and tossed it onto the table in front of the reporter.

'But here, I'm feeling generous. Get a bag of nuts as well.'

He had the enormous satisfaction of seeing Pocket Billiards' look of disappointment as he turned and headed for the door.

# Chapter Thirty-six

'Good news and bad news,' Mike said, to start the morning briefing.

Jezza had not yet arrived or sent word. They'd waited a few minutes for her to appear, then the DS had started without her.

'The good news is that we now have a name and address for Angela. She's Angela Mortensen, widow of a man who died in hospital while waiting for a bed in intensive care.

'The bad news is, I've been round there and couldn't find hide nor hair of her. She lives up a lane, the back end of beyond, near Otterspool. There's just a few cottages down there, a little cluster of semis, spaced out, along a lane which goes towards the river. A no-through road. It's like the land that time forgot. I'm not sure they know the war's over yet.'

At that moment, the door opened and Jezza came in quietly and headed for her desk.

'Nice of you to join us, DC Vine,' Mike said sarcastically.

She did at least say sorry, not soz, before she sat down. Ted had not thought it possible for her to look any more tired. He had been wrong. She looked on the point of collapse from sheer exhaustion. He really needed to have another word.

'So, Angela Mortensen exists. I was a bit suspicious of the name at first. I thought it was another alias. It sounded too like her Angela Mortis identity. But no, she's on the electoral register as Mortensen. And Steve checked the name out for me.'

'Of Danish and Norwegian origin. The twentieth most

common surname in Denmark. Means son of Morten,' Steve chipped in, not taking his eyes off his computer screen.

'There was just no sign of her at her house,' Mike continued.

'Was there a car outside, Sarge?' Rob asked.

'No signs of any vehicles at any of the cottages, and no one about to ask. All the curtains were drawn in Angela's. It looked a bit deserted, as if she might be away. We'll just have to keep going back at different times of day until we find her.

'So it's down to you, Jezza,' Mike turned towards where she was stifling yet another yawn. 'If we're not keeping you up?'

She shook herself, as if trying to wake up, and said sweetly, 'No worries, Sarge. Bright-eyed, bushy-tailed and raring to go.'

'Right, for now, Steve, dig up everything you can find about Angela,' the DS told him. 'Vehicle licence check, National Insurance, credit cards, anything.

'Already on it, Sarge.'

'Should we get back to the law firms?' Rob asked. 'Now we have her real name? It's just possible she may work at one, perhaps not as a solicitor, but as something else.'

'Surely, when we were ringing round asking about an Angela Mortice someone would have had the gumption to say no, but we have an Angela Mortensen?' Jezza asked, but Ted noticed that there was none of the usual sarcasm in her question.

'It's worth trying,' Ted put in. 'We're the closest we've been yet, so let's not leave any stone unturned, not even the most unlikely. Law firms are not always known for giving out information freely, if we don't ask the right questions.

'Now, where are we up to with Mandy Griffiths?'

'She claims not to know anyone called Angela Mortensen,' Sal said. 'When I mentioned the episode at the hospital, she admitted talking to the woman, but said she didn't know her name. She's sticking to her story that that's the only contact she's ever had with her. We know Angela changes her appearance, so it's just possible Griffiths would not have recognised her anyway, even if she saw her at Snowdon Lodge. She may just be telling the truth.

'She's being as cooperative as anything, clearly desperate to avoid any implication in a murder case. She's admitted to robbing her neighbour. We can safely charge her with that, I think, boss, if you're happy. But I don't know that we can justify keeping her in custody much longer, without charging her.

'We're going through her phone records, with her permission, to see if we can find any connection to our Angela. But there's nothing incoming or outgoing that we can identify as anyone other than her family, friends and work.'

'I'm inclined to agree with you, Sal,' Ted said reflectively. 'Let me have a quick look at the file before you charge her and we'll decide what to do from there.

'Right, you all know what needs doing. Let's get on with it. Let's hope this is the day we finally get hold of Angela and see what she has to say for herself.'

He stood up and headed towards his office, throwing over his shoulder, 'Jezza, I'd like a word, please.'

This time, at least, he did not leave her standing. He was worried she might fall asleep on her feet if he did. He nodded to the spare chair, then sat down opposite her.

'Right, DC Vine,' he began formally. 'Without wishing to be critical of your appearance, or to pry into your private life, you look dreadful. Should you even be at work?'

Now he was looking at her more closely, he was sure she had lost weight. She did not really have any to lose. The dark smudges under her bloodshot eyes were even more pronounced.

'I'm fine,' she said, attempting a breezy tone. 'I'm not ill. I just don't sleep very well.'

'Frankly, you look as if you haven't slept in a week. What you do in your own time is your own business. Up to a point.

Once it starts impacting on your work, then it becomes my business. Can you not take something to help you sleep?'

She shook her head emphatically.

'I don't do medication. And I don't do drugs, if that's what you're thinking.'

'I don't make assumptions, Jezza,' he said calmly. 'I try not to judge people. But you are a member of my team, therefore you are my responsibility. And something is clearly affecting your ability to do your job as required.'

'I can do my job,' she protested. 'I'm just a bit tired. And I can't take any medication. I really can't. It's … it's complicated. But I can't.'

Ted looked at her hard for a long moment. As usual, she had no trouble in holding his gaze. Behind the defiance he could see something else. Determination? Desperation?

'Right,' Ted said finally. 'Go and start on your appointed tasks, then get off to Cottage Row. And don't let me down, Jezza. I've already given you far more rope than any of your previous senior officers have ever done. I don't want it to come back to hang me out to dry.'

His words were still ringing in her ears as she set off for Cottage Row later that day. She was so bone-crushingly tired she had no idea how she was going to get through the day. She had already fallen asleep at the wheel of the Golf at a red traffic light. Only the angry honking horns of the cars behind her had jolted her awake. And then she had stalled the car in her haste to drive off.

Her cursing, as she crashed the car into first gear and pulled away, tyres squealing, was mostly directed at her new boss. Ted bloody Darling. Not because of his words to her, but because, for the first time in her police career, she had finally found a boss she could respect.

He was clearly passionate about his work and scrupulously fair in the way he ran his team. Damn him. Despite her prickly shell and determination to stay aloof, she found she wanted to prove something to him. Nothing to do with her usual bloody-mindedness, but because she actually valued his opinion.

Being short, gay and called Darling must have caused him so many problems in his police career. But perhaps because of that, she had never met anyone who could command such respect without ranting, raving and resorting to disciplinary hearings.

She did not yet feel part of the team. They were too wary of her to let her in. Too protective of their boss, and disapproving of the way she behaved towards him. But she had never before worked in a team where she had not encountered lewd, blokey remarks which, if she challenged them, were put down to humour which she had misunderstood. Or accusations that she was a dyke.

'You need shagging, darling,' she had been told so many times by sneering male colleagues, when she had objected to their comments.

She now desperately wanted to be the one to bring Angela to justice, to prove to Ted that she was a good copper. And when she did, she was going to ask for a day off – a weekday off – and she was going to sleep the entire day.

The team would have been surprised once more at the total transformation she underwent as soon as she arrived at Cottage Row. The ripped jeans had already been replaced by neatly tailored trousers, the boots by comfortable shoes. The rebellious hair was gelled into submission. Carefully applied make-up covered most traces of the dark shadows under her eyes.

Her entire posture changed as she approached the door of the care home and rang the bell. The slouch was gone. She stood up tall, light on her feet, and appeared brimming with energy and ready for her shift. At least the rain had stopped and the sun was trying to appear.

One of the carers let her in and she went in search of her pale pink tabard. Her name badge showed her as Jessica.

Once she was wearing it, she breezed over to where an elderly woman was sitting in a shaft of weak sunlight which streamed through the stained glass side panels of the porch. With her walking stick, she kept stabbing at the moving patterns of light on the carpet.

'Hello, Lucy, how's my favourite person today?' Jezza asked brightly, bending down to make eye contact with the woman.

'Oh, hello, love, how lovely to see you,' Lucy Lee said, her rheumy eyes blinking up at her. 'Is it our Doris?'

'No, it's Jessica,' she said, then, seeing that she had not been heard, she repeated more loudly, 'Jessica.'

'Yesterday?' the woman asked in confusion.

Jezza laughed.

'You've not got your hearing aid in again, have you, bless you? I'll go and get it for you. I won't be a moment.'

When she came walking back up the corridor from the bedroom, hearing aid in hand, there was a woman standing next to Lucy. Jezza knew instinctively that it was Angela.

The CCTV from the hospital had not been clear enough to be helpful. But this woman matched perfectly the description Maurice had been given on an earlier visit to Cottage Row. A smart, expensive-looking tailored skirt and jacket, black hair neatly pulled back into a French pleat, sober glasses with dark frames.

Jezza had rehearsed this scene so many times in her head. Don't do anything to panic her. Act naturally. Find a way to get some information from her, even if it was only her car registration number.

'Hello,' she began brightly. 'You've come to see Lucy? That's lovely, she loves to have a visitor. I'll just pop her hearing aid in for you, then you won't have to shout. Would you like to take a seat?'

Jezza fought to keep her hands steady as she fiddled the hearing aid into Lucy's ear, while Angela sat down. There was a small table between her and Lucy. Jezza could see that she had put a bakery box on it.

'You've brought her some cakes, too. That's great. She has a very sweet tooth,' Jezza went on. 'I'm sorry she can't have them this afternoon, though. We have to monitor her blood sugars today, so nothing sweet. Shall I pop them in the fridge for you, then she can have them another day?'

'No, don't worry,' the woman she knew as Angela said, slightly too quickly. 'I'll just go and put them back in the car. I know I'll forget them otherwise and I do enjoy watching her eat her little treats.'

'What are these on the floor? Are they mice?' the older woman was saying, poking determinedly at the light patterns on the carpet with her stick. 'They're very quick. I can't catch the little beggars.'

Angela had stood up and was holding the bakery box almost protectively as Jezza said, 'Honestly, it's no trouble at all, and I can remind you to take them,' then, to Lucy, 'No, sweetheart, it's just the light, shining through the glass.'

'I'll just do it now, then it's done,' Angela said. 'Perhaps you could organise a cup of tea for us while I do? That is, if Lucy is allowed tea this afternoon?'

'Back off, Jezza,' she told herself mentally, trying to keep calm, keep control of the situation. Aloud, she said, 'Yes, of course, I'll see to that right away. Just as long as Lucy doesn't have sugar.'

'Are you sure they're not mice? They keep scampering about,' Lucy said, poking more vigorously.

Something about Angela's body language as she went out of the door, still clutching the cake box, told Jezza she had blown it. She had spooked Angela into flight and she was not coming back in.

She decided she just had time to rush to the bay window to get a glimpse of Angela's car before she drove out of the car park. She took a step forward. Lucy's prodding walking stick went between her legs and she crashed to the ground, her head hitting the small side table, hard, before she reached the floor.

Jezza had always thought the expression 'seeing stars' was just poetic licence. She quickly discovered it was not. For the moment, she was not going anywhere. She tried her best to reassure Lucy, who had become extremely agitated and was wailing loudly. Her cries quickly brought help in the shape of a carer and, shortly behind her, the home manager.

'Whatever's happened? Are you all right, dear?' the manager was saying anxiously.

Jezza's head was spinning. She decided she would much prefer to lie where she was for the time being. Angela would be long gone by now. She had completely blown it, so she may as well stay on the floor, where her morale already was.

'I'm fine, honestly. Just give me a minute. It's nothing serious,' she tried to reassure everyone. 'Lucy tripped me up with her walking stick. I think I head-butted the table on the way down. But you need to phone my boss.'

Ted was working at his desk when his mobile rang. It was the care home manager, clearly anxious. She outlined what had happened and added, 'Jessica was most insistent I should phone you directly, not her sergeant.'

'Is she all right?' was Ted's first question.

'We've checked her out carefully and she appears to be fine,' the manager assured him. 'But I think it would be advisable if she didn't drive home, after a bump on the head. She's very upset, worried that she let you down.'

'I'll send someone round to collect her, and please tell her not to worry. This is clearly not her fault, from what you've told me.'

When he disconnected the call, he went out into the main office. Only Mike and Maurice were in, working at their desks. Perfect. Despite appearances to the contrary, Maurice was the best person to deal with anyone hurt or anxious. He was naturally the fatherly type.

He quickly outlined what had happened. As he expected, Maurice's first reaction was to ask if Jezza was all right.

'Mike, take Maurice over to the home. Maurice, you drive Jezza back to her place in her own car, then either come back with the DS or jump on the bus. Make sure, both of you, that you let her know I understand none of this was her fault.

'Tell her only to come in tomorrow if she feels up to it, and then to tell me what happened. Maurice, when you get back, you report to me first, please. I don't want this gossiped about until I know exactly what has happened.'

Mike and Maurice replied with a brief, 'Sir'. They both knew what it meant when the boss used that tone of voice.

# Chapter Thirty-seven

Mike and Maurice got back to the station together and, as instructed, Maurice headed straight for the boss's office. Ted had just made himself a mug of tea, so he made coffee for Maurice and put it in front of him as they both sat down.

'Bloody hell, boss, I don't like to speak out of turn,' Maurice began.

Ted could not suppress a smile as he said, 'It's never stopped you before, Maurice. Tell me first how she is. Is the injury serious?'

Maurice shook his head.

'The home checked her out and I did too,' he said. 'She's going to have a nasty bump on her forehead by tomorrow but I think she's fine. She was very upset, poor lass. I was nice to her. I did my daddy hen bit,' Maurice said with a wink, then went on, 'No, but seriously, boss, Jezza must be minted. Do you know what car she drives?'

'A Golf, she told me,' Ted replied.

'Not just a Golf, boss. A GTi cabriolet, top of the range. Custom paint job, leather seats, the works. Must have cost more than thirty grand,' Maurice told him. 'And her place? She's got a flat in one of those big posh buildings on Heaton Moor Road. The ones that go for two or three hundred grand. She didn't ask me in,' he said, with a twinge of regret.

'Are we sure she's not moonlighting as a high-class hooker? I mean, you saw the way she was dressed up in the pub. It would explain why she's always falling asleep …'

Ted held up a hand.

'Stop right there, Maurice,' he said sternly. 'That's totally unacceptable. You can't make assumptions about a colleague behind their back. Especially not ones like that.'

'I know, boss, but if she was a suspect, we'd be thinking that,' Maurice said stubbornly.

'She isn't a suspect, she's a valued member of this team,' Ted replied shortly. 'Even if she was a suspect, there are all sorts of other perfectly plausible explanations. She may have independent means. So, how did you leave it with her, about coming in tomorrow?'

'She was really worried about coming in to face you, boss,' Maurice said. 'I told her you were a pussy cat really, very fair. And that the best thing about this team is that there's no blame culture. She said she hoped to be in late morning.'

Ted nodded.

'Great, thanks, Maurice, you did well,' he said. 'Just remember though, this particular pussy cat doesn't like gossip about colleagues. Keep your theories to yourself, please. If I hear any talk within this station, I will know where it's come from and the consequences will be dire. Do I make myself absolutely clear, DC Brown?'

'Perfectly clear, sir,' Maurice said formally, but he was grinning widely as he left the office, after gulping down the rest of his coffee.

Ted was not at all surprised that Jezza did not appear first thing the following morning. She must have been left with quite a headache from her fall, if nothing else.

There had been another small breakthrough. Rob had succeeded in finding out that an Angela Mortensen did work part-time for a firm of solicitors in town, but as a legal executive, rather than a solicitor.

'She works mornings, but she's been signed off on the sick for a couple of months,' Rob told the team. 'Obviously they wouldn't give me any confidential information. They did say she cut her hours from full to part-time after her husband died, but she's still not been coping well.

'Reading between the lines, it sounds like she had some sort of nervous breakdown and is still suffering from depression. I did persuade them to give me the name of her GP, by pointing out that we were seriously concerned for her well-being. I thought I'd talk to him next. Again, although he will certainly wave the confidentiality card, if I can persuade him we are anxious about her, he might help. It's possible, for instance, she may have given some indication if she's staying somewhere other than at her home at the moment.'

'I'm going to go back to the cottage again later today,' Mike chipped in. 'If she's not around, I could perhaps have a scout round the garden, just to see what she's growing there.'

It was not long after the morning briefing that the manager from Cottage Row phoned Ted to ask after Jezza. She spoke highly of how well she had been carrying out her role there.

'It really wasn't her fault, Inspector. Lucy is a menace with that walking stick. It's a real Health and Safety hazard. Jessica is not the first person she's tripped up with it. We've tried taking it off her but she gets so upset we keep having to give it back.

'Do please give Jessica my best wishes and say I hope she'll come back and see us all again soon. Such a lovely young lady, so bright and cheerful.'

Ted thanked her and rang off, surprised. The description didn't tally at all with the truculent side that Jezza presented in the workplace. He was all the more determined to try and find out more about her and why she was always so prickly at work.

Later on that morning, Maurice knocked and came into Ted's office.

'Jezza just phoned me from the car park, boss. She's here, but she's really worried about facing you. I told her it would be fine, but in the end I said I'd go down and get her.'

Ted nodded as Maurice disappeared. He was seriously

concerned to hear that Jezza was so worried. He did not consider himself particularly intimidating and he had certainly been careful with how he had handled her so far. He stood up and put the kettle on. He could certainly do with some tea and he thought it might be useful for Jezza, too.

Before long, Maurice reappeared and ushered a subdued Jezza into the office. As predicted, she had a formidable lump on her forehead. She looked marginally less tired but Ted was troubled to see that she looked as if she had been crying.

'Come in, Jezza, please sit down,' he said as gently as he could. 'Would you like Maurice to stay?'

She shook her head, just sitting there looking thoroughly miserable.

Ted nodded his thanks to Maurice, who withdrew quietly. He could be surprisingly tactful and sensitive when the occasion required it.

'Would you like some green tea? I'm just having some,' Ted asked, wishing he was better at this sort of thing.

To his astonishment, Jezza blurted out, 'Don't be nice to me, for fuck's sake. I can cope with anything but that.'

None of the other team members would ever have used such strong language in front of the boss. They knew he didn't appreciate it and never said more than the odd 'shit' or 'bloody hell' himself in public. Ted was just about to remonstrate with her when, to his further surprise, he saw big, fat tears well up in her eyes and start to trickle down her face.

Wordlessly, he reached into his pocket and took out the clean, neatly ironed handkerchief Trev always insisted he carry with him at all times. He handed it across his desk to Jezza, then busied himself making the tea, giving her the chance to cry without him looking at her.

Only when her sobs had subsided somewhat did he put the mugs on the desk and sit down opposite her.

'So, first things first,' he began quietly. 'How are you feeling? Are you all right to be in work?'

'I had to come in,' she said miserably, studying her hands. She was wringing the now wet handkerchief as if trying to dry it. 'You're obviously going to kick me off the team, so I needed to get it over with.'

'Why would you think I was going to kick you out?' Ted asked, astonished. 'The manager of Cottage Row told me that what happened was an accident. She also spoke very highly of you.'

'But I let Angela get away,' she wailed forlornly. 'I'm rubbish at my job.'

'If people got kicked out for every suspect they allowed to get away, I'd never have made DI, believe me,' Ted told her. 'Whatever gave you the idea that I would make a decision like that, without at least hearing your side of the story?'

'You try being rational on less than four hours sleep a night,' she said, sharply.

Now they were getting to it. The real reason why Jezza was as she was. Ted knew there was something troubling her. He doubted that Maurice's theory was the correct one. He certainly hoped it was not.

'Perhaps if you explain the reasons …' he suggested, and left it hanging in the air.

'Why are you so understanding? Every other senior officer I've had would have put me on a disciplinary by now.'

'In case you hadn't noticed, I'm not like every other senior officer,' Ted said wryly. 'Try me.'

For a moment, he thought she was going to refuse to talk. Then she began. Hesitantly at first. Soon the words were tumbling over one another, in their haste to get out. Ted was a good listener. He just sat quietly, sipping his tea, letting her talk.

'I have a kid brother,' she began. 'Tom. Tommy. He's eleven and autistic. Very bright, very intelligent. Just very … different.'

She took a swallow of her tea before continuing.

'A couple of years ago … ' there was a slight catch in her voice. She drank some more tea. 'Our parents were killed in a car crash. We have no other family. Just me and Tommy.

'I made a big mistake. I thought the best thing would be for Tommy to come and live with me. Our parents were well-off, with a big house in Prestbury. I expect Maurice told you about my flat? They bought me that. It was a bribe, really. I wanted to become an actor. I did drama at A Level and took acting lessons. But they wanted me to do the whole settle down, have a decent career thing. So I joined the force. It was my attempt at rebelling.

'I thought they would be horrified, but they weren't. They were very supportive, in their own way, that's why they bought me the flat. And the car. No one was more surprised than I was that I turned out to be quite good at being a copper. Up to now.

'Anyway, after they died, I sold their house and moved Tom in with me, into the flat. He needs someone to keep an eye on him all the time. He's in mainstream education but he struggles. He has no social skills at all. But there's a trust fund for him. I can easily afford paid childcare to cover when I'm not there. I thought I could manage.

'I have a really good friend who looks after him on the rare occasions I get a night out. She can't do it often, as she's busy. But I make the most of it when she can. Sometimes I let my hair down a bit too much and get drunk and punchy in the street, with complete strangers.'

She risked a wry smile over the rim of her mug as she said that. Ted returned the smile but made no comment.

'But I didn't realise how bad Tommy gets with any unexpected change in his routine. If the person he thinks is coming to look after him has to be replaced at the last minute, he goes into meltdown. I can't always leave on time to come to work if a different person turns up to take him to school.'

She drank more tea. Looked warily at Ted to see how he was reacting. He nodded encouragingly for her to continue and prompted, 'Weekends would be worse, I imagine? No school, change of routine?'

'Exactly,' she said. 'Moving house was horrendous. I thought he'd never settle down again. But he does have a coping skill. It's what stops me sleeping.

'Dad always used to play Trivial Pursuit with him. Tom knows the answer to every question on every card in every edition of it that exists. So he decided to start making up his own questions. He comes and tries them out on me, whatever time of day or night it is.

'He doesn't seem to need to sleep, like I do. He thinks nothing of just wandering into my bedroom, at any time of night, to ask what was the pattern on the china in the first class dining room on board the Titanic, for instance.'

'Or who scored the winning goals in the 1966 World Cup?' Ted surmised, remembering her knowledge of it. 'Why have you never mentioned this before, to any of your previous senior officers?'

'Yeah, right,' she scoffed. 'Because the force just loves officers with childcare issues. Especially women. So now you know, what with that, and me letting Angela slip away, I suppose I'll be on the move again?'

Ted leaned back in his chair and looked at her thoughtfully.

'Isn't that you being more than a bit judgemental of me?' he asked mildly. 'I've told you, I'm satisfied that what happened with Angela was an unfortunate accident, nothing more. Not your fault. Could have happened to anyone.

'As far as childcare issues go, now I know, I can understand, perhaps even help in some way. I wish you'd trusted me with this sooner, but I can understand why you were reluctant.'

Jezza was sipping her tea, still looking warily at him over the mug, holding it protectively in both hands.

'You're not going to kick me out, then?' she asked, seeking clarification.

'I like a challenge,' Ted told her, with a grin. 'I'm not so keen on bad language though, if you could avoid that in the future.'

'Message received and understood, boss,' she said, with no apparent trace of irony.

'Now, there's something I want you to consider, which you may not like,' Ted told her. 'You're not yet really an integrated member of this team.'

Ted held up a hand as she started to interrupt him.

'That's not a criticism. I'd like you to tell the team some of what you told me. Just mention that your brother gives you some problems. None of us much likes talking about our private lives, but you might be surprised,' he said. 'We work well as a team because we help and support one another. At least if they know, they'll be more understanding. Will you do that?'

'I don't want pity,' she said defensively.

'You won't get it,' Ted assured her. 'We have a serial killer to catch. If one team member is struggling, the others need to get behind them. It's how we roll.'

She nodded reluctantly. Ted went to the door and put his head out.

'Mike, can you get the team together in, say, half an hour? Jezza needs to talk to everyone.'

Ted suspected that it was her drama training that got Jezza through a difficult few moments, talking to the rest of the team.

'I just wanted to say sorry for being a bit of a cow since I joined the team, and not pulling my weight. And sorry I let Angela get away yesterday. Not that it's any excuse, but I've been a bit light on sleep.'

She proceeded to tell the team, briefly, a bit of what she had told Ted about her younger brother. Once she'd finished, she looked round hesitantly, as if not sure Ted had been right in asking her to tell them.

Maurice spoke first.

'You should have said, bonny lass. I'm not much good at most things but I'm good with kids. Maybe I could babysit some time? I have two lasses myself.'

'Tommy's not very good with other children. They think he's weird. He's better with adults, though he's not always good with them. He's very geeky,' she said.

Maurice laughed.

'Geeky? Send him round to mine, then, he and Steve were clearly separated at birth.'

'A few of us might be able to help, Jezza, now we know what the problem is. Some of us might prefer looking after Tommy to working extra shifts to cover when you can't get here,' Mike said with a laugh.

'Right, that's more like it,' Ted said. 'We're a team, we need to look out for each other. Now, a swift half in The Grapes for lunch, because Jezza can join us then but not in the evenings, because of getting home for Tommy. And then let's get on with finding Angela and bringing her in.'

# Chapter Thirty-eight

Angela seemed to have gone well and truly to ground. On the positive side, that meant no more killings. The downside was that it also meant that they did not have a prime suspect in custody, nor even in their sights.

The team now had plenty of information about her, including her car registration number and bank card details, thanks to Steve's computer work. But there was no sign of the car anywhere and her credit cards had not been used for several days.

None of the neighbours could throw any light on her absence. They knew very little about her, other than that she was a widow whose husband had died a few months ago. She had always been, they told the officers who asked the questions, aloof to the point of being anti-social. It seemed she and her husband were more than happy in each other's company and had no need of anyone else.

The story was the same both at the firm of solicitors where she worked and at her GP's surgery. She was a person who kept to herself and no one knew much about her at all.

Ted had sent the team round the care homes once more to ensure the food ban stayed in place and to ask that any sightings of Angela, in any of her different guises, were reported immediately. They were still not sure how she usually looked, when not disguised, but had tried showing the CCTV stills from the hospital, the best they had to date.

'So I presume you're now considering putting her house

under observation in the hopes of finding her?' the Ice Queen asked Ted, as he brought her up to speed in her office.

'It's tactically tricky, ma'am,' Ted told her. 'There's nowhere even an unmarked car can park and stake it out without being seen. It will mean extra hours. Officers in the field, literally, watching the place, then two teams in unmarked cars on the road if she makes a break for it. Assuming she does eventually turn up there.'

'In view of the pressure the Chief Constable is putting on both of us, I don't see the extra hours as a problem,' she said dryly. 'Speak to Inspector Turner about a few extra officers as and when you need them. I think at the moment it is our best chance. Sooner or later, she's bound to head for home, surely? And you don't want to go public with an appeal for help in finding her, yet?'

Ted shook his head emphatically.

'I'd prefer not to,' he said. 'I'd like us to try to bring her in. I'm trying to persuade her employers to give us information from her personnel file, but you know how cagey solicitors are. It may take a warrant.'

'Very unfortunate that she slipped through DC Vine's fingers.'

'Not her fault, ma'am,' Ted said, instantly on the defence of his team.

'At ease, Inspector,' she said with a smile. 'That was an observation, not a criticism. I know by now about your unswerving loyalty to your team. How are things going now with DC Vine?'

'Now we know what the problem is, the rest of the team are all rallying round.'

With Jezza's permission, Ted had explained her circumstances to the Ice Queen, whose only comment had been, 'We must be seen to do all we can to be supportive of a promising young officer.'

To Jezza's surprise, her brother had hit it off well with both

Maurice and Steve. Steve in particular was hugely popular, with his endless patience at searching out complex answers for Tommy on the Internet. She had even found that, as a result, he was starting to sleep better. It gave her an extra option for childcare and meant that she could start to do more shifts outside his school hours.

Now the team knew what the problem was, they were being more tolerant of Jezza and were even including her in some of the gentle banter. She was still desperately hoping to be the one who finally collared Angela. Only then would she feel she had truly earned her place as one of them.

Ted was better able to concentrate on the task in hand, now he knew that Trev was all right. In fact, Trev was on sparkling form, free from the worry of possible serious illness. Literally fighting fit. At their last judo session together, Ted had, unusually, found himself on the mat right at the beginning of their randori.

His breakfall technique had saved him from any ill effect, but he still took a second or two to adjust to the unusual turn of events. Trev, meanwhile, was bouncing round him on the balls of his feet, eyes sparkling, shamelessly air-punching, and gloating in his phony accent, 'Down is where you went, uncle!'

Ted had included himself on the rota which Mike had drawn up to cover a watch on Angela's cottage. A few days into the surveillance operation found him sitting with Jezza in her Golf on the main road near to the cottage, facing in the direction of Romiley. The hood was well and truly up as it was raining heavily and looked set to continue throughout the night. Jezza's brother Tommy was round at Maurice's house, safely installed in front of the computer with Steve.

Virgil had drawn the short straw and was crouched miserably, binoculars trained on the cottage, in the sparse shelter of some trees, which dripped persistently down the back of his neck. He was a couple of fields away, in the only cover suitable. An officer from the uniform branch was keeping him company, wearing dark civilian clothes and grumbling a lot.

Rob was sitting in his car further down the main road in a lay-by, facing the opposite way to Ted and Jezza. He was accompanied by PC Susan Heap, also in plain clothes.

It was early evening, still daylight, but the visibility was not good because of the persistent rain. They were further hampered by the spray thrown up by the steady stream of traffic heading past, going home at the end of the working day.

'Do you think we make a likely courting couple, boss?' Jezza asked conversationally.

Ted smiled indulgently.

'An unlikely one, perhaps.'

'What, are you saying you wouldn't fancy me, if you were straight?'

She was clearly feeling very much more at ease in his company.

'People would be more likely to think I was your dad dropping you off to meet your boyfriend,' he suggested.

'Boss, there's a dark Fiesta, same model as Angela's, heading in your direction,' Rob's voice came over the radio. 'We couldn't see the number for the amount of spray being thrown up.'

Jezza was keeping watch in the rear view mirror for any traffic turning into the lane where Angela's cottage was.

'Got visual on it now,' she said, 'and it's turning into the lane.'

'Virgil, do you copy'? Ted asked.

'Copy, boss. I can see lights coming down the lane, heading towards the cottage. The car's turning round in one of the parking spaces. Backing down to Angela's cottage.'

There was a pause, then Virgil continued, 'Someone has just got out but it looks as if they've left the car running. The lights are still on.'

'Quick visit to pick something up, ready for a speedy getaway?' Ted mused.

'Something from the garden, perhaps? Ready for her next victim?' Jezza suggested.

They had already had a discreet look in the garden when no one seemed to be around. They'd found foxgloves and aconite plants, a hedge of yew and an oleander shrub, growing in a sheltered corner against a wall. Full house of the poisons used in the killings. A look through the a corner of the kitchen window, where the curtain did not quite reach, had revealed an impressive shelf of books on the healing and harmful properties of plants.

'Everybody stay in position. Let's not spook her at this stage,' Ted cautioned. 'What's happening, Virgil?'

'A light's gone on in one of the upstairs windows,' Virgil reported. 'The car's still outside, with the lights on. Damn!'

'What?' asked a chorus of voices.

'Sorry, just a massive big trickle of cold water down the back of my neck,' Virgil apologised. 'Hang on, the upstairs light has gone out. Front door is opening again. Suspect has come out, carrying a small bag. Put the bag in the car. Got back into the car. Now she's driving off. It's over to you guys now, I'm just about to lose visual.'

Jezza started up the engine, just in case Angela turned in their direction. She imagined Rob would do the same in his vehicle.

Ted was also looking behind them, glancing through the back window, one arm casually on the back of the driving seat behind Jezza. To a casual onlooker, it would hopefully look like an affectionate gesture, not one which would suggest undercover cops at work.

'We have her in sight now, heading our way,' Ted announced, as Jezza let the Fiesta go past then pulled into the traffic behind it, three vehicles back. Luckily there were enough cars to make trailing Angela less obvious.

'Keep her in sight but don't press too close,' Ted advised. 'Rob, are you following?'

'Not far behind you, boss, but the traffic's building up, so give me a clue if you turn off.'

'Traffic is slowing down here now,' Ted told him. 'I think there are roadworks ahead. Temporary traffic lights, with single file traffic.'

The lights were just changing to amber as Angela's car went through. Jezza held her breath, willing the cars in front to go for it. They did and she followed them, tailgating the one in front as the light turned to red.

'Shit!' they heard Rob shout over the radio. 'Some twat's just driven right into the back of me. Sorry, boss.'

'Are you both all right?' Ted asked, his first concern as always for his officers.

'Yeah, fine, but I'm not sure my car is,' Rob said ruefully. 'Keep us posted with where you are and we'll catch you up.'

'Do you want me to stay put here or come after you, boss?' Virgil asked. 'We've got a bit of a walk to the car so we won't be quick.'

'Negative, Virgil, you two stand down,' Ted told them. 'Go and get dry. Jezza and I will try to keep her in sight. If I had any clue where she was going I could get someone up ahead, but we'll just have to follow her for now.'

'She's turning off,' Jezza announced, as Angela swung the Ford into a narrow lane, without indicating. 'Unless this is a known rat-run, we're going to stick out a bit like a sore thumb, following her along here.'

'Hang well back,' Ted told her. 'I've no idea where this goes. I must have driven past it dozens of times but I'm none the wiser.'

'We could ask the GPS,' Jezza suggested.

'I'm rubbish with anything like that, I find it too distracting. Let's just keep following her and see where she leads us. She should have no reason to suspect who we are, unless she's really paranoid.'

The lane was narrow and twisting. If they met any

oncoming traffic, it would be uncomfortably tight to squeeze by another vehicle, unless there were any passing places. They had not yet seen any.

Angela seemed to have speeded up somewhat. Whether it was the lack of any other traffic, or she was feeling uncomfortable with another car behind her, they couldn't tell. Jezza was careful to keep back as instructed.

They lost sight of her for a moment on a particularly tight bend. When Jezza rounded it, she suddenly had to hit the brakes, hard. Angela's car had stopped dead in the middle of the road, just before a bridge. The impressive braking system on the Golf brought it to a smooth halt, not too close.

Angela had got out of the car and was standing next to it in the pouring rain, clutching something to her chest. She was shouting towards them, but they couldn't hear what she was saying, from within the cocoon of the vehicle.

'Wait in the car. I'll go and talk to her,' Ted said, opening the passenger door to step out, reaching for his warrant card.

'Be careful, boss,' Jezza said warningly.

'Don't worry,' he said, hitching up the collar of his trench coat against the rain. 'If she whips out any cake, I won't eat it.'

He took a step forward and said calmly, 'Mrs Mortenson? Please don't be alarmed, I'm a police officer.' He held up his warrant card, although she wouldn't be able to see much through the rain.

'Why are you following me?' the woman's voice was hysterically shrill.

'I'm sorry if we alarmed you, ma'am. We've just been trying to contact you,' Ted continued in the same tone. 'We were concerned about your welfare. No one's seen you for a few days. Could we just have a word with you, please?'

'You've been spying on my house,' she spat. 'I've been watching you, watching it. And you've been in my garden. I left markers, so I'd know if anyone had been in.'

'Mrs Mortensen, could we please have a word, somewhere

in the dry?' Ted asked reasonably, rain teeming down his face, droplets forming on the end of his nose.

'Get away from me!' she shouted, backing up a few steps. 'I know what you're trying to do.'

'Mrs Mortensen, all I'm trying to do is to get us both in out of the wet. Would you like me to get into your car, or would you like to come and sit in ours?' he asked, wondering what Jezza would think about them both dripping all over the leather upholstery.

'I just need to ask you a few questions, please,' he continued, keeping his tone as non-threatening as possible.

He took one step forward. Angela immediately screamed at him to stay away, then turned and ran up the slope towards the bridge.

Ted still had the radio in his hand. He said quietly into it, 'Jezza, stay in the car, call specialist back-up. We may need to talk her down. She's clearly very agitated and irrational.'

He walked after Angela as calmly as he could, then caught sight of her, standing on the stone parapet of the bridge above the river, which was swollen from all the recent rain. He stopped as soon as he saw her. She was swaying precariously, still clutching whatever it was she held in her hands.

'Mrs Mortensen, please come down from there,' he said evenly. 'You have nothing to be afraid of. I'm not going to harm you. I just need to ask you some questions. Somewhere out of the rain, in the warm, over a nice cup of tea.'

'My Robert,' she said, her voice much lower, holding up the object, which Ted could now just make out was a framed photograph. 'He was so wonderful. Such a lovely person. They couldn't find a bed for him. Yet some stinking, useless old crone who should have been dead long ago got a bed. And my Robert died.'

'Mrs Mortensen, your husband was very seriously ill,' Ted was still trying to keep his voice calm and reasonable, to buy himself some time. There was no way he could get close enough to the woman to snatch her to safety. He would just have to try to keep her talking until expert help arrived.

'He died, just so some old person could live a few more miserable weeks or months. They could have saved him, if they'd tried. If they'd wanted to. But I've been evening up the score. There's not so many old people left now, blocking beds in hospitals which younger people could have.

'I did it for my Robert. I miss him so, so much. And now I'm going to be with him.'

Ted lunged forward as she took a deliberate step off the parapet and disappeared from sight. He was hauling off his trenchcoat and shoes when Jezza reached him, shouting, 'Boss, no, what the hell do you think you're doing?'

'Going in after her,' Ted said, heading towards the parapet.

'Are you mad? If she doesn't drown first, she'll get sucked into the hydro and chopped to pieces.'

She put out an arm to stop him, which he shrugged off and turned back to the bridge. This time, he totally missed her roundhouse kick which came from behind him and knocked his feet out from under him. He did feel the weight of her as she leapt onto his back, kneeling on his shoulders to pin him face down.

She grabbed his radio and shouted instructions into it.

'Suspect gone into the river near Otterspool, probably swept away downstream. Need urgent Fire and Rescue Service, probably divers.'

She added the coordinates which the GPS had given her while she was waiting in the car as instructed.

Ted could so easily have unseated and immobilised her, but he didn't even attempt to. In a sense, he was relieved. He was no swimmer at all, useless out of his depth, and would probably have drowned. He had just felt that he should at least try.

'DC Vine,' he ground out, 'would you please stop kneeling on me so I can get up and we can both get in out of this rain.'

She leapt up, but she was grinning, especially at his dishevelled appearance. Ted noticed the state of his work suit. Trev was not going to be pleased.

He got to his feet and tried to put his shoes back on. His socks were soaked through, so there seemed little point. Instead he just squelched wetly back towards to car, carrying his sopping shoes, to await the arrival of the cavalry.

'You do know there are probably screens to stop even fish, never mind bodies, getting sucked into the hydro, don't you?' he asked.

Jezza opened the boot and produced a towel, which she threw at him, telling him to get into the car.

'I had to say something to stop you jumping in,' she grinned. 'The team would never have forgiven me if I'd let you drown.'

'And you do know I have black belts in four martial arts?' Ted asked her with mock severity.

Jezza was still grinning widely. 'Good job one of them isn't kickboxing then, eh, boss?'

# Chapter Thirty-nine

'I think I might just give myself six out of ten today,' Ted said, surprising Carol.

It was the highest mark he had awarded himself to date in any of their therapy sessions. She was even more surprised that he said it while looking directly at her, rather than staring at the carpet.

He said it with a boyish grin. It made him look both attractive and vulnerable at the same time. It lit up his hazel eyes, with their hint of green. She was pleased to be able to see more of his face, rather than the top of his head as he bent forward.

She had spent a lot of time thinking how thick his hair was and how beautifully kept, always clean and shiny. He had probably been blonde as a baby, now the colour had the slightly dusty look of corn left standing too long before harvest.

'Maybe seven,' he said, on reflection, then, hedging his bets, 'six and a half'.

She knew his recent difficult case had come to an end. Not quite the end he had hoped for, but at least it was finally over and there was closure, of sorts.

Angela's body had been found not far down-river from where she had gone into the water. The post-mortem revealed that she had hit her head as she jumped in, and been knocked unconscious. She had drowned, and her body had been caught on rocks further down, quickly recovered by the Fire and

Rescue Service.

'There will have to be an internal enquiry into the circumstances of her death, of course,' the Ice Queen had warned him. 'It's routine, but merely a formality. Neither you nor DC Vine are under suspicion of any irregularity. It's a pity we could not have brought her to trial, but the likelihood is strong that she would have been found unfit to plead in any event. Grief can do terrible things to the human mind.'

Ted had at least been able to close the file on the killings. They had strong evidence against Angela which would probably have convinced a jury of her guilt. But he agreed with the Ice Queen. Any halfway decent defence team would have been screaming unfit to plead, in view of what were her obviously serious mental health issues.

He had spent some time figuratively beating himself up that they had missed an important link. The first victim chronologically, though not the first they had heard about, Lilian Protheroe, had been in hospital at the same time as Angela's husband, though not on the ICU. It was an angle they had not thought to explore, after the CEO's assertion that no elderly patients were blocking beds which might otherwise have been available to Robert Mortensen.

It had emerged, from later questioning, that Mandy Griffiths had given Angela Mrs Protheroe's name and told her which home she had come from, when Angela had been screaming her protests that the elderly lady had been allocated a bed. She'd given her the information before the reporter arrived on the scene, and he'd been quickly moved on to his appointment so had not heard all the details.

Angela had started to visit Mrs Protheroe in the home after her discharge from hospital. She had established her presence as not suspicious, then taken her chance to poison her. Presumably, once she had found how easy it was to do, she had tried again, then kept on going, until a chain of events made her realise the police were on to her.

It was clear that the articles about the case in the local paper had pushed her over the brink, where she had been teetering since the death of her husband. She must have been worried the police were getting close. Then the incident with Jezza at Cottage Row had clearly sent her into a panic, probably suspecting the police were on to her, and had driven her into hiding.

They found out that she had been staying in a B&B not far away, returning from time to time to keep an eye on her house from a distance. From her vantage point, she had seen what she deduced must be police officers looking around and had realised that the net was closing in.

'If I may give you one piece of advice, Inspector,' the Ice Queen said, in a tone which left Ted in no doubt that it was an order, not a suggestion. 'If ever it were to get out in the public domain that you were related to the first victim, I suspect that having resolved the case would not protect you from the further and terrible wrath of the Chief Constable.

'I would therefore suggest that you take the local reporter out for a decent lunch somewhere, ply him with food and drink of his choice. I would not be averse to signing an expense claim for doing so, in the circumstances.

'I'll get the Press Office to draw something up, a crib sheet for what you can and can't tell him about Angela and about the Mandy Griffiths case. We'll feed him some titbits no one else will get. Put your best charm offensive into operation, then he won't feel the need to go digging any deeper.'

'I shall look forward to it immensely, ma'am,' Ted said with heavy irony.

'Keep your friends close and your enemies closer, Inspector,' she said, with the hint of a smile and a twinkle.

Ted was back on good terms with Jim Baker once more, which pleased him enormously. He had huge affection and respect for his former boss, both as a colleague and as a good friend. The return dinner party had made sure that his behaviour at their table was forgiven and forgotten.

Ted and Jim had taken the opportunity of a break in the rain to stroll into the garden and talk shop, leaving Trev and Bella at the table.

'A result of sorts, Ted,' Jim said. 'I imagine you're pleased with that, at least?'

'We should have got her sooner,' Ted said ruefully. 'No wonder the Chief Constable was jumping all over me. I had my eye off the case and we missed a thing or two.'

'Random serial killers are the hardest of all to catch, you know that. And you had good reason to be distracted. How is Trev now?'

Ted looked towards the house, smiling fondly.

'He's great,' he said. 'Better than his old self. He's so full of energy.'

'You know, you really should put in some flowering shrubs along this part of the fence.'

Jim always got uncomfortable when Ted talked about anything to do with his relationship with Trev. His changes of subject were often clumsy. Ted laughed to himself.

Trev and Bella were watching them through the open French doors.

'Is it as difficult as people say, living with a policeman?' Bella asked.

'They don't make a very good plus one, that's for sure,' Trev laughed. 'You get used to being stood up, rather a lot. And to eating on your own.'

'So how do you manage? James says you two have been together for a long time.'

'If you love someone enough, you can make anything work,' Trev smiled.

'Will you two ever get married?'

'Ted wants to. It's always me who refuses. He has enough difficulty introducing me as his partner in police circles. I don't want to make it awkward for him by being his husband.

Coppers are not generally known for being an open-minded lot.

'Jim's used to us now. He's accepted us, after his fashion. But I'm not sure how he would react if he got invited to our wedding and had to make a best man speech,' he told her with a smile.

Ted was still holding his therapist's gaze as he continued speaking. It was the longest eye contact he had ever maintained with her.

'You've helped me enormously, Carol, and I can never thank you enough,' he said. 'I've always been rubbish at talking about myself. But I've learned to do it, a bit, and it's helped.

'The other day, I took my mother out for the day. Trev was off playing Hell's Angels with Bizzie Nelson. I took her up to Roman Lakes, where I used to go fishing with my dad. She loved it. I did, too.

'We walked all round the Nature Trail and the History Trail, we ate and drank in the tea rooms. Above all, we talked. I found I was able to tell her all about what happened to me at school. I think I'd subconsciously been blaming her most of my life. Not for what happened. I realise she couldn't have prevented that. But for not being there to make it better afterwards. We hugged a lot and we both cried a bit. I think we're all right now. I think I'm all right now. Hence six and a half out of ten.'

'You know where I am, Ted, if ever you feel there's still more that you need to work through,' she told him.

He stood up and they shook hands warmly. They both maintained the contact slightly longer than was strictly necessary. Carol wondered once again if he knew just how attractive he was.

'Thanks, Carol, but I don't think I will need to,' Ted said quietly. 'Now I know that Trev is going to be all right, I think that I'll be all right, too.'

**The End**

Lightning Source UK Ltd.
Milton Keynes UK
UKHW041824061019
351114UK00001B/159/P